Praise for *Atlanta Burns*:

"[Atlanta Burns] is like Veronica Mars on Adderall. Chuck Wendig knocks this one out of the park as he so often does." —Stephen Blackmoore, author of *City of the Lost*, *Dead Things*, and *Broken Souls*

"Give Nancy Drew a shotgun and a kick-ass attitude and you get Atlanta Burns. Packed with action and fascinating characters, [*Atlanta Burns*] is a story that will captivate both teens and adults and have them clamoring for the next installment." —Joelle Charbonneau, author of The Testing Trilogy and *NEED*

**Praise for *Under the Empyrean Sky*,
Book One in the Heartland Trilogy:**

"This strong first installment rises above the usual dystopian fare thanks to Wendig's knack for disturbing imagery and scorching prose." —*Publishers Weekly*

"Wendig brilliantly tackles the big stuff—class, economics, identity, love, and social change—in a fast-paced tale that never once loses its grip on pure storytelling excitement. Well-played, Wendig. Well-played." —Libba Bray, author of The Gemma Doyle Trilogy, *Going Bovine*, *Beauty Queens*, and The Diviners Series

"A tense dystopian tale made more strange and terrifying by its present-day implications." —*Booklist*

THE
HUNT

THE HUNT

ATLANTA BURNS, BOOK TWO

SKYSCAPE

SKYSCAPE

Text copyright © 2016 Chuck Wendig

Published by Skyscape, New York

www.apub.com

Amazon, the Amazon logo, and Skyscape are trademarks of Amazon.com, Inc., or its affiliates.

ISBN-13: 9781503953390
ISBN-10: 1503953394

Cover design by Cyanotype Book Architects

Printed in the United States of America

To everyone who helps make it better for everybody else

PART ONE:
TRIGGER WARNING

"They say it gets better," Atlanta says into the camera. "That bullies come and bullies go and eventually everything sorts itself out. It doesn't. That's not how the world works, and it won't ever work that way. Somebody's always going to be there to hold you down against the ground and kick you while you're there. I'm saying it doesn't get better on its own. But I am saying you can make it better. You can fight back."

CHAPTER ONE

Way the crying comes through the woods, Atlanta thinks, *I'm too late*. The sound of Ecky sobbing slides around the trees like a snake looking to eat, and Atlanta puts some pep in her step. Twigs snapping under her feet, and under Whitey's feet, too—the big dunderheaded dog trots alongside her, with his one ear and one eye gone, his skull underneath his soft white skin dented in like a run-over soup can. He usually has a look on his face that's just dumb as bricks: empty eye, mouth gaping wide, tongue out, love coming off him in waves. Now, though, he's on the hunt. He knows something's wrong.

Atlanta's got the squirrel gun cradled to her chest, barrel to the sky.

She hears a voice, mean as a wasp. "Take a bite, Icky."

"I don't wanna," Ecky—Joey Eckhart—blubbers.

Dangit. Late, late, too late. She had her phone on mute, missed the text because of the stupid vice principal. Ecky hired her, and heck if she's not messing this up. Atlanta hurries through the brush—past trees twisted up with poison ivy, through spiderwebs and the spiders that sit in their centers—nearly tripping over a shattered boulder spongy with moss.

"Bite it, or I stick you the way I stuck that frog." The mean voice again. She knows it. Hank Crayley—known by most folks only as Crayley. A nobody. Just another bully. World's full of the likes of him. Only three weeks into the school year, and already he's been suspended for throwing a chair through a window. Probably his plan all along. He's what Atlanta's daddy would've called *smart-stupid.* Too stupid to do much good, but smart enough to do a world of bad.

Ahead: colors. People colors. Shirt, shorts, skin.

She raises the gun and steps into the clearing.

Ecky stands there against the pale trunk of a paper birch. The makeup he wears is running, black, bleak streaks through muddy blush. His hair is usually a thing of controlled chaos—shaved on the sides with the top looking like a wave about to break on a beach. Now, though, it's mashed flat. Sweat-slick.

He's got a lump of something dark skewered on the shaft of an arrow.

A frog. A dead frog.

Across from him, two assholes.

Jed Carver: a short, stumpy little thumb of a guy. Big, puffy baby cheeks and a military buzz-cut so sharp and so precise it looks like someone used a ruler to get it that way.

Hank Crayley: the opposite. Handsome in a way that Jed isn't. Tall where Jed is short, lean where Jed is thick. Everything in Crayley's face comes to a point: sharp nose, chin like a chisel, a stare on him like a pair of bull's-eyes on a dartboard.

Crayley has a compound bow nocked with an arrow. The bow is camouflage, but wrapped up in swatches of blaze orange tape.

The bowstring is taut. The broadhead arrow points right at Ecky.

Whitey's shoulders go up. His head drops. A low growl comes from his throat like the idling rumble of a truck engine.

"Jesus *shit*," Crayley says, seeing her.

She brings up the gun. "Hey, Crayley. You ought to put that down."

"You," he says.

"Yup."

"Atlanta, you seem to be in everybody's business these days." He still keeps the bow drawn, the arrow ready to slip. "Don't you take a break? Go do something else. We got this covered."

Atlanta gives a side-eye toward Ecky. "You good, Ecky?"

Ecky takes a second, but nods slowly. Tears on pause. "I'm fine. Now."

"What's that you're holding?" she asks.

"Frog."

"Frog?" she asks Crayley.

"Lot of 'em in the swamp across the road," Crayley answers with a half shrug. "I shoot frogs, turtles, sometimes a possum or a cat. I freeze 'em because they keep better." He laughs like this is a joke, a funny joke, but then the laugh turns black and dies, because nobody's laughing with him. Even Jed looks scared. "Icky here said he was hungry. Didn't you, Ick?"

"Sh . . . shut up."

"Let's just get this done," Atlanta says. "Put the bow and arrow down, Katniss Everdeen, else I pull this trigger."

Crayley hesitates. Jed says nothing, just reaches out and gives the other boy's shoulder a gentle touch, as if to say, *C'mon, let's go.*

Thing is, Crayley's got a whole lotta not much going on in his present or his future. His daddy owns a junkyard. His mama ran off with a propane salesman, or so the story goes. He's in and out of suspensions, probably because he wants to be. Best you can say about Crayley is he's got a fairly good-looking girlfriend, another go-nowhere type by the name of Patricia Mebs. Patty.

So maybe it shouldn't surprise that he's not so keen to ease off on the bow and arrow. But what does surprise is when he pivots—

—and points it at Atlanta.

Whitey tenses. His growl deepens.

"Easy," she says to Whitey. To Crayley, "You sure you wanna do this?"

"You think you're a real bad-ass bitch. Some tough hick twat who shows up and starts pushing people around. Protecting a bunch of nerds and homos and freak-shows. You know that people are scared of you?" He thrusts out that sharp chin of his. "Not me. I hunt. My father hunts. That gun you got there, it's worthless. A one-shot .410 is good for killing a squirrel, *one squirrel,* and not much else. But *this*?" He pinches one eye shut, and with the other one open, he stares down the long, lean shaft of the arrow, the point never wavering. "I'll spear you right through the heart." He lets the tip drift higher. "Or maybe your eye." Then, he tilts it downward and to the side—right toward Whitey. "Or maybe I'll stick one through that fugly-ass dog of yours. Whaddya say?"

She sniffs. Her blood, hot as a coal furnace. Sweat drips along her brow—summer still has its teeth out, and she's really feeling it now, like it's biting down, chewing her up. Part of her thinks, *Just put the gun down and go. He's crazier than you. You have to stop messing around with people who are way more cuckoo-canary than you could ever be.*

But she keeps that gun pointed.

Flies buzz. Mosquitoes take their taste.

Atlanta sets her jaw, tries not to let her voice shake when she says, "Here's what I say: I say you kill my dog, I shoot you, then maybe beat you to death with the gun. I say you shoot *me*, you probably kill me. But I'll still get off a shot, and worse, Whitey will have your crotch for an early dinner. And my .410 is pointed right at that smirking mug of yours. Birdshot will make an awful mess of your face. Blind you in one eye. Blow off your lips. Maybe part of your nose. You got a pretty girlfriend. Patty, right? You think she's gonna want to stick her tongue in that ruined mouth of yours? She'll probably jump Jed's bones instead."

Jed flinches when she says his name. He says to Crayley: "Hey, c'mon, man. We don't have to do this. Let's get outta here."

"Shut *up*, Jed." Crayley's got the doubt. She can see it creeping in like mold on bread. The arrow point trembles, dips. "Why you gotta be such a bitch, Atlanta Burns?"

"Because bitches get shit done."

He lowers the arrow. Then there's a moment when it's like . . . he doesn't seem to know what to do. A few seconds of embarrassment, maybe confusion, before he suddenly turns and bolts through the woods like a spooked whitetail. Jed, caught off guard, follows after—though not before tripping and almost breaking his ankle on a fallen branch. Jed yells, "Sorry!" and then he's gone.

Atlanta lets out the breath she didn't realize she was holding. She yells after: "You mess with my friends again, I promise to end you, Hank Crayley!"

Whitey goes over to Ecky, nuzzles the boy's hip.

"C'mon, you two," Atlanta says, popping the shell out of the gun and pocketing it. "I'm getting bit up."

———

They come out by Bauman Road, and to get there they have to pull through some gnarly briars—Atlanta hops the ditch, then holds out her hand for Ecky. Ecky takes it, jumps, almost falls. Whitey sniffs around the ditch like a pig looking for a half-buried apple core.

Just down the way is a four-door sedan the color of a pine tree: a Saturn, which apparently they don't make anymore. Shane is down there, leaning against the hood, using his phone to—well, with Shane, who knows what. He might be playing *Minecraft*, but he's just as likely to be looking up birdcalls or Mesopotamian history. She whistles, gives him a wave, then starts walking over.

"Everything okay?" Shane says, looking up.

"It's cool," she says. Then sighs and adds, "We were late. Almost too late."

Ecky shrugs, his makeup still in streaks. "It's fine. Thanks."

"Here," she says, pulling out some money. In her head she counts out a handful of twenties. "There's three hundred back. I'll keep two."

"You don't have to—"

"No, no, hey, that's on me. You hired me. I wanted the money up front. I kinda messed up." She rolls her eyes. "I had to stay after school to see Planet Wilson." Wilson, the vice principal. "Planet" Wilson, not just because he's fat but because he's almost perfectly round, like a beach ball, or like a well-fed tick.

Which reminds her—

"Tick check," she says, and starts patting herself down. Hands under her shirt, along her belt line, up the back of her neck, and through her hair. There—the feeling of a teeny-tiny-something crawling. Sure enough, one such bloodsucker. She drops it on the asphalt and grinds it with a boot until it's just a smear. "I hate ticks. Sometimes I pee on 'em before flushing. Sometimes I burn 'em with fire, or cut 'em with a knife."

Ecky says, "How's that different from what Crayley does to frogs?"

"Last I checked, frogs don't latch on and try to drink my blood like vampires. If they did, well."

"They're just creatures. Doing what they have to."

"Are you trying to make me feel bad about killing a tick? You ever meet somebody with Lyme disease?" She shakes her head. "You know, never mind. You want ticks on you, that's your business. You need a ride home?"

"I'm good," he says. A small shrug.

He seems sad. Not just *now* sad, not just shook up, but something fundamental—it's crept into him like a long damp.

"Hey, sorry that punk wanted to kick your ass." *Or make you eat a frog or straight-up kill you.* Though she's not sure it ever would've gone that far—she doesn't think Crayley's an actual sociopath. "Just because you're gay doesn't mean—"

"I'm not gay," Ecky says.

"Oh." Atlanta blinks. "Sorry, I kinda thought—with the makeup and, y'know." She twists her face like she's trying to solve a math problem. "Hold up, are you one of those boys who wants to be a girl?"

"Not really."

"A girl who wants to be a guy?"

A shrug. "Not that, either."

"So are you a boy or a girl or what?"

Ecky looks irritated now. "File under *or what.*"

"I don't—" Atlanta feels like she's got her feet caught in a boggy mire and she's sinking fast, and she knows that struggling is how you sink deeper and yet here she is, struggling. Words line up and push one another out of her mouth like buffalo pushed over the edge of a cliff. "So you have both sets of parts?" Ecky's face becomes grimmer. "No parts at all?"

"It doesn't matter what parts I have."

"It kinda matters. Like, when you wanna pee."

Shane, for his part, observes this back-and-forth with some combination of fascination and disgust. Like he's watching a train hit a deer in slow motion.

And Ecky, well, he's got a fire stoked now—gone is the sadness, and in his (or, uh, her?) eyes, there's a flash like light on coins at the bottom of a fountain. "It doesn't matter when it comes to how I see myself. Or how I identify myself. But other people don't like it. They like putting things in neat little drawers. It's why they call me Icky. Because it's gross to them. *I'm* gross to them. Does that bother you, Atlanta? Is it gross to *you*?"

She takes a deep breath and chews on it for a second. "It confuses me, but that's not your fault, it's mine. Lots of things confuse me. Calculus. Manga. Snapchat. I mean, with Snapchat, you take a picture and then it's gone? Like, it self-destructs? I don't get it. But that makes *me* weird, not anyone else. Way I figure it, you have the right to be called whatever you want: boy, girl, something in between. You wanna be called a cat on a washing machine, then it's my job to respect that and call you what you wanna be called."

Ecky seems suddenly unsettled. As if that wasn't what he or she expected to hear. "Oh. Okay." Then he says, again like he's on the offensive, "You're supposed to ask me about my pronoun."

"Which one's a pronoun again? That the thing you're supposed to not end a sentence with?"

"That's a preposition, and you just ended a sentence with a preposition."

"Oh."

"No, like, do I want to be a *he* or a *she* or what."

"I'll bite. What pronoun do you like?"

Ecky hesitates. "I . . . don't know yet. I think *she/her* for now."

"Okay. You let me know if it changes. Otherwise I'll just call you Ecky."

A moment of hesitation. "Actually, I'd prefer Joey."

"Joey." She thinks, *Could go either way with that one: boy or girl.* "Okay, Joey."

"Thanks."

"It's cool. You're good walking home, then?"

"Yeah."

"See you on the flipside, Joey."

————

"They call it 'genderqueer,'" Shane says in the middle of driving.

"Huh?"

"What Joey is. I think they call it genderqueer. Or maybe genderfluid?" He frowns, suddenly—probably because Shane doesn't like not knowing things. Little Shane Lafluco. Not a hair out of place. Nary a wrinkle in his plaid shirt. He's taken lately to calling himself a *nork*—a nerd and a dork. He says it's the "age of the nork," with geek stuff suddenly becoming cool. She told him, good luck with that, you'll still get your ass kicked if you run around school talking about *Doctor Who* instead of football or cow-tipping.

"I thought *queer* meant 'gay.'"

"I dunno. I think it just means 'strange.' Or 'to change something.'"

"Oh."

He drives for a while, past the road that would take you up to Grainger Hill, to the trailers and rinky-dink ranchers where you can buy weed and meth and old lawn mowers and older washing machines. Atlanta can see on Shane's face that he wants to say something. He doesn't hide it well. He gets this look like he's tasting something funny, or like maybe he's gotta go to the bathroom. Even Whitey knows something's up. From the back, the dog pokes his big-ass head between the seats and just stares at Shane, unblinking. Stern and stoic.

Finally she says, "Oh, just spit it out already."

"Well—uh."

"Say it. Lay it on me." She pats her chest.

"Uhhh." He visibly swallows. "What are you doing?"

"Like, right now?"

"Like, with all this. With what just happened back there."

She squints an eye, raises one eyebrow above the other. "You know what I'm doing. You were with me when we made the video." Before school started, she and Shane got together, made a YouTube thing about how no, it doesn't get any better, you have to *make* it better. And one way you make it better is by calling Atlanta Burns.

Helper of the downtrodden. Defender of the underdog. Friend to freaks, foe to bullies. "That was you, right?"

"It was me, yeah, duh, I know." A flare of irritation in his voice. "It's just, I didn't know you were going to ask for money."

She shrugs. "Nothing wrong with money."

"No, yeah, it's just—it cheapens it somehow."

"Money does the opposite of cheapening something."

"I guess I'd just rather you be doing this because you want to, not because it's a job. When you get paid for it, it's like . . . you're some kind of mercenary."

"Rather than what, a superhero, like in your comic books?"

"I guess." He scrunches his face. "That sounds dumb, huh?"

"Well, uh, I dunno—" *Oh, hell with it.* "You know, yeah it does. Because the world isn't like that. *I'm* not like that. There are no superheroes and I'm sure as shit not one of them. Okay? Jeez. I do want to help people, but at the same time I gotta get what's mine, too. I provide a . . . service. And people pay for it. Same as anybody doing any job, even a job they believe in, a job they love."

"Lawyers do pro bono work all the time."

She snaps, "Well, I'm not a dang lawyer, am I? I'm just . . . me. Dumb Southern girl in the middle of Pennsylnowhere, carting around a one-shot scattergun and attended to by the Venezuelan Charlie Brown and a dog so big and so dumb that he doesn't know a gunshot to the head should've killed him. I swear, he's so stupid he's probably dead and just hasn't figured it out yet." Whitey, for his part, pants and nuzzles her ears with his sloppy muzzle.

"I miss Chris," Shane says suddenly. And it's like a thunder-clap—silent, but still felt deep inside her. A pit of grief. A sucking chest wound like a bullet straight through her lung.

"I know. I do, too."

"I just want to make sure we're honoring his memory."

"Yeah." She nods. "Yeah. Listen, no harm, no foul you don't wanna do this anymore. Or if you want a cut of the money—"

"It's okay. I'm good. I just—I dunno." He gnaws on his lip. "What are you going to do with the money?"

To that, she just shrugs, like she doesn't know the answer already. Like it's not a key to a lock. Like it's not a ticket to ride.

CHAPTER TWO

They drive past the barns and tractors and the bent-elbow sharp turn sign that the drunk in the pickup took out last month. They go past the fading corn and the Cat Lady's house, past a rusted combine, past a pile of bones that used to be a deer. Shane drops her off at the foot of her driveway where she can grab the mail (bills, junk, junk, bills, someone else's mail, bills). Then she huffs it down the driveway on foot, mail in one hand, shotgun in the other. Whitey trotting alongside—him snuffling and snorting as he slaloms between invisible tentpoles, like he's got the scent of something and can't shake it.

A low growl rises in the back of his throat.

Atlanta sees why.

There, parked by the house, a well-abused Crown Vic.

And sitting on the front porch: Detective Holger.

"Hello, Atlanta."

Her guts tighten. "Hey, Detective Holger."

"No need to be so formal. You can call me by my first name."

"I don't know it."

"Cherry."

A scowl. "Cherry? That sounds like a stripper name."

"Well, in this case it's a cop name. Cherry Holger."

"Oh. Sure. I'm still gonna call you Detective Holger, though. I was taught to respect my elders."

There—a moment of hesitation on the cop's face before a slow smile breaks out. "I'm sure that's true." A hint of sarcasm, maybe. Atlanta thinks suddenly, *This ain't gonna be a friendly visit, is it?*

Holger, she always looks like she's hung on the line to air-dry—everything rumpled and wrinkled. No idea how old she is—once someone hits about forty, Atlanta kinda figures they're a short hop, skip, and jump from the funeral home—but smart money says she looks older than she is.

Every time Holger shifts—a lean forward, a swipe of dirt off her denim—Whitey lowers his head and stares. Like he's ready to make a move when necessary. Atlanta can't blame him. Last time Whitey saw Holger, it was at the police station—just minutes before another cop, Petry, shot Whitey in the head.

Petry. The name crawls up inside her like a cockroach.

"You out shooting?" Holger asks.

"Oh. This?" She looks at the gun like, *Oh, hey, who put this funny shotgun in my hand?* "Just shootin' cans."

"You being safe?"

"I am."

"You do any hunting?"

"Sure," Atlanta answers. True, maybe, from a certain point of view. But she doesn't like where this is going so she changes the subject: "Mama know you're here?" Atlanta asks. "She should've gotten you something to drink. Sweet tea, some Crystal Light, glass of ice water maybe. Though our water's been tasting funny, lately, I'll be honest."

"I'm good, thanks. Your mother's at work."

Atlanta's laugh is husky and rough. "Work. That's funny." She offers her left leg. "Pull the other one and candy will come out."

"Maybe you should talk to her more, because she has a job."

Narrowed eyes. "Really?"

"Mm-hm. At the Karlton." The little coffee-and-bakery place by the Sawickis' Polish food stand? Huh. "She's been working there about a week."

So that's where Mama's been going.

"Great. Good for her. How'd you know it?"

"I eat there."

"Oh."

"Take a seat."

She scuffs her boot against the stones. "I'll stand. I sit all day in school."

"Can we talk?"

"Kinda what we're doing right now."

Holger laughs a little. "I like you, Atlanta. You're tough. Most people who go through the kinds of things you've gone through, they don't make it out okay, if at all."

"I haven't made it out yet."

"And that's what I'm worried about. You've spent some time at Emerald Lakes. And the thing with Ellis Wayman and the Farm, and then your friend, Chris—it's a lot for an adult to handle, much less a girl like yourself." A pause. A moment of calm before the lightning. "Then there's the video."

Yup. Here it comes.

"I don't know what you mean," she says, playing dumb.

"C'mon, Atlanta. I've seen it. Everyone in town has seen it. It's on YouTube, for Chrissakes. And though nobody has made any official calls to the department about it, people talk. We know you're . . . making good on your promises. Like the thing with Tim Schmidt?"

"Shitty Schmidtty." Atlanta sucks a little air between her teeth. "Such a shame. Crapping his drawers in gym class? I mean, it's right there in his name, you'd think he'd be more careful. Maybe he had a stomach bug."

"Or maybe someone slipped laxatives into his school lunch."

"I can't imagine why anybody would do that."

"Maybe because he was threatening a girl at your school. Do you know Dolores Kimpton?"

"Name's familiar." Familiar because Dolores—Dolly—hired Atlanta, not that she'd admit it here and now. Tim Schmidt, that weasel-dicked chode, was making all kinds of suggestive comments to Dolly about what he'd do to her if she didn't go with him to Homecoming dance. He's one of those types with bigger balls because he's backed up by a crew of bros and buddies: the haw-haw types, a bully's chorus, folks who give him power by laughing at his jokes and egging him on. But he fouled his gym shorts thanks to Atlanta—and, story goes, it got bad. *Real bad.* Ran down his leg, into his socks, and onto the gymnasium floor. Another kid, Gary Moynihan, stepped on it and slipped. Now nobody will talk to Tim. And now he's Shitty Schmidtty all the way home.

"How about Alberto Willis?"

"That one I don't know."

A lie, because she does. Little Alberto. Twelve years old. Perpetually picked on by another kid at his bus stop, Colin Strauss. A richie-rich shit, same age. Alberto said nobody else would help him. At first she wasn't sure how to deal with that one—because how do you intimidate a twelve-year-old like Colin Strauss? Turns out, twelve-year-olds get spooked lickety-quick. She told him, "You ever pick on Alberto again, I'll kill your mother, your father, and your guinea pig." She'd never do any of that, of course, but it's so easy to lie to a twelve-year-old. You can tell them Bigfoot will show up on the back of the Loch Ness Monster with Slender Man riding shotgun, and they'll buy in.

"What about Mitchell Erickson? John Elvis Baumgartner? Gordon Jones? Virgil Erlenbacher?" Those names. *She knows. Something.* Maybe not everything.

"Sure, I know some of them. Just from school."

"Just from school."

"I'm not real social. Kind of an introvert."

Holger stands, changes the subject. "What are your plans, Atlanta?"

"Thinking of having some dinner. There's a can of Campbell's Chicken and Stars in our pantry that I've had my eye on for the better part of a week."

Another step closer. "I mean . . . long-term. After school."

"Guidance counselor and vice principal both asked me that same question today. Must be something in the water. Maybe that's why it tastes funny."

"You're a senior now. It's time to think about it."

"I'll tell you what I told them: I take it one day at a time."

Holger steps close now. Whitey's hackles are up—fur like the bristles of a brand-new toothbrush. Atlanta steadies him with a hand, and he eases.

"Listen," Holger says, lowering her voice. "You have to look farther down the road. Find a future for yourself. High school's short, much shorter than you think. Your best bet to make it out alive is to have a plan."

"Sorry. Don't know what to tell you." That's what she says. What she thinks is, *I have a plan, Cherry, don't you worry your frumpy head about it. But I'm not going to tell you what it is, because it's not your dang business.*

"I'll see you later, Atlanta."

"See you. Thanks for the talk."

"Oh, one more thing," Holger says, turning around just as she's about to pop the Crown Vic's door. "Officer Petry."

That name again. Like an ice pick right in her middle. Atlanta tries not to flinch, but she's not sure she managed.

"Him I remember. Hard not to, since he shot my dog."

"He's been missing for some time now."

"I'm sorry to hear that." Her words don't match the sound that they make—much as she tries, Atlanta cannot inject sorry-feeling into that statement.

"We found his cruiser not far from here. Parked up the road. Nobody's seen him."

"Weird."

"You haven't seen him?"

"Mm-nope."

"He didn't come here?"

"Should he have?" Atlanta asks, knowing full well that he did come here. To kill her. And she shot him in the hand, sent him packing.

"I guess not. If you ever hear anything, let me know?"

Way she asks, it almost sounds like, *I know something already.* Maybe that's paranoid. How would she know? In the past Atlanta figured Holger for one of the good ones. Maybe it's time to reconsider that.

For now, she just says, "Sure thing," and gives a little wave as Cherry Holger slides back into the car and heads down the driveway.

———

Upstairs in her room, Atlanta reaches under her bed, straining at the shoulder. Her fingers search the floor and push through junk: an old sweater, a CD case, a tangle of hangers, an opened bag of off-brand Doritos (Coolritos). All of it put there on purpose, debris in the way of what she's trying to hide. What she's hidden so well she can't even find it herself.

Unless it's not there.

Worry lances through her like a hot pin. *No, no, no, c'mon, now*—the hangers rattle, the bag of chips shakes, and then—

There it is. Her fingers feel the edge of the shoebox.

She slides it out. An old Florsheim shoe store box bound up with bungee cords. Atlanta undoes the cables, pops the lid, and looks inside. Couple stacks of bills now. Almost two grand in there. That money sits next to a little red notebook. She touches the notebook—not sure why, really, maybe just to make sure it's still there.

Then she throws Ecky's money on top of the other money before quickly binding it up again.

Back under the bed it goes. Behind the debris and hidden from sight. The shotgun is the final piece; she slides it there, just near the edge. Ever in reach.

———

By the time Atlanta goes to bed, Mama Arlene still isn't home. The Karlton closes at, what, seven on a weeknight? Mama may have a job, but it isn't the end of her night. Something else is going on.

Atlanta lies there in the dark for a while. Thinking on it, on how her mama is hiding something. She has been acting skittish lately. Cheeky, like she's got something she wants to say but can't or won't or doesn't know how.

Her brain tosses it back and forth, over and over again. A hot potato bouncing around. She thinks about Ecky. And Shane. Her mind drifts to school and her future, because right now everyone seems to want to talk about that: *what's next, what do you want to be when you grow up, hey, why don't you go ahead and plan your next fifty years, gee gosh golly won't that be a hoot.* As always, her mind drifts back to the place it always drifts; she thinks about her friend, Chris, and how he won't have any future at all. So why does it matter?

His voice finds her there in the dark sometimes, the sheets tangled up around her legs like slick seaweed trying to drag her down deeper underwater—his voice, always just a whisper: *You could've saved me.* Sometimes it's *You did this to me,* or *Why can't you just quit picking scabs, Atlanta?*

It doesn't get better, and you can't make it better.

So why even try?

Outside the room, a squeak of a floorboard.

Sweat laces the lines of her palm. Her mouth goes dry as a wad of cotton. Atlanta tells herself to just ignore it, even as her heart starts to beat so hard she can see the faint shape of the bedsheet over her chest bouncing like the front of a kick drum. A high-pitched whine in her ear. The smell of gunsmoke.

Another squeak. Footsteps. Something clicking (like the hammer of a gun).

Nobody's there. She knows it. This happens every night. But it doesn't matter because the idea seizes her just the same, grabbing her like a pair of big hands closing around her neck. Everything is tight—jaw, chest, throat, thighs.

A foolish thought hits her: *I'm having a heart attack.* Of course she's not. She's just a teenager. But maybe it's a heart defect. Or maybe someone is really in the house. Or maybe her brain is just broken.

Faint footsteps.

Someone's here. Here to hurt her. *It's not true, dangit, stop thinking about it,* but then there's a long creak—a foot falling on a floorboard, and that one seemed real, real as a brick thrown through a window, real as a gun heavy in the hand, and she thinks back to that story of the boy who cried wolf. What if, this one time, this isn't just her brain crying foul? What if it's not some cruel pairing of insomnia and a panic attack, and it's real?

Whitey may not know it. He sleeps out in the garage, and that dog sleeps like (wait for it) he's been shot in the head (rimshot), or worse—maybe he's already been killed. Maybe whoever it is— Petry or one of Ellis Wayman's people or some neo-Nazi bastard she hasn't even met yet—killed Whitey already.

A warning goes off in her head: *You need to take this seriously, girl.*

The dam breaks. She hops up and casts her foot under the bed. Atlanta hooks the tips of her toes around the Winchester .410, slides it out, and picks it up. It's already loaded. Because of course it is.

Then she's marching forward, gun up—she's creeping forth on the balls of her feet, breath held in her chest as if to let go of it is to die. Thumb on the hammer of the single-shot, easing it back with a soft click—

In the hall, she hears it. Whispering.

Is it real?

Or all in her head?

No time like the present to find out. She whips open the door, the barrel of the gun thrust forward—a square of bright light there in the darkness, floating like a tiny window. A whoop of fear rises up. A man's voice: "No!"

Atlanta thinks, *Pull the trigger.*

But then, her mother's voice yelling, "Atlanta! *Atlanta, wait!*"

Her hand flies to the plaster wall in the hallway—there she finds the switch and she flips it on. A man stands revealed in front of her, stubble-cheeked, lean, a little rangy like an underfed hound. He's got a phone in his hand—like he was using the light from it to navigate his way upstairs.

Behind him on the steps is Arlene Burns.

Her hair's all a-frizzle. Coming up with her are the mingled stinks of fresh cigarette smoke and stale beer. She's got two more beers in her hands, Yuengling lagers. The pair of them—Arlene and what must be her new beau (suddenly Atlanta can guess at what her mother has been hiding)—stand stock-still on the steps like a couple of raccoons caught in the beam of a flashlight.

"Atlanta, baby," Arlene says, her words mushy like gravy-soaked bread. "Put that gun down, 'kay? It's just me and my . . . friend, Paul, here, and—"

"Gosh*dangit*, Mama," Atlanta growls. "Shit!"

Then she backpedals into her room and slams the door hard enough that the whole house rattles and shakes with it.

Arlene tries for a while, knocking on the door. "Baby. Baby. Sweetheart, open up. Let's talk this out real quick, okay? Super quick." Then, a fast turn into parental authority, something Mama's never been particularly good at: "Atlanta, I said to open this door right now. Right now. Come on."

A show for *Paul*, probably.

Atlanta locks the door.

Turns out the light.

Eventually, Mama drifts away like a dead frog pulled toward a pool filter.

Atlanta hears murmuring from the hallway or another room: Paul and Mama talking. About what just happened, probably. About her.

Atlanta hopes that Paul pissed his Wrangler's. *Not getting laid tonight*, she thinks. It's cold comfort for a long, sleepless night.

————

Sometime late, or maybe it's early, Atlanta thinks:

I need to go see Guy tomorrow.

I need new drugs.

CHAPTER THREE

The smell of bacon might be supernatural. You got a dead man on the ground in front of you, cook some bacon—the smell might wake him up.

But no matter the magical properties of salted, cured, smoked pork belly from the Amish market, Atlanta Burns is in no mood for it. Her stomach whines like Whitey does when he gets a bone stuck under the ratty pull-out couch, but her head and her heart aren't having any of it. She stays in her room long as she can, putting her books in her book bag. Time keeps on ticking, though, and soon she's either gotta go or gotta skip school, because Shane will meet her at the end of her driveway in about ten minutes. *Maybe I could skip . . .*

No. Too many eyes on her right now.

One thing Holger had right: she has to get out of this thing alive. And even more important than alive is graduated. (Though even now she thinks, *I could just get a GED. Is school really that essential?* But she shoves that thought away.)

Downstairs, then.

In the kitchen, Arlene has her head buried in her folded-up arms. It's not her doing the cooking. It's *him*. Paul, standing there in pajama shorts and a firehouse T-shirt. He looks over with those sleepy hound-dog eyes and says, startled, "Hi there."

At that, Arlene's head perks up. "Atlanta. Hey, about last night—"

"No" is all Atlanta can muster.

Then she grabs the first thing off the counter and ducks out the door.

Of course, what she grabs off the counter is a can of baked beans, and she's not sure why she grabbed it. She curses under her breath, says good-bye to Whitey (who is outside, taking one of his epic dumps), and wings the can into the nearby cornfield. Whitey runs after the can. Atlanta goes to school.

———

Wham.

Atlanta jerks her head up and sniffs. "Whuzzit," she says.

She's in an empty classroom.

Mr. Lovegrove is standing in front of her desk. He's holding a book. A history book, as he is a history professor—American history, actually.

"Usually," he says, nasally and droll, "these books put kids like you to sleep. But turns out, you slap one against a desk, it wakes them up. This book is a multitasker. I wonder what else I could do with it. Hit a baseball. Mash a potato."

"Hey, Mr. Lovegrove," she says, her mouth tacky with dry spit. Her words sound like her mother's this morning: gluey, gooey, still half-drunk. (And suddenly she wishes she really *were* half-drunk.) "Wha' happened?"

"You fell asleep."

Her eyes narrow. "For the whole class?"

"For the whole class. Even through the bell."

"The bell's loud."

"Very."

"Oh."

"I think it's your lunch period now."

She blinks. *Is that right? Wait, yeah, it is.* "Okay, thanks."

As she stands up, Mr. Lovegrove clears his throat—the teacher has a goaty vibe about him, what with the wispy gray beard and the bumpy forehead and the long nose with big nostrils. Looks like he'd be right at home eating a can or munching a mouthful of grass.

"Atlanta," he says. "You all right?"

"Peachy. Can I go?"

"Before the school year, the vice principal made sure to have a talk with all your teachers. Last year, given . . ." He chaws on it for a minute like he's trying to find the right words. "*Extenuating circumstances*, I'm to understand that your teachers all received instructions to give you a B plus across the board."

"Uh-huh."

"That grace period is over."

"It shouldn't be. I'm still traumatized." She hears the words come out of her mouth, and therein lurks a paradox, because on the one hand, they're true. On the other hand, they're an excuse.

"Be that as it may, the word from on high is, no special treatment."

"Fine, whatever."

He leans in. "And you're not doing well in this class. You're hovering a hair's breadth above a D grade."

"Yeah, fine, I said."

"That's okay with you? Don't you want to do better? Not just sleep through your classes? Through life? What are your plans—"

Oh, good gravy, not this again.

"I gotta go," she interrupts. "My blood sugar is so low right now it's like a snake's belly in a wheel rut. Lunch calls. See you, Mr. Lovegrove."

———

She carries a lunch tray through the caf, hair pulled close around her face—a curtain to hide the windows of her eyes. She knows people watch her. They've been watching her since she got back from Emerald Lakes last year, but now the look has changed. It's different. She can't quite peg how, yet.

Other side of the room, her table. Once, she sat alone, but now she's collected a beautiful sideshow. Shane, of course, looking primped. Chomp-Chomp (Steven), his hair a mess, the shirt of some local hardcore band—Cold World—hanging loose on his bony frame. Kyle Clemons, the geek with the doe eyes and the puffed-out goldfish cheeks. Eddie Peters, one of Chris's friends from the La Cozy Nostra gay mafia days—though since this school year's started, it seems like they aren't really much of a thing anymore. Next to Eddie is Josie Dunderchek, who Atlanta was pretty sure is a lesbian—she kinda dresses in this 1950s rockabilly roller derby way—but after the thing with Joey Eckhart, Atlanta's not so sure anymore. (Shame, she thinks, that Joey has another lunch period. He'd fit right into this crass menagerie.) She doesn't see Damita Martinez at first, but then—

There she is, at another table.

Huh. She and Shane were getting cozy for a bit. Wonder what happened there.

Atlanta keeps moving. But suddenly, someone pops up in front of her like a deer running in front of a car.

Mandy Newhouse.

Hair the color of the sun on autumn wheat. Lips as pink as a Barbie car. The smell of money comes off her like she's got fresh-printed hundreds lining the inside of her too-tight jeans, her fuzzy boots, her weird little puffy vest.

"Atlanta!" she says. She's either feigning excitement or somehow manufacturing the real thing. "You wanna sit?"

One of the popular girls is asking her to sit. At her table. *Their* table. Kids who belong to the seventh heaven, the UAF (uppity-as-fuck) types with rich, divorced parents and new cars on their sixteenth birthdays and vacation homes either in the Poconos or down the Shore, or even up in the Hamptons. They ski. They have the parties. They have the coke, the Molly, the good prescription stuff.

Sitting there, the usual crowd: the brooding Danny Decker; the cheekbone twins Jason and Joshie Barford; the human tree trunk, Moose Barnes; the pit viper (and some say school bicycle), Samantha Gwynn-Rudin; and of course, two of Atlanta's once-friends, Petra Bright and Susie Schwartz, both of whom have apparently made it to the Big Leagues now.

All the gang's accounted for but one:

Becky Bartosiewicz. Atlanta's first friend in school—a friend who abandoned her once the shit hit the fan and Atlanta took a trip to Emerald Lakes.

"Where's Bee?" Atlanta asks.

"What?"

"Bee. Becky. Where is she?"

Mandy just gives a snooty shrug and a small laugh, like she knows something. "Well. I dunno. But she's not sitting here."

Moose, who's a linebacker on the football team, looks up from a hoagie and with a mouthful of meat and shredded lettuce says, "What do you care?"

"Moose, shut up," Samantha says. And he shuts up fast.

At that, from the table, Petra says, "She's off campus." And then Samantha shoots Petra a glare, and the girl withers like a marigold after first frost.

You do well in school, you might earn a few off-campus lunches per week. Get in your car and drive somewhere to eat, Burger King or Applebee's or whatever. Maybe that's what it is. Maybe she's off with the likes of Mitchell Erickson somewhere. Dang, wouldn't they be a pair. Ugh.

Still. Something weird going on here. Atlanta gets the sense that the herd has shouldered together and pushed out one of their own into the wild.

Well, maybe Bee deserves it. She did that to Atlanta, and now they're doing it to her. Daddy used to say, *Sometimes, you gotta eat the cake you bake.*

No matter how it tastes.

"Sit?" Mandy says.

"Yeah, no," Atlanta says, then pushes past her. She figures it for some kind of trick, a trap, a joke—they want her to sit and then they'll do something to make fun of her, knock her down a peg. And she can't have that. Even if it was a sincere offer—well, heck, why even entertain that idea? No way it's sincere.

"Wait," Mandy says, but Atlanta's already moved on to have lunch with her friends. Her real friends. The freak-shows, the fuck-ups, those who won't fail her.

That's what she tells herself. She has to believe in somebody, because believing in herself just isn't enough.

———

Later. Seventh period. She's in precalculus with Miss Prasse. *Math sucks.* This one period above all the others pulls the day like taffy— it stretches minutes into hours. And so she sits there, belly full of square lunch pizza, trying again not to fall asleep as Prasse snoringly lazes through sine, cosine, and tangent. Whatever those are. Atlanta's trying to find some reason she might use these in real life.

She's coming up short.

Time comes that she starts to drift off again—but before she does, something tickles her brain stem, an old caveman paranoia that tells her she's being stared at. It tells her that because it's true. Someone *is* staring at her.

It's the new kid. Damon something-or-other.

He's staring at her with a set of dark eyes. And smiling at her with those thin lips and bright white teeth. He's one of a few new kids this year—Atlanta was new not long ago. She's not sure about his story. Maybe it's a problem with changing district lines. Or maybe he's like her: the child of a parent who decided to pack up everything and move.

Damon gives her a wave.

"Quit staring at me," Atlanta says, loud. Too loud. On purpose.

Prasse stops the chalk line across the board. She's a little thing, Miss Prasse—an itty-bitty skeleton of a woman with hair almost perfectly triangular. She turns and purses her lips. "Atlanta, do you have a problem?"

"Smirkybutt up there won't quit lookin' at me."

"Mister Carrizo, do you have a problem?"

Damon holds up both hands in surrender. "Nope."

"Good. Now eyes forward. This math is important. You need to learn this for the job market."

Atlanta almost laughs. *Sure, lady. Sure.*

———

He comes after her in the hall. Atlanta winds her way through, trying to get away because she doesn't like being cornered or followed or stared at.

But he's calling after her. Damon.

Ahead, she gets blocked by a bunch of kids standing around a bulletin board, ogling it like it's a brand-new stone tablet huffed down the mountainside by Moses hisownself—looks like some kind of audition results for a musical.

"Move!" she says, trying to push on ahead, but the cows won't budge, so now Damon is right behind her.

"Atlanta—"

She wheels on him. *"What?"*

"I just wanted to say sorry."

"Super. You said it. Bye."

"Wait! Slow your roll."

"You don't tell me to slow my roll. I don't even know what that means, but I'll slow my roll when I want to, not when you say so."

She turns and uses her backpack as a battering ram to push through the theater nerds, knocking them over like bowling pins. But Damon, this kid's like a burr on a dog's ass. "I thought you might wanna get together."

"And why would I want to do that?" she says, not stopping.

"You were new once. I'm new now. I don't have a lot of friends here. You seem cool and pretty and all—"

Again she stops and again she turns. "I don't give a hot sack of cat crap whether you think I'm cool or whether you think I'm pretty. What I care about is your ass respecting my ass when I say I don't want you to stare at me in the middle of class and stalk me in the hallway. Now, I'll give you the benefit of the doubt and let this go because you're fresh fish and you haven't heard the stories. But I don't do well by men and boys who don't respect my personal fuckin' space. You hear?"

He smirks. The asshole *smirks*.

"I hear you, okay, okay. I surrender."

But he doesn't look like he is. That's not surrender in his eyes. That's something else. Determination.

Still. When she storms off, he doesn't follow.

————

Guillermo Lopez—Guy, or Guy-Lo—sits outside his trailer just outside of town, sipping a Corona with lime and reading a beat-ass paperback book, a Megan Abbott. A few other crime novels lie strewn in the grass near a cooler: Laura Lippman, Joe R. Lansdale,

Iris Johansen. He looks up over his beer, sees her coming up the path, and he laughs.

"Hey, 'Lanta, there you are! Been a little while, eh?"

She comes up, grabs another folding beach chair, and pops it open. Drops her body in it like it's a bag of milled flour. Atlanta puts out her hand. "Beer me."

The clink of bottles until one hits her hand. Wet with ice melt.

Top popped, long sip. "So, hey," she says.

"Haven't seen you in . . . well, damn, I dunno. Few weeks. Month or more, maybe. Where you been?"

"School started back up again."

He laughs. "Oh, ho ho, yeah, shit, I forgot that you do that. I dropped out of school by your age." He lifts his chin and looks snooty for a second and affects a comical, rich-white-person accent: "I am the proud owner of a GED, I will have you know. Only the very best schooling for me, my dear. *The very best.*" Another laugh, then a loud gulp of beer. "How is it? School, I mean."

"Sucks. You know. The usual. It's like, they teach you a bunch of stuff you don't really need to know and don't teach you the stuff you *need* to know. I mean, who cares which king came after which other king? Tell me how to . . . pay taxes, or fix a toilet, or become a CEO of a major corporation so I can exploit my workers long enough to send my business to China."

"Normal, basic life shit," he says.

"Exactly. I'm just talking *life skills.*"

They both laugh now.

He says, "That dog of yours still keepin' on?"

"Whitey?" She sips the beer. "You bet. One eye, one ear, head like a package too big for the mailbox but the postman shoved it in anyway."

"You got a thing for strays and runaways, huh?"

"Birds of a feather and all that."

The breeze kicks up. Does a little, but not enough, to scatter the heat slicking her brow. The sun's drifting down over the horizon now; its light is broken by the trees, but its intensity remains whole.

Finally, she says, "I need some pills."

"Adderall run out?"

She shrugs. "Not on that anymore."

"No shit?"

She'd started taking the Adderall because it helped keep her awake—because sleep meant nightmares. Nightmares that stayed with her all day, like cigarette smoke in your hair and your clothes. "I got the opposite problem now. I don't sleep." *Instead,* she thinks, *I just lie there, shaking like a leaf and sweating like a pig looking at the butcher sharpening his cleavers. I hear things in the house. I see shadows standing at the door—shadows of men, evil men, coming to kill me.* She doesn't say any of that, though. All she says is, "I need something to knock me out."

"You still got the Ambien I gave you?"

She scrunches her nose. "Dang, I forgot about those. Yeah, maybe. I'll probably need some more, just in case I can't find 'em. They safe enough?"

"They're pills. Pills are never safe."

"I guess screw safe, yeah?"

He offers his bottle. She *tinks* hers against his, neck to neck. "Amen."

CHAPTER FOUR

Atlanta's back home, a new pill bottle rattling in her pocket like dice. Whitey's outside when she gets there, and he comes bounding up the gravel driveway to meet her—it's like this every day when she gets home. He runs, fast enough that she always thinks, *He's gonna slam into me like a runaway dump truck.* But then he circles behind her and comes up alongside of her. He trots with her the rest of the way, matching her pace, never getting too close—but never drifting too far.

He respects her personal space. Some jerks could learn a thing or two from him.

(Whitey, she figures, is better people than most people.)

It's about seven p.m. when she gets there. Mama's car is in the driveway. So is a pickup truck, a Chevy Silverado that's clean but has some miles on it. Next to that, a third car: an orange hatchback. Looks pretty new. Atlanta gives it a long look, sees a little stuffed panda bear dangling from the rearview. A girl's car, if she had to guess. Huh. *A new client*, she thinks. And then she gets to wondering when she started calling them "clients."

She heads inside, trying to guess what the hell is going on, but it doesn't take long to figure it out—because as she pitches her backpack on the nook table in the kitchen, she sees into the dining room at the same time the smell of dinner hits her.

Table's covered in a finished dinner: plates of mostly eaten food, a bowl of mashed potatoes, another of green beans, a long serving tray of pulled chicken. (It smells good, so she dang sure knows Mama didn't make it.)

Sitting there is Arlene. Next to her is the new beau, *Paul.*

Atlanta steps into the dining room, and then she sees the third person. The driver, she guesses, of that girly car out front.

It's Bee.

Becky Bartosiewicz. Her best friend. Once upon a time.

She's sitting there, a plate in front of her, food picked at a little. A glass of Mama's sweet tea—so sweet just a half glass will give you diabetes—sits in front of her, sweating like a perp. Long, straight hair framing her face. That innocent look she wears so well.

"What is this?" Atlanta asks, venom in her voice. "Some kinda intervention?"

"Hey, Atlanta," Bee says.

"You're late, missy," Mama says.

Atlanta says, "Don't play parent with me. Ten times out of ten you don't care where I am or when I come home." She thinks but doesn't say: *Just putting on a show for our guests, huh?*

Arlene frowns and is about to say something, but Paul speaks up. "Atlanta, you shouldn't speak to your mom like that—"

"Just because you're sticking it in my mother doesn't mean you get to be my daddy," she seethes. "Word of advice, Paul: shut up."

"You're grounded," Mama says.

"I'd like to see you enforce that."

Mama stays silent, sitting there quivering like a plate of Jell-O on a wobbly table.

Bee says, "It's okay. Atlanta, maybe we can go somewhere to talk."

"You can talk to my *ass*," Atlanta says, and she's not even sure what that means, really—but it's out there now, and the best thing she can do is drop the metaphorical mic and walk out of the room. So she does—she turns tail and heads for the steps, Whitey trotting along behind.

———

She sits and stews in her room for a while. Puts on the fan in the corner—it whirs and clicks as it turns. Whitey pants loud—*hah, hah, hah, hah, hah.*

From her pocket, she fetches her pills. Rolls the bottle around in her palm. Thinks, *Maybe I take one now, maybe I just pass out.* Heck, she is tired. *Exhausted.* It's like she's got concrete in her blood and mud in her shoes. And yet, her heart is beating a tom-tom in her chest, a timpani roll.

Soon, footsteps outside the door.

The pills go back in her pocket as someone knocks.

From outside, Bee says, "Can I come in?"

"No."

"Please?"

"What's the password?"

Without a beat, "Pistachio."

And that is, indeed, the password. The two of them used to get high and eat pistachios—whenever Bee smoked weed, that's what she craved. (Sometimes the joke became crasser: "You like salty nuts," Atlanta would say. Bee'd ramp it up, licking the pistachio shells and her fingers: "I *love* salty nuts, mm-mmm. I'm going to pop these nuts in my mouth." Then they'd laugh so hard they coughed and cough so hard they saw stars. Bee said that was good, because coughing made the high better.)

With the password spoken, Atlanta gets up, opens the door.

"'Sup, A?" Bee says, and hovers there.

"'Sup, Bee."

Then, a big empty canyon of silence separates them. A silence so epic, it's almost loud—like it generates its own kind of noise, a white noise that fills the ears, a blood noise. Atlanta's about to say something—something dumb like, *Hey so what's going on* or *Boy, school is stupid* or maybe something serious like, *Oh hey, thanks for abandoning me and leaving me feeling all alone in a great big abyss, that was real awesome of you.*

But Bee speaks first. "I'm pregnant," she says.

Atlanta feels like she just got slugged. "Whoa."

"Twelve weeks," she says, and those two words have a tremble to them, a vibration like a teacup in a palsied hand. Bee's eyes suddenly go shiny, and Atlanta thinks, *She's about to cry, isn't she,* but she doesn't have to wait long to find out. It's like an earthquake breaking a dam: the ground booming, the river roaring, because suddenly Bee is sobbing as if her whole extended family just got killed and eaten by wolves on live television—her body shakes, her shoulders tighten in so far she might fold up into a wad. The grief rolls through her.

Atlanta wants to get up, hug her. But something keeps her rooted to the bed. Anger, still. Resentment. Some little part of her that says, *You deserved this.*

All she can do, then, is wait it out. Bee stands there, alone, sobbing in a way that is emotional, physical, and maybe even spiritual all at the same time. Whitey stares as if to say, *I don't understand what this human is doing.* Eventually, though, he's the one who plods over and sits right next to her, his one good eye looking up at Bee, his nose nuzzling her hand.

Maybe that's what helps to end it.

Like with all storms, this one drifts back out to sea, and soon Bee is left standing there, puffy-cheeked and pink-eyed, her face wet, her nose plugged. She sniffs and Atlanta tosses her a tissue box from her bedside.

Blow, honk, sputter. Two tissues, then three, then a fourth before all the demons are exorcised from her grief-struck sinuses.

Bee sits, staring off. Atlanta wonders if this is why the popular crowd ditched her. Pregnancy isn't sexy. Nothing popular about being preggo. Still—she's not showing yet, by the looks of it. Still a thin slip of a girl.

"So, ahh—" Atlanta starts to say.

"I want to hire you."

"Pardon?"

"I want your help. And I don't ask as a friend because I know that . . . that ship has probably sailed so far it's in Bora Bora by now. I can pay."

"I don't really get it," Atlanta says, but then all the sudden she *does* get it. She heard stories when she came back from Emerald Lakes. Bee was with the popular crowd by then, and the popular crowd sleeps around. She went through a handful of boyfriends

and she probably wasn't chaste with them. "You don't know who
the father is, do you?"

A slight, small shake of the head.

"And you want me to find the father?"

A small nod.

"No" is Atlanta's answer.

"What? Why . . . why not? I need your help."

Tiger won't stay caged for long, and here it comes, jumping
through the grass. "Right now, you need me because you think
I can do something for you." She hears the volume of her voice
going up, up, up. "Let's say those words again: you *need* me. But
when I needed you—where were you, huh? When my mama's last
boyfriend . . ." Her jaw clenches. It hurts to say it, so she doesn't.
"When I got sent away for months on end to some cuckoo cracker
factory, and I had to sit there day in and day out in group, and
take meds, and watch girls go deeper into crazytown, where were
you? Did you come and visit? Or was I just too bombed out of my
gourd, too much of a space-case, to remember?"

Bee stares down at her lap. "I didn't."

"No, I didn't think so. What *were* you doing while I was gone,
hmm? You and Petra and Susie. Huh, *Becky*, what were you doing?"

"Nothing, I—"

"Oh, you were doing something. You weren't just sitting on
your hands. You weren't stitching me a sampler that said *Welcome
home, bitch.* You were off making new friends. Shiny, popular
friends. You care to sorta . . . pick that apart for me? How'd that
happen, huh?"

"They . . . they just . . ." Her nostrils flare. She's having trouble with this. *Good,* Atlanta thinks. *This should be hard for you.*

Atlanta's anger is like a nail sticking up through her shoe. She can't shake it.

"They just *what*?"

"You were like a . . . celebrity. Like an, a . . . a what's the word? An infamous one. And . . . I was here. You left me alone and—"

"I left *you* alone? Oh, girl, you did not just say that."

"Wait! Wait, I don't mean it like that. I mean it like—I was just here, and they wanted to know more because of, I dunno, morbid curiosity. And, like, they thought it was cool. That I was cool. For having known you."

"They wanted to watch the car accident from behind a window. And you were supposed to be that window, right?"

Bee shrugs.

"Well, I'm glad I was able to be your stepladder. Even if that means I have to clean your boot print off my back."

"I'm sorry. Okay? What do you want me to say?"

"Nothing. I don't even want your apologies. I just want you to go."

"I said I'll pay."

"And I said no. Now go. Your money's no good here." She gets up, holds the door open.

Whitey whines.

And Bee, blinking back tears, hurries out of the room.

Door: *slam.*

———

Outside. Nighttime. Whitey's gotta go do his business—so he darts off, a white flash, looking for a place to deposit his leavings.

Atlanta stands out there for a while, thinking about when would be the right time to pop an Ambien, but then the breeze turns and a smell reaches her nose—a whiff of cigarette smoke. Every part of her tenses up as Paul comes walking up from the direction of their shed—a shed that looks half-collapsed like Whitey's head. "Hey," he says.

"Uh-huh" is all she says.

"You wanna talk about it?"

"Talk about what?"

"What happened at dinner. Or after. I heard some yelling."

"Just a spirited game of Connect Four is all."

He takes a few steps closer. He's got a screwdriver in his hand. "She was crying when she left."

"You know us womenfolk. Always on our periods, crying at every dish-soap commercial or country song."

Paul drops the cigarette butt, puts a foot on it, and does the twist. "I think we're maybe getting off on the wrong foot—"

"Throwing your cigarette butt on the ground like a careless shit won't do you any favors. You think I want my dog eating that? That's trash, and trash doesn't belong on the damn ground." *Or with my mama.*

A small, stiff smile, and he stoops over and fetches the butt before sliding it into his pocket. "You're right. I'm sorry."

"Whatcha need the screwdriver for?" She narrows her eyes.

"The door to your mother's bedroom. Hinge is loose."

"So, you're gonna fix it."

"That is the plan."

"Just gonna swoop in and fix everything."

"It's just a door hinge, I promise."

"Right. Sure." Out in the dark, near the edge of the corn, another flash of white lightning as Whitey follows a scent. "Then it'll be something else. The freezer in our cellar, maybe. Or the pipes in the bathroom that bang like a poltergeist when you turn on the shower. But I also know that eventually, that shit will turn around the other way. There'll come a point where you'll start messing things up instead of fixing them, because my mother? She has terrible taste in men. The last three men she dated, in order: One was a coke dealer in Virginia. The next was an alcoholic who was not a funny drunk but rather the kind who got angry, angry enough to punch a defenseless woman and knock out one of her teeth. The last of the lot was this smooth cut of rope who, as it turns out, had designs on the daughter instead of the mother. Turns out the daughter didn't fancy him very much and he paid a *very* steep price for his mistake."

Paul's silent for a while. It means he knows. Not that it should surprise Atlanta, because it was in the news, and likely Mama said something anyway. But there he is, shifting nervously from foot to foot.

"I'm a good guy," he says finally. "I'm a fireman."

"That don't make you a good guy. It just makes you a fireman. Something will come up and out, and when it does, I'll be there to see it. And I'll be there to deal with it and pick up the pieces of Arlene that you scattered all around."

"It's not like that. This will be different. How much you wanna bet?"

"It's never different. And I don't bet." Whitey comes snuffling and snorfling back over. He lifts his head, suddenly, staring at Paul, and then to her, and then back to Paul, as if he's not quite sure if he should be on alert or not. "Good night, Paul."

Atlanta puts Whitey in the garage, then goes back inside. Soon as she's in through her bedroom door, she dry-swallows an Ambien and waits for it to kick in. Eventually, it does. There on her bed, it's like she sinks into it at the same time her head floats separate—like something is drawing her down to little pieces, as if she's a soft dinner roll being pulled apart by probing hands. Part of her thinks to fight it. Panic arcs through her, quick as an electric current, but then she realizes: *This is what is supposed to happen.* For a moment, the room seems to be moving—furniture sliding around like it does on those cruise ship videos where the ship lists and tilts in a hard wave, and then she's down, down, down, zoned out, gone off the deep end and—

CHAPTER FIVE

Waking up is clean. Like a toothpick poked into and pulled out of a batch of fresh-baked brownies: there's nothing stuck there, no lingering feeling of oogyness, no baggage from sleep. The sleep itself felt . . . complete. Dreamless, dark, and deep.

It did the job. Whitey nuzzles her hand. Mama must've let him out of the garage early. He tends to whine and want out and Mama, she lets him.

It's time to go to school.

———

The day goes all right. She's not sleepy in class. Atlanta can actually sit there and pay attention. It doesn't make any of it *more interesting*—good as Ambien is, it can't make her care more about SOH-CAH-TOA or the Yorktown Campaign or Newton's Laws. But at least she stays awake long enough to be bored. That's something.

The one class she does like is English with Mrs. Strez. That surprises her. But it was something Mrs. Lewis said to her last year: *Poems and stories have a way of helping us make sense of things.* More and more, she's finding that true. In the little notebook she keeps in the shoebox under her bed, she's jotted down lines of poems she likes, or sentences from short stories they read in class. She's not sure she has it right, what the authors really were laying down, but she's also not sure it matters. Because once the writers are done with it, it's not theirs anymore.

It's hers.

(Plus, it doesn't hurt that Strez isn't docking her any points for failing to turn in her assignments. She's supposed to do homework, isn't she? Oops.)

In the computer lab, Shane and Kyle try to show her the stats on her YouTube video. Shane says, "Been a month since it posted, and now it has five thousand hits, and over a hundred comments." Kyle adds: "A lot of them are pretty nasty." Shane adds: "Never read the comments," and Atlanta agrees. She tells them she doesn't much care about any of this. The video's the video, and it's either gonna reach people who need it, or it won't.

"I have no time for people who aren't my people," she says.

Later that afternoon, Atlanta sees Bee winding her way through the crowded hallway between periods. A thought hits Atlanta like a hammer to the head: *It's like watching myself from last year.* The crowds part, almost imperceptibly, to let Bee pass. Nobody stares at her directly—no, that'd take too much moxie. That'd be too direct, too aggressive. But they shoot off a whole lotta side glances, heads turned one way, eyes looking back.

Which means they know she's on the outs.

Do they know she's pregnant?

Bee gets to her locker. Pops it open with a clang.

Something white pops out. She shrieks, steps back. Atlanta's not far, only ten feet away, and the stink hits her—it's shit. She smells bona fide feces. There, at Bee's feet, is a wadded-up diaper. A bit of brown at the edges.

Somebody went and dumped in a diaper. Or maybe put some dog crap in there. Then wadded it up, broke into her locker, and left her a present.

They *do* know.

Huh.

Again that dark thought hits Atlanta: *Serves you right.* She's not much for spiritual beliefs—at least, not any she understands in a Ten Commandments sort of way. But karma, that's something she can get behind. What you do comes back at you, like a whip biting you on your own chin, or a boomerang circling through the air. That's one of those phrases she has written in her notebook, actually. Something from Chaucer. Translated and paraphrased away from his old-timey way of writing: *And often the curse returns again to him that curseth, as a bird returns again to his own nest.* Chickens, home, roost.

Bee doesn't cry.

But she does turn around and see Atlanta watching her. She gives Atlanta a plaintive look. *See what they did? Now I'm just like you.* Or maybe Atlanta's reading too much into it.

Both of them turn away and go in opposite directions.

———

Day's over. Atlanta heads out to the school parking lot. She feels alert and aware. A change from the last couple weeks, where it's felt like she's just been drifting—floating like an old fast-food cup down a flooded gutter.

A football corkscrews through the air over her head. The smell of car exhaust fills her nose. A rumble from a nearby muscle car. A dull booming bass from some jumped-up Honda. Everybody's laughing or making out or just horsing around—some are yelling, some are arguing. Others still are posturing and preening.

Some folks say hi to her now. It surprises her even still, though it probably shouldn't. They've seen the video. They heard the stories. She's not the poison pill she was at the end of last year. But it still doesn't feel real.

(Or maybe it's that it doesn't feel earned. If that even matters.)

No real engagement, yet—nobody's asking her how her day went or saying they wanna hang out after class. But a lifted chin. A *hey* here and there. A guy from the wrestling team, Wes Newman, a guy she doesn't even know, walks by her and gives her a set of fingerguns and says, "'Sup, Atlanta." First she thinks, *How's he even know my name,* but then she remembers: *Everybody knows my name.*

She's not sure if she likes it or if it freaks her out. Maybe both.

Far end of the lot is Shane's car. He always parks on the fringes, always at the very edge—"I don't want anybody opening their door and dinging the paint," he says, and every time he says it, she just shakes her head. A little dinged paint, so dang what. Life is all about dinged paint.

But as she's walking, she sees a familiar car. Orange hatchback. Bee's in the driver's seat. Just sitting there, hands on the wheel, car engine idling.

Atlanta thinks, *Well, okay, whatever,* and keeps on walking. But then she catches it.

Someone's keyed a message into the side of Bee's car.

PREG MEANS YOU PUT OUT

Nearby, she hears laughing. It's all too familiar: Mitchell Erickson's smooth, car-salesman laugh. He stands there at the back end of his sports car, watching Bee's hatchback like a hungry vulture. Next to him stands Russo and Lanky—two more of his baseball buddies—and Samantha Gwynn-Rudin. They're all having a blast, smirking like mean little kids, chuckling and sharing looks and elbowing each other like, *har har, haw haw, ain't we a clever batch of assholes.*

And then it all falls apart. All the bad feelings Atlanta has built up for Bee—this is the knife that cuts that knot clean in half. If Bee's on the receiving end of misery from these chuckledicks, well, that puts them, by extension, on the same side of things. Atlanta pulls her bag high on her shoulder. She feels naked without any weapons—they got metal detectors at the school, so it's not like she can bring in a knife or a can of bear mace or anything—but she thinks, *I got my words, and right now that's all I need.* She starts to march toward them.

Mitchell looks over, sees her coming. His smile falls away like the last shingle blown off an old roof. His face twists. The others follow his gaze.

Then comes the revving of an engine.

Bee's engine.

The hatchback suddenly guns it—wheels spinning, spraying up gravel in every direction before suddenly lurching backward like a drunken horse. It bolts in reverse toward the gathered chuckledicks. Mitchell yelps, and the other three cry out and hurry away—

—just as Bee's hatchback slams the ass-end of Mitchell Erickson's red Lexus.

Metal crunches against metal.

Mitchell stares, gaping in horror. "You whore!" he screams.

Bee rolls down her window, and something pelts him right in the chest.

A diaper. A full-on, shit-brimming diaper.

It leaves a little brown mark on Mitchell's Abercrombie shirt. Samantha Gwynn-Rudin cracks up.

Bee peels away in another cloud of gravel and exhaust. As her little car speeds off, the bumper from the Lexus groans—

—then drops off into the stones with a *crunch-clunk*.

Atlanta laughs so hard she almost cries.

———

When she gets home, she calls Bee, leaves her a voice mail: "I'm in. Tomorrow's Saturday, so meet me at my house around the crack of noon."

CHAPTER SIX

They walk along the tree line out back of Atlanta's house. Sometimes the trees break and they can see the plumes of smoke or steam coming off one of the PP&L power plants. Atlanta keeps her eyes up—wary, like a wolf, she tells herself. (Though a small part of her thinks: *Scared, like a deer.*) Bee keeps her head down, kicking at stones and dandelions. Any stone or flower she kicks, Whitey goes after it and eats it. Just gobbles it down like the whole world is kibble.

"I want a cigarette so damn bad," Bee says. "I don't even smoke. Just, like, at parties sometimes. But man, now that I'm all ... stuffed up with this baby, I just *want* things. Things I can't even explain. Yesterday, I wanted a Tastykake—a Butterscotch Krimpet—soooo fucking hard. I just couldn't shake it. Couldn't get it out of my head."

Atlanta glances over. "You get one?"

"I did." Bee hesitates, then smiles all guilty-like. "I got a whole bag."

"A whole bag? Dang. You sure that's a baby in there and not some kind of starving wolverine?"

She shrugs. "After eating that many I think this baby's turned into a Butterscotch Krimpet. I'll give birth and eat it right up." She pats her belly. "Sorry, baby." Then she says: "I miss this. You and me talking like this. I couldn't say weird stuff like that to the other girls. They'd stare at me like I had a second head growing out of the middle of my chest."

"Don't," Atlanta says. "Don't do that. Don't try to lather my ass up. I'm here for the job, not anything else." She hears the meanness coming out of her, lashing like a stingray's tail. "You gonna take care of that thing?"

Bee stops walking. "What?"

"Take care of it. Go to a doctor and—you know, the baby vacuum."

"An abortion?"

"That is what they call it, yeah."

"No." She stands, aghast. A wind kicks up. "Atlanta, I go to church."

"So?"

"They don't . . . we don't agree with that."

"You're having this baby, then."

"Damn right I am."

"Oh. I just figured . . ." Her words get lost coming out of her mouth. Instead she asks: "How'd everyone know?"

"That I'm preggo? Susie and Petra. Had to be them." She sighs and scowls. "I went to the appointment with my mom and then after I called Susie bawling. I told Petra the next day and then the two of them told . . . well, whoever. Probably Samantha. Nobody keeps a secret from her."

"Shit."

"Yeah."

Gossip at school is like a disease. It's in the air. You can't help catching it and sharing it.

They keep on in silence for a little while. Whitey chases, and eats, a few flitting cabbage moths. Then, just inside the trees—a couch. Old white leather, like something out of the eighties or nineties. The couch has lost most of its definition: a sagging blob now, which Atlanta thinks of as an old stripper's boob. But it's still comfy, even if it smells like the mold of a long damp. She steps through a bit of briar, twigs snapping underneath her feet. Then she plops down.

Bee walks over, plops down, too. "Been a while since I've sat here."

"Yeah." Atlanta doesn't want another trip on the Nostalgia Choo-Choo, so she changes the subject back to the one at hand: "I don't know why you need my help. I'm not some kind of baby wizard—I'm not Obi-Gyn Kenobi, I don't have Jedi powers to help you figure out which guy you slept with stuck a proper acorn into your dirt. Get a paternity test. Call Maury, get on his show. Why do you need me?"

Bee leans forward on the couch, hands on the sides of her head. Her thumbs run along her jawline, up to her temples, massaging circles. She breathes in, out, in, out, like she's having contractions—but while Atlanta is no *baby doctor*, she's pretty sure it's hella early to be having those.

"Sorry," Bee says. "Feeling a little queasy."

"Oh. Morning sickness, right?"

A half shrug from Bee. "Sorta."

"What is it, then?"

"I don't . . ." She blinks back tears. "I don't know who the father is because I don't know who had sex with me."

Bee sits back, stares at Atlanta. A hard, unblinking, unswerving stare. A look that says, *This is how it is, this is how I gotta get through this,* like she's rooting down and pressing on the accelerator even though she knows she's about to drive off a cliff.

"Bee, are you telling me—"

"I went to a party. End of summer. And everything was going good. But I got drunk. Real drunk, I guess. I . . . blacked out and . . ."

"Oh, Bee. Jesus."

"Yeah. Jesus." She sniffs. Pulls out a tissue, wipes her nose. All dainty. Bee could be like that. She could hang with Atlanta and they could make funny, horrible jokes. And they could smoke weed and listen to eighties hair metal or Kanye (Bee wouldn't listen to country), but always in there was the good church girl. Just a hint of being proper. A rusty pickup with a shiny chrome bumper.

"Did you . . . talk to the cops?"

"Why?"

"Last I checked, rape is illegal."

"I dunno that it was . . . rape."

"It's rape. You get drunk, somebody sticks it in you without your sober and enthusiastic say-so, that's called *rape.*"

Bee stiffens. "I don't like calling it that."

Atlanta feels her own heart going like the leg of an itchy rabbit. She hears a high-pitched whine. A smell hits her. *The* smell. The sharp, skunky tang of expended gunpowder. She hears the *bang* right in her ears, like a gun going off just inches from her head. She visibly flinches. Whitey senses it. Comes over, nuzzles her knee, and puts his chin on her thigh, staring up at her with that one soulful eye. It's enough. She goes from feeling like a boat lost in a storm-churned sea to dropping an anchor—the ocean is still crashing against her, but at least she can stay in one place and not get swept away.

"You call it what you like," she mutters. "I'll help you."

"What's the cost?"

"A thousand." She just makes that number up. Then she adds something she's heard in detective stories: "And expenses."

Bee nods. "I got the money."

"Good."

"Where will you start?"

A long sigh. She doesn't really know because, again, this isn't her bag of tricks, is it? Protecting someone from a bully is easy enough. You stand between the human monster and their target, and you put some rebar in your spine and plant your damn feet as deep in the dirt as you can. Then you put your gun up—metaphorically or literally—and you say, *This far, no further.* But solving mysteries like she's part of the Scooby gang—it feels uncomfortable. Unlikely.

Maybe even impossible.

Still. She said she'd do it, and so she'll do it.

"The party," she says. "Guess I need to know about that."

———

As she walks, the barns and fields she passes become houses—at first, just a few ranches, or a couple small developments tucked away in areas once all green or all trees, but then the houses get nicer and nicer. The road gets steeper, too, and Atlanta thinks: *This is what it's like to go to Rich Person Heaven.* Climb higher and the trees get prettier, the barns become decorative, houses with brown siding become houses made of old stone. And those houses give way to bigger and bigger ones until they're up in the minimansions: houses with whole extra wings, with swimming pools and balconies and lawns sculpted by teams of ill-paid immigrants. Until there, up on a hill all its own, is Samantha's house.

Samantha Gwynn-Rudin lives, of course, up on Gallows Hill. At its very peak. Moneyland. Richie-rich-ville. Her father's a lawyer, her mother a self-help "guru," whatever that is. Atlanta figures anybody who calls themselves a guru is a know-nothing no-how con artist who just wants to make money pretending to be an expert. When she was in Emerald Lakes, some of the counselors seemed keen to get the girls to read self-help books, but those books always seemed too wispy, too hippy-dippy, to make sense to Atlanta. Eat more kale, they say, except who wants to eat an ugly ornamental plant? Meditate and do yoga, except nothing's more stressful than trying to twist your body up into a knotty shoelace. One book just said, *Love yourself,* as if that's the easiest thing in the world. Just love yourself. Just do it. As if the reason you don't love yourself is your own darn fault—gosh, if only you'd flip the Happy Little Light Switch inside your brain, you'd feel better.

Idiots.

Of course, the other side of it is that they drug-bomb you into bliss or unconsciousness. Try to medicate your demons back into their cage. That doesn't work much, either. It's like the bodies that serial killers try to hide in lakes and rivers—they always float back up. You can't just hide the bad feelings or forget about them. Most of the kids Atlanta knows at school are on some pill or another.

Then half of them sell their pills to each other—or back to a dude like Guy, who then resells for a profit.

Anyway. Samantha's house isn't a regular house so much as it is the White House. It really looks like that. The columns out front. The big white toothy face—the door the mouth, the windows the eyes—with wings on both sides of it. Roses along each end. A mix of pink and red, like the colors of skin and blood.

A garage sits off to the side—a garage with four bay doors, all closed. One car sits parked outside: a lemon-chiffon Mercedes convertible.

Must be nice, she thinks. Same thing she always thinks when she sees how the other half lives—though, not really the other *half* so much as *the other tiny fraction of humanity.* Whatever.

Atlanta pulls her bag over her shoulder, heads to the front door.

Ding-dong. It's literally one of those doorbells that goes *ding-dong.*

The door opens. A little Latina woman stands there in a blue blouse and jeans. Ruby-red lips and eyes pinched behind wrinkled pockets of skin. Her lips are puckered up like a too-tight coin purse. "Yes?"

"Uh. Hi."

The woman gives Atlanta an up-and-down look, then visibly dismisses her. "We don't want any. Thank you." She starts to backpedal and close the door—

Atlanta sticks her foot in. "Whoa, hey, hold on. I'm looking for Samantha."

"Miss Samantha is in the back. Are you one of her friends?"

"Let's say yes?"

A moment of hesitation before a curt nod. "Come."

She waves Atlanta on, then heads into the house. The woman moves like a tiny locomotive: legs pistoning into an aggressive shuffle, arms like the wheels running along parallel tracks. Every step looks like she's thinking, *I think I can, I think I can, chugga chugga woo-woo.*

Steam should be coming out her ears.

Atlanta has to hurry to keep up.

The house is—well, if the outside is mostly white, the inside is mostly peach. Or almost peach—the floors are white marble shot through with threads of blush. Pink roses on a nearby table. A mirror framed in warm gold. A family portrait hangs opposite: a mother with severe bangs so sharp and so black they look cut with the devil's own straight razor; a mustached father gone bald on top, a big goofy grin on his face like he's got a steady marquee of dad jokes running through his head at all times; a little sister with puffy cheeks and braces; and finally, Samantha. Looking like murder is on her mind, like the family photo is so miserable she'd rather be sipping on a cup of cat pee.

(The Latina woman is not in the photo.)

They go through the house, through the kitchen, to the back door—which opens onto a huge stone patio the color of dirty snow. It's so big that Atlanta's pretty sure there's more square footage out here than in her own house. Got a grill built in. Tables. Umbrellas. Automated awnings.

And a pool shaped like a long stick of gum.

Samantha sits out back in a cherry-red two-piece. Sunglasses with white frames that almost wash out against her porcelain-pale face. She's got a cell phone in her hand turned sideways, the phone resting on the flat of her tummy. Her thumbs move fast on the keyboard, twitching like the antennae on an irritated ant.

"Miss Samantha," the woman announces, "you have a guest."

The thumbs stop typing. Samantha cranes her head back.

She lifts her sunglasses and a big smile crosses her face.

"Atlanta. Wow. You. Here. *Huh*."

Atlanta just shrugs. "Wonders never cease, I guess."

"Yeah, no kidding." To the woman, Samantha says: "Delfina, you can go now. Go on. TTFN."

"Yes, Miss Samantha."

Delfina turns, and Samantha calls after her: "Don't forget. I need socks. And if you're going out later and my parents aren't coming home for dinner, I want Thai food. So get me Thai food. But not from the close place. The other place. With the good noodles."

"Yes, Miss Samantha."

Then the woman is gone, back inside the house.

Samantha says, "Delfina's our house manager. Which is a fancy shorthand way of saying nanny, maid, personal assistant, blah blah blah. I love her. I do. But she's like a robot you program. She's only as good as the instructions you give her. And her name means *dolphin*, which, y'know. Bitch, please. Dolphins are long and lean and beautiful. She's short and squat, like a fire hydrant. What's Cuban for 'fire hydrant'?"

"I sure don't know."

Samantha shrugs. "Welcome to my *casa*. There's some Spanish for you."

"Thanks."

"Sit down."

Atlanta thinks, *No, I'll stand*, but that feels somehow more awkward. She hates that she feels awkward at all. But it's hard not to. Samantha's got bank in the accounts and junk in the trunk. She's thin where she needs to be, thick in the other places, sharp at the edges. Skin so pale it might as well be a saucer of grass-fed milk. Atlanta feels dumpy in her presence. Her hair, too wild. Her freckles, too strange. Hips thick, arms think, skin soft, too soft, like a kangaroo pouch.

Ugly and poor. That's how she feels.

She hates Samantha for that. More than a little.

Still, she takes a seat on a lounge chair. Leans forward. Can't get comfortable in part because everything about this situation makes her feel uncomfortable. She starts to say something, but Samantha interrupts:

"You wanna get high?" From the far side of her lounge chair she grabs a bong. Tall glass stem—hot pink glass. The bottom of it a round bulb filled with water. "This is super primo stuff. Hydroponic. This stuff is called . . ." She pulls out a little baggie and scrutinizes the printed label. "Eternal Sunshine. Ugh, who names these things?"

"I'm good," Atlanta says, staring at the door, suddenly nervous. "Delfina doesn't know that you have that out here, right?"

"She knows. She doesn't care. It's my dad we have to worry about. He hates that I smoke this stuff. He's such a dong."

"And your mom?"

Shrug. "God, I get the stuff from *her* dealer. She's cool with it. Believes it's all part of the *psychic repair* process." She snorts. "It's bullcrap. For me it's just part of the *getting really freaking high* process." Samantha, looking disappointed, sets the bong down. "So. What's up? Why are you here, exactly?"

"You had a party."

"I have had lots of parties."

"I'm interested in one in particular."

"Oh?" Then she sits forward, suddenly. "*Ohhh.* You're here on *official business.* This is a Very Special Atlanta Burns visit, isn't it?"

"You make it sound kinda douchey when you say it like that."

"It's a gift. What party?"

"End of summer."

Samantha nods. "I remember it. So?"

"Well, I was talking to—"

Delfina pops the sliding door again. "Miss Samantha?"

"God, what?" Samantha says, sneering.

"A man is here to see you. He says he's your teacher?"

Atlanta frowns. "Teacher?"

But the look on Samantha's face changes. Her confident, take-no-shit veneer shows cracks—and panic comes shining through. She shoots Atlanta a look: "Hey. What time is it?"

"I dunno. I got here around five, I think."

"*God.*" To Delfina: "Two minutes. Then bring him back."

"Okay, Miss Samantha." Then the woman is gone.

Atlanta starts to say, "Why would a teacher—"

"It's not a fuckin' teacher. You need to go."

"Now?"

"I don't mean later. Don't go through the house. Go around the front." She waggles an impatient finger toward the gate at the far end of the patio. "Gate's unlocked, just go out that way."

"I still need to know about that party."

"Now's not a good time!"

Atlanta stands, hikes her bag over her shoulder. "When is?"

"*Later.*"

Something scratches at the back of Atlanta's mind like a raccoon pawing at a trashcan, hoping to knock it over. For now, she nods, doesn't bother saying good-bye, and heads out the back gate like she's told.

She starts to round the house—alongside another run of roses, these as white as a unicorn's innocence—but then she stops.

Her way of doing things and getting stuff done isn't about just letting stones sit there. Atlanta likes to turn them over. One time she was poking through the woods with her daddy and she found an old piece of plywood rotting into the ground. She started to lift it up, and her father warned her, said she might get splinters, might not like what she found underneath. She did it anyway. Found the usual suspects: pill bugs, earthworms, ants.

And a cat skeleton. Skin draped over it like a blanket that had gone stiff and brittle.

She got a couple splinters, like Daddy warned. Didn't matter. She hasn't learned since. (And truth be told, finding a cat skeleton was kinda cool.)

So, now, she thinks: *I don't get things done by taking other people's advice.* She wants to know what's going on, that means getting her hands dirty and splintered and seeing what hides underneath.

From the back patio: voices. Samantha. And an older man.

Atlanta heads back in through the gate. "Hey," she starts to say, "I think I forgot my—"

There stands Samantha, arms crossed, almost like she's cold even though the day is warm. A man stands across from her. Atlanta doesn't recognize him. Pink polo shirt. Nice khakis. White sneakers like you'd see on some golf asshole.

He's got a beard, but it's cut so short and his hair is so blond that it almost looks like part of his tanned face. He turns toward Atlanta. Looks, what, late forties, maybe? He smiles big and broad, slides his hands into his pockets. Atlanta can feel his gaze going up and down her like he's measuring her for something.

"Well, hey, now," he says, not taking his eyes off Atlanta. "Who's this, Samantha? Friend of yours?"

"I *guess*," Samantha answers. The way she says it—face scrunched up like a wadded-up Kleenex—says how much she believes it. "Atlanta was just leaving."

"I forgot something," Atlanta says, improvising. "I think I maybe left my phone here or something."

Samantha narrows her eyes. "I don't see it. Sorry. Bye."

"Hold on, hold on," the man says. To Samantha: "Is she cool?" Then to Atlanta: "Are you cool?"

Atlanta shrugs. "I'm all right, I guess."

He laughs. But again he returns his gaze to her. It's a dissecting stare—like she's a crab claw and he's looking for the meat.

"She's not cool," Samantha says. "And like I said, she was just—"

But the guy, he reaches forward. He's got a card in his hand. Like a business card. No name on it, just a phone number printed there.

"You ever want work," he says, "call me."

Atlanta stares at the card like he's handing her a turd. But then she conjures a fake smile and an empty stare and takes it. "What kind of work?"

"Sammy here will fill you in."

"Sweet. Looking forward to that, *Sammy*."

Samantha says: "Uh-huh. Now, time for you to *go*."

"Uh-huh," the man says. "Run along now. But keep that number close."

Atlanta holds up the card and shakes it at him like it's a winning Lotto ticket. "You bet I will, mister. You bet I will."

———

"You got an admirer," Mama says when she comes in the door. Mama, who's pinballing around the kitchen, pulling toast out of the toaster and popping it in her mouth, leaving crumbs everywhere. There, on the kitchen nook table, is a big bouquet of flowers. Red roses. Little white flowers, too—baby's breath.

"Who're they from?" she asks as Whitey comes up, sits so close he can lean his head against her lip. She scratches him behind his one ear.

"I don't know, sugarbear," Mama says, whirling about—grabbing car keys, taking a bite of toast. Around a mouthful of food she adds: "I might've peeked. Like the kids say, *I don't want to spoiler it for you.*"

Atlanta cocks an eyebrow. "Pretty sure the kids don't say that. Hey, where are you headed, anyway?"

"Off to work. Evening shift."

"You didn't tell me about this job before."

"Oh. Well. You've been so . . . busy." And that last word hangs there funny, like a painting dangling cockeyed from its last nail on the wall. It's a word with a lot of weight to it, a sponge soaked through and made heavy. Mama knows. She knows what Atlanta's been up to, maybe. Hasn't said a word about it. Which both thrills and hurts Atlanta at the same time. Thrills her because, *yeah, stay out of my dang business, lady*. But it hurts her, too, because, shouldn't she care? Shouldn't she actually play the I'm-Your-Mother card and at least try to stop Atlanta from putting herself in danger? Suddenly, it hurts more than it thrills.

"You didn't tell me about Paul, either."

"I didn't want to . . . surprise you with it."

"And yet, that's exactly what you did." She leans in, squints. "You were trying to hide Mister Fireman, weren't you?"

"'Lanta, I gotta go."

"Yeah. Okay. Go, then."

Mama Arlene scoots by, gives Atlanta a little kiss on the cheek, and tornadoes her way out the door.

The flowers, then.

Atlanta fishes through them, sees the card, reaches for it—

A thorn pokes the tip of her pointer. She recoils. A bead of blood swells up like a bubble at the end of her finger, and she pops it in her mouth to suck on it. She grabs the card with her other hand.

Atalanta—
Wanted to say sorry for bein a creeper.
Wanna go to homecoming?
—Damon

Go to Homecoming? With him?

"Learn to spell my name first, jerkwad," she says. She flicks the card in the trash. Then dumps the roses in there, too.

CHAPTER SEVEN

Fire crackles. Embers pop and whirl.

"Pull!" Atlanta yells. Chomp-Chomp (oops, *Steven*) hauls back with the clay thrower, which is this flexible plastic rod that holds a clay pigeon in its grip. Atlanta doesn't know why the heck they call it a clay pigeon, because it doesn't look like a pigeon at all: it's just a round disc, like a small and brittle Frisbee.

He lets it fly. The disc spins through the dark. It's bright enough that she can see it in the night—she whips the shotgun up and doesn't bother doing much aiming. Not enough time to think about it. You overthink it? You miss. Instead, she kind of lets her mind go blank. Like she's just an extension of the gun tucked tight against her shoulder, and so she sucks in a breath and leads the front bead at the end of the Winchester ahead of the disc and—

Bang.

The little .410 bucks against her.

The journey of the clay pigeon is interrupted—the orange disc jerks in midair like someone tugged on it with an invisible wire. Bits fall away. All of it tumbles into darkness out over the corn.

"I got a piece of it," she says.

Some half-assed applause from behind her, from the usual crowd of miscreants: Shane, Kyle, Josie Dunderchek. Eddie's out— got some sorta stomach bug, said he just wants to sit on the couch all night and binge-watch *Arrow*. (Atlanta asked what that was, and Eddie just said: "Two words: Stephen Amell. Two more words: salmon ladder." None of that made any sense, so she thought it a good time to end the call.) No Damita (she reminds herself again to ask Shane about that). No Guy, either—he's working, he said.

Josie hops up from her chair by the fire, and she picks up a stick Whitey had been slobbering on earlier. She pitches it into the darkness. The dog takes after it fast—he's a ghostly streak.

"Kinda dog is this?" Josie asks.

"A Dogo Argentino," Atlanta says, breaking the barrel. Wisps of gunsmoke drift up as she plucks the shell out and tosses it into the grass. It clatters against the dozen others there. The smell still brings that night back to her, the night she first learned what power this weapon had—or, maybe, what power *she* had. But she presses on. Can't let the memory control her. "Argentine Mastiff. People think they're fighting dogs, but that ain't quite right."

Josie pitches the stick. "Seems like a sweetheart to me. What the heck happened to his head?"

It's Shane who speaks up: "You really don't know?"

"What? Uh-uh, no," Josie says.

He starts to go into it: "Dog got shot in the head. By a *cop*. This guy named Petry—oh, man, I should start at the beginning—"

Atlanta plunks down by the fire. "No, you shouldn't. I don't wanna talk about . . . any of that." Doesn't want to think about it, either. The fear hits her when she goes to sleep and when she wakes—wondering suddenly if Whitey is okay. Did she forget to bring him inside, and is he out dead on the road somewhere, or shot by some hunter, or strung up by Petry and cut into like he's a slab of beef made for steaks? She thinks: is Mama okay? Is Shane? And then the worst thought of them all: is Chris okay? And that answer, always and forever, is *no*, no he is not. Chris is dead and gone. That, thanks to Petry.

Maybe thanks to her, too.

She reaches down, grabs the bottle of cheap pink wine from underneath her chair—stuff is supposed to taste like strawberries, but mostly it tastes like Kool-Aid mixed with some stripper's perfume. Still, it's fuzzed up the edges and softened the sharp corners of all her ugly thoughts. Drinking is good sometimes for putting corks on the ends of forks. So she's less likely to poke out her own damn eye.

"Sorry," Shane says.

"Question I wanna ask," she says to Shane, "is where's Damita?"

He just shrugs.

Steven says: "Uh-oh."

"I dunno where she is," Shane says, staring into the fire.

"They broke up!" Kyle offers, because that's Kyle. Most folks have a bouncer at the door between their brain and their mouth, someone to make sure that all the thoughts inside don't make it into the air where actual human beings can hear them. Kyle doesn't have that. He just *says* stuff. Some folks say he's got Asperger's. Either way, Atlanta likes him. He's a good old-fashioned dorkus.

"Spill it," Atlanta says. She passes the wine bottle around the fire. Everyone takes a sip, the pink not-quite-wine sloshing around.

"She wanted to . . ." He clears his throat. "Make love."

"Oh, so she was DTF," Josie says.

"I don't get it," Steven says. "What's the prob?"

"The *prob* is," Shane snaps, "I'm not ready."

Atlanta leans forward, elbows on her knees. "For real? Most teen boys I meet are pretty much ready all the time. You dudes are like shook-up pop cans. It's kinda why most of you suck, actually. It's like you can't just be *people*, you gotta be these jumped-up hormone tornadoes."

Josie offers a high five for that. Atlanta's not sure what she's high-fiving, exactly, but she's not one to reject a proper high-five opportunity. They slap hands. Pow.

"Okay, okay," Shane says. "I'm ready. I'm just not *ready*. Like, I want it to be special. Dinner. Dancing. Roses."

"Uck, roses," Atlanta says.

He gives her a quizzical look but keeps talking: "I just want it to be right."

"You want to make love, not just . . . y'know. *Bang*," Steven says, with some almost surprising insight. He makes grabby hands and Kyle passes the wine over. He plugs the bottle to his lips, glurk, glurk, glurk. "I totally get it, dude."

Josie says: "I say, hell with all that. Just go over there. Bring your suave little-man self, and lay her down and—" She pounds her fist into her palm. "You nail her to the floor like she's carpet."

"That's very . . . aggressive," Atlanta says.

"Yeah, wow," Shane says. "I just want her back. You think it'll work?"

Josie shrugs, takes the bottle. "Sometimes the ladies want dudes who are . . . forward. They want someone who's confident. They want to be *wanted*."

"Yeah," Atlanta says, "not me. That's creepy to me. I mean, it sounds good on paper and all, but most guys are too dipshitty to figure out where the line is between asking for what they want and just . . . taking it. Besides, what do you know? You like girls. You're a lezzie, right?"

Everyone goes silent. Firelight flickering in all the eyes that turn toward Atlanta. Jaws go slack. Nobody blinks. *Uh-oh.*

"Can I not say that?" Atlanta asks. "I just thought . . ."

"Who told you that?" Josie asks, suddenly gruff. She stands up, maybe a little tipsy. "I'm not gay."

"I just heard—"

"Heard what?"

"That you were?"

"From who?"

"From *whom*," Shane corrects, and Josie flicks him in the ear. He yelps.

"I dunno who I heard it from," Atlanta says. She stands, too, holding up both hands as if in surrender. "You just *hear* things. Rumor and whatnot."

"Oh, good. Believe *rumor*. I thought you were better than that."

"Well, that, and you kinda seem gay. Maybe a little butch?"

"*You* seem gay, too. You ever think about that? You with your . . . fuckin' damn Army jacket and your big hips and carrying a *gun*. Shit, do you wear makeup? Do you even *own* a makeup brush or know what concealer does? I rock makeup, man. My lips are red like dynamite. You know how much time it takes to make my eyelashes look longer and thicker than they are? God, I own an *eyelash comb*."

"I didn't even know those existed," Atlanta says. She chews on the inside of her cheek as Josie stands there, her fists relaxing back into hands as her chest rises and falls. "So, you're not gay, then."

"Ugh," Shane says. "Atlanta, let it go already—"

"I am," Josie says, suddenly, eyes wide. A sharp gasp comes out of her mouth, and this look crosses her face: something between exhilaration and fear. "I am a lesbian." Another gasp. She covers her own mouth as if to stop words from coming out.

"I am so confused," Atlanta says.

"Wait," Shane says. "Did you just come out?"

Josie, still covering her mouth, gives a small nod.

Atlanta feels it. Oh. *Oh*. Whoa-dang.

"You ever told anyone else?" she asks Josie.

"No," Josie says, quiet as a mouse fart. Then, louder: "It just . . . happened."

Atlanta holds up her hand: "I think *now* is the time for the high five."

Josie laughs—a mad sound, an uncontrolled noise, a combination between a giggle and a cackle—and then gives a helluva high five. Atlanta's palm is left stinging from the slap. They recirculate the bottle back to Josie and she takes a long celebratory glug-glug-glug.

———

She's inside looking through her mother's secret, not-secret liquor stash (seriously, it's just an unlocked cabinet in the downstairs bathroom), picking out another bottle of too-cheap, too-sweet wine.

A floorboard creaks behind her.

Her blood pressure shoots up—all parts of her clench.

Then Steven clears his throat noisily. "It's just me. Just me."

"You have *got* to learn to stop sneaking up on people. And by people, I mean me. I about brained you with one of these bottles."

"Sorry."

"It's fine, what is it?"

But he doesn't say anything. In the half-light bleeding in from the kitchen, she can see the look of eagerness on his face. Like a man summoning courage. Like maybe he's gonna jump off a cliff or try to make love to a grizzly bear or something, or maybe like—

Oh, no.

"Last time we found ourselves here, we made out," she says.

"Yeah."

"And you were thinking of maybe trying out that move again."

"Worth a shot?" He quickly hurries more words out of his big-teethed mouth: "But, but, but—really, what I wanted was to ask you a question."

"Shoot."

"You wanna go to Homecoming? It's, uhh, it's next week and—"

"I do not," she says without hesitation. "Not with you. Not without you." Even just the *thought* of going to a dance makes her skin crawl like it's covered in breakdancing roaches. Being close to so many people. All of them swaying like zombies to music that sucks so hard it could pull a baby through a garden hose. All in the half dark, with hands and heat and—a lurch of nausea derails that train of thought. It's the wine, in part: she's feeling fuzzy and strange, still high off Josie trusting them all enough to share what she shared. But it's sitting sickly-sweet in her stomach now, too. "Sorry, no dance."

"Well, um, maybe we—"

"Maybe we could be friends."

"But we kissed."

"And like I said then: it was a big step. Huge! I didn't hate it. It didn't make me throw up. That sounds like an insult but it isn't. It's a compliment of the highest order, dude. But we're not a thing. Not gonna happen. Okay?"

"Okay."

"And you'll drop it? Because I'm asking you to drop it."

He mimes dropping something, like a brick. "Dropped."

She holds out her hand, pinky thrust out like a knife. "Pinky-swear?"

They pinky-wrestle, and he agrees.

And that's when Shane starts screaming her name from the outside.

———

It's Ecky. Joey Eckhart.

One half of her face is swollen and black, like a gone-rotten pumpkin. The firelight highlights the rime of crusted blood around her nose, the split lip, the one eye forced halfway closed by swelling. Joey's been crying but isn't now, and she has this faraway look in her eye. A look of cold, dead iron.

She came walking down the driveway like the stumbling undead, according to Shane. Just shuffling along, beaten to hell and back.

Didn't take long to get out of her who did this. Because it's not much of a surprise. Hank Crayley. Jumped Joey about a mile away from the Sheetz gas station—Joey was taking a walk down there to buy some snacks and one of those machine-made cappuccinos, and then a junker pickup pulled up, and they just held her against the tailgate and beat her ass good. Joey lifts up her shirt and man, all those bruises. Like wine soaking into a white carpet.

All Joey says is, "At least they didn't kill me." But her lip is fat and so it comes out, *Least dey diddit gill bee.* Then she sits down at the fire and asks if she can just hang out for a while.

But Atlanta, she's got her blood tumbling in her ears, pounding at her temples like war drums. A heat comes off her. She's mad, too mad, scary mad—part of it is the wine washing away any second thoughts she might have, the way waves pull sand away from the beach and strip it bare.

"You need the hospital?" she asks Joey. Even in that simple, innocuous question she hears the serrated edge in her voice.

Joey shakes her head. "No. Just wanna sit here. Can I have some wine?"

Shane passes Joey the wine.

Atlanta says, "Okay. You guys stay here." She picks up the shotgun and a handful of .410 shells that she shoves into her jacket pocket. "Steven, you and me, c'mon. Let's take a ride on your quad."

———

They wait in the darkness of the junkyard. Heaps and mounds of rusted, forgotten things making a maze out there in the darkness. Cars and washing machines and scrap piles of corrugated tin and copper. It's junk, but it's worth money, too, which is why you get kids and junkies hitting up houses under construction and pulling out the pipes and wires to sell. Atlanta figures that explains the tall fence and loops of razor wire surrounding it all.

A few lights on around the perimeter, but it's easy enough to hide in a patch of tall grass and weeds. Steven said that sometimes Crayley and his boys come here to hang out, drink, smoke, shoot that bow and arrow of his at makeshift targets—targets that sometimes include cats, he says.

Right now, it's dark, and comes a point where her blood starts to cool and the wine buzz starts to wear down like a worn pencil eraser—she thinks, *Well, screw it, let's just head back*, but then: headlights cut through the night.

A pickup truck. Hank Crayley's pickup: a pitted, pocked thing. Loud and grumbling, the muffler hanging low like a dingleberry off its ass. It drives up to the front gate and waits a few seconds, the truck idling with an occasional *bang*, some kinda death metal coming out of the open windows. Then the gate buzzes and clicks. The chain-link rattles, and the whole thing turns out to be mechanized—triggered, she guesses, by a control inside his truck. It groans and squeaks and opens slowly, dragging a furrow across the ground, scattering stones.

"Stay here," she whispers to Steven. "Anybody comes? *You run.*"

"Wait," he says, but she's already off like a shot because time is ticking.

The pickup is already in the junkyard—and the gate starts to close behind it. She hurries sideways just as it rattle-clacks shut.

Atlanta sneaks up alongside a two-stack of refrigerators lying on their sides. She ducks down, out of the range of light coming off the truck and from the bulb dangling loose from a telephone pole not far from what must be the junkyard's "office." The truck's engine finally cuts, and Crayley hops out.

The red cherry from a cigarette glows. Smoke above his head like a hovering ghost. "Dad!" he calls. "Yo! *Dad.*" No answer. Mumbles: "Asshole."

He pulls a set of keys, then heads over to a nearby wrecker parked not far from the office, in the shadow of a stack of cars smashed flat like apple fritters. Pops the door. She thinks: *This is my chance.* Again her blood boils. She thinks about Ecky and those cuts, those bruises. Hank's alone.

Doesn't get any better than this.

She keeps her head low as she pops the breach and thumbs a shell into it. She tells herself she doesn't know what she's gonna do here, and that's true to a point: but it's hard not to think about the power she has in her hands.

The cold trigger. The long barrel. The bead at the end that tells you where your enemy stands.

Atlanta runs across the open space, gun up at her shoulder. She gets near, starts to slow—and the scuff of her heel is enough.

Crayley turns. "Dad, goddamnit—" Then he sees. "You."

"Me."

The look on his face is clear. He's got no friends here. No father. He's alone in the dark with a girl who made a promise. A promise to end him if he went and messed with one of her friends again. Now that debt has come due.

"We didn't hurt him too bad," Crayley says and shrugs. "Doesn't seem right. A dude who wants to be a chick. I don't get it. It's not natural."

"Doesn't seem your place to judge." Her jaw, set. Teeth grinding against teeth. The pain of it goes all the way up into her skull.

"Seems like she's not hurting you any, but you sure are hurting her. Or him. Whatever. That's not the way it ought to be."

"We were just having some fun. He's—she's fine."

"She's not *fine*. She's beat to hell. It's not the marks on her face that matter. It's the ones down deep. A far worse infection will find its way into her heart because of people like you. And years from now, or maybe months, or maybe even weeks, when she swallows a load of pills or steps out into traffic and kills herself, it might just be you that ends up as her last living thought."

He's nervous, shifting from foot to foot. Looking left, right, for any way out of this. No exit, though, for him. "Yeah, I . . . I don't want that. I just thought maybe he—*she!*—she was tougher. People gotta be tough. It's a hard life out there. We're just . . . toughening her up."

"It's hard out there *because* of people like you."

She hugs the gun close to her shoulder.

Her finger flirts with the trigger.

There's a moment where she knows what's coming next.

And the only scary thing is how little it scares her.

Crayley's eyes flit to just behind her. Over her shoulder. The realization hits her far too late: *Somebody else is here.* Then something hard, metal hard, presses against the middle of her back—there's a *click* that follows a half step later. "Put that gun down," someone growls.

"No," she says, the tendons in her neck pulled taut like hanging ropes.

"You pull your trigger, I pull mine."

Shit.

She stoops low, sets the gun down.

A big boot steps on the stock of the gun, swipes it out of reach. Fear climbs through her like spiders on a web. She feels suddenly, woefully powerless. The worst thing. Being subject to other people. Other *men*. They could do anything they want, now. Crayley says: "Thanks, Dad."

His father answers: "Shut the hell up. You dumb-ass. What is this? What did you *do*?"

"He hurt someone," Atlanta says, but then the man behind her pushes forward with the gun again. Hard enough against her spine that it hurts.

She risks a look up, sees a scruffy older man with mussed-up hair—long at the sides, half-bald on top. Looks like he just woke up. He says as much, then: "Hank, you turd, this is what I wake to find?"

In the distance, sirens.

Oh no.

Hank says, "Did you call the police?"

"Damn right I did," his father answers. "Better hope they don't find some reason to haul you in, too, because I won't bail your mummy ass out."

Red and blue lights wipe away the darkness.

Two cop cars come up to the fence, and Hank's father tells his son to get off his ass and go open it.

CHAPTER EIGHT

Sometime near morning, a cop comes and gets her out of what must be the drunk tank at the Maker's Bell police station. A place that haunts her—walking through its halls, the gray carpet, the bleachy too-clean smell, all of it reminds her of the day that Petry shot Whitey in the head. The day that dog almost died.

"You made bail," the cop—a sludgy, jowly blob of a man—says. "But first, you gotta visit the principal's office." That, he says with a chuckle.

He leads her into Detective Holger's office.

Ah, hell.

Holger sits, stone-faced, at her desk.

The cop closes the door behind her.

"Sit," Holger says.

But Atlanta doesn't sit, not yet. "How much trouble am I in?"

"None. Mostly."

"I don't get it."

"I'm in my late thirties, so I remember playing the unholy heck out of *Super Mario Bros.* when I was a kid. And the best things in that game were those 1Up mushrooms, because they made sure you got another life. Another *chance.* Well, this is that. This is your 1Up mushroom, and I don't know that there are any after it. We like you here, Atlanta. We do. You shut down a dog-fighting ring that we couldn't touch with a ten-foot pole. You've been through hard times. Your dog got shot by one of our own right here in this building. You've built up some credit. But that credit is now spent."

"So what happened?"

"Sit, first."

"I kinda wanna stand."

"Sit, or I'll have Officer Dale put you back in that cage."

Atlanta sighs, nods, sits.

"The slate is clean," Holger says. "The ledgers are zeroed out."

"For me."

"For everybody."

"Including Hank Crayley?"

"Including him."

Atlanta's hands form fists. "But he did something bad. He needs to *pay.*"

"The law doesn't think so. Nobody's pressing charges against him. Same as how his father, Henry, isn't going to press charges against you for trespassing on his private property."

"But Hank hurt somebody."

"That somebody being Joey Eckhart." Atlanta's silent, because she doesn't necessarily want to throw Joey into this. "Joey won't confirm. Won't press charges. This is just how it is, Atlanta."

"That bully needs justice."

"What you're talking about isn't justice. It's something much meaner."

"Maybe the law and justice don't agree. You ever think of that?"

Holger shrugs. "It's true. They don't shake hands as often as I'd like. But life rarely presents clean solutions and—" Here Atlanta's about to file yet another protest, but Holger interrupts her sharply: "Hey. *Hey.* You need to think real hard about what went down last night. Seems to me you might've been planning to use that gun on Hank. Maybe to injure him. Maybe something worse. This is you at the edge, Atlanta. Standing right at it, the ground crumbling underneath the toes of your shoes. Stop staring down. Start looking ahead."

She grumbles: "I don't know what that means."

"You do, too. And there comes a point when if you keep ignoring the warning signs and the flashing lights and you drive through all the barricades people have put up—you're gonna head off into oblivion. You're seventeen years old. At eighteen, they can bring the adult judgments down on you. Right now, though, you're still a kid . . . so, I'm going to issue you one punishment, just one, and it's barely punitive and is good common sense."

Atlanta likes common sense. Her own version, not anybody else's.

"Oh, crap, what?"

Holger slides a piece of paper across the table. It's a form— some kind of police equipment requisition form by the look of it. But that's not how the detective is using it. On it, she's written in permanent marker using big words:

HUNTER SAFETY COURSE
MANDATED!!!

"The heck is this?" Atlanta asks.

"Just what it says. You are to take a hunter safety course, immediately. You wanna use a gun, you're going to learn to respect it. It's a six-hour class spread out over three weeks. You do that, I'll give you back that shotgun of yours. Oh, and you will need an adult to accompany you."

"Well, who the heck is that gonna be?"

"Maybe the person who paid your bail." Holger looks up at the wire-mesh window behind Atlanta's chair. Atlanta follows her gaze.

There at the window stands Paul. Her mother's boyfriend.

He waves.

"What's he doing here?" Atlanta asks.

"Mister Miller paid your bail, which to his knowledge was five hundred bucks but I have reduced to nothing. Still means he's here to pick you up. And given that he is a licensed hunter, I'm saying he's the one who should accompany you on your hunter safety training."

"Dangit, no, *no*, I'll find someone else—"

"You won't. It's him. Have a nice day, Atlanta. And *stay out of trouble.*"

———

She's buckled up in the Silverado and not saying much. Paul seems to be taking a long way back to the house. Instead of cutting clean through town he goes up and around, by the old mill, the collier, past that old quarry where kids sometimes swim but they also tell stories of some lake monster that lives down in the watery dark. The day is gray, rain spitting against the windshield.

Finally, Paul speaks. "You could say thank you," he says.

"Why?"

"Oh, come on, now. For coming to bail you out."

"You spent literally no money because they dropped the charges." She leans her head against the window with a *thunk*. Stares out at the passing trees and fields of corn, the corn already being cut down in places, mashed flat like a giant came down from his beanstalk and started stepping on everything. "So, thanks."

"I *was* going to spend money. My mom, rest in peace, always said that it was the thought that counted." He leans across, and as a conspiratorial aside says: "I handmade a lot of my gifts. And, hand to God, I'm not very good at it. I remember I made this mug in ceramics class in junior high, and it didn't look like a mug so much as a glazed-over cow pie with a handle—"

"That's a cute story, Paul."

He sighs, sounding exasperated. She feels kinda bad about it, but kinda happy about it, too.

"Fine," he says. "Then thank me for not telling your mother about this."

She sits up. "What?"

"She doesn't know."

"And how is that, exactly?"

"Phone rang. She told me to take it, so I took it. Had a nice conversation with Holger, but didn't let on what was being said. And then I set out."

Atlanta tries to be suspicious. She works at it, like the way you might snort real hard to hawk up a loogey. Because, she tells herself, it's a little odd. Here's this guy, this *adult male*, and he's hiding something from her mother. Hiding something about his relationship to Atlanta. He hasn't said the classic words, yet—*it's our little secret*—but feels like that phrase might be in there somewhere, buried under the dirt. And yet, it's just as likely—*likelier*, even— that he's doing this to score points with her.

Hot dang if it isn't working.

"Oh" is all she says, still processing it all. It's like pulling a wolf's teeth out through his hiney-hole, but finally, it comes: "Thanks, Paul."

"I hear we're going to hunter safety together."

"I hear that, yeah."

He leans back as he pulls up to a stop sign at a four-way inter-section where Sunbury and Hopcatong Roads cross, and lets the truck idle. "I have good memories of hunter safety when I was a kid. My dad took me because he wanted me to go out deer hunting with him that November. I mean, it was thirty years ago, but back then the whole thing had a 1950s vibe about it—all the filmstrips and pamphlets were all from that era. Dick and Jane type of stuff. My dad was a real mean dude sometimes. He'd whip my ass with a belt just for looking at him wrong, but during those classes, all that went away. He'd muss my hair and put his arm around me and help me take notes. And I still remember the smells of the place, too. His cologne—Old Spice, or sometimes, Stetson. Gun oil. Dust, too, because the animals on the walls of that old gun club were damn near ancient—"

"Gun club?" she asks. Panic seizes her by the wrists, holds her tight.

"Uh-huh."

"The hunter safety. It's being held at the gun club?" That's Orly Erickson's stomping ground. Ground zero for some racist, neo-Nazi trashbag ideology. First and only time she was there, she and

Chris ended up tied to chairs and beaten. "The one on old Gun Club Road?"

Paul suddenly laughs. "That place? Oh, jeez, no. Those guys there are fuckin'—" He clears his throat. "Sorry, excuse my French. Those guys there are pretty scummy. Buncha slimy, racist douche bags. No, we're going to the course up near Danville. Nicer group of people, I think."

And *that*, she thinks, is how you score points with Atlanta Burns.

———

Arlene's drinking coffee and flipping through a *Cosmo* when they get back to the house. Smells a little like cigarette smoke, like maybe she's been puffing in the house again, which means Atlanta will have to have a talk with her. But now isn't really the time. She sees Atlanta come in with Paul.

Her eyes light up like a Macy's display at Christmas.

"Hey. Look who's making fast friends," Mama says, suddenly beaming. Then she smirks and narrows her eyes. "You two look like a pair of cats that just killed the first spring robin. What are you up to?"

"Nothing," Atlanta says, feeling suddenly self-conscious.

Paul says: "Me and Atlanta are gonna try to do something together. Kind of a bonding thing. We're gonna take a hunter safety course together."

Mama looks to Atlanta as if to confirm that it's real, that this isn't just some dream going on during a particularly pleasant nap. Atlanta rolls her eyes and gives a small nod. Then Arlene hops up, gives them both a big shared hug, and then says, "Well, I think this calls for a little Irish in my coffee."

CHAPTER NINE

Monday morning. School again. *Seems like this happens every week,* Atlanta thinks, *ha ha ha,* because of course it does. (She laughs about it because it's the only thing that stops her from crying.)

After homeroom but before first period, she catches sight of Samantha—she slides through the halls like a shark slipping through the busted hull of an old shipwreck, always looking like she's on the hunt. Mandy Newhouse is with her.

There exists a social code in high school. Nobody ever tells it to you—it's not like there's a class where they break it down with an overhead projector or a PowerPoint slide show, but there's a system in place. She remembers reading about India in tenth-grade global studies class with Mrs. Wanamaker, and how this caste system existed there—like, you have your richie-riches and your working class and your religious folks and the dirty beggars, and each caste isn't supposed to drift into the other. One can't become the other.

And they don't even talk to one another because to do that is just, nuh-uh, no-no, no-how, no way.

That's high school in a nutshell. At least here, at this school.

She's not sure what caste she's in, but she's not up there with Samantha and Mandy. But Atlanta, she doesn't much care for social codes. Propriety can go dunk its head in an unflushed toilet.

She cuts a line through the crowd, steps in front of Samantha.

Atlanta knows what's coming. The disdainful looks. The disgust at one of the unclean coming to speak to the two royals.

Except, that's not it.

Samantha smirks. Mandy beams.

"Heard you got into some shit the other night," Mandy says.

Samantha leans in. "So you *are* cool."

"Wait, how the—" Atlanta starts to ask.

"My uncle Tyler is a cop," Mandy says.

"Which means we can get away with anything short of *murder*," Samantha says, smiling but sneering, too. Her eyes are wild, wide, full of crazy.

To Samantha, Atlanta says: "We have unfinished business—"

"Oh, *that*," Samantha says. "Is it boring? I bet it's boring."

"No, it's about the party—"

At that, Mandy gets excited. "Next week's party? Are you coming?" To Samantha: "Is she coming?"

"She is," Samantha says.

Atlanta scowls. "Am not."

"You *so* are."

"So not."

"You want me to help you?" Samantha asks. "You want me to tell you what you wanna know? Then after the game, after the dance, you will come to my party. Then, and *only* then, will I help you. Deal?"

"No deal," Atlanta says, and walks past.

———

"You don't remember anything?" Atlanta asks.

Bee seems cagey about it. The two of them sit outside school between fifth and sixth period. Easiest shortcut between math and English is to go outside—and so there's a steady stream of kids marching past like a line of ants following a food trail.

"No," Bee says, hands on her knees. She's watching the people go by. Like she's self-conscious. Nervous.

"Is something wrong?"

"No, I just . . . I'm just a little queasy. The baby. Morning sickness. Ugh."

"Sorry."

Atlanta wants to ask, but doesn't: *Is there something you're not telling me?*

Bee says, "I don't remember anything. I blacked out, woke up in one of Samantha's bedrooms at her house, and . . . I knew someone had, y'know." She sighs. "And now I've got *this.*" She pats her stomach as her nostrils flare.

"Dang, dang, dang, *dang,*" Atlanta says. "That means I'm gonna have to go to Samantha's . . . goddang Homecoming party next week."

Dang.

Dang!

Bee sits up. "You're going to her party?"

"Yeah."

"Be careful there."

Atlanta cocks an eyebrow. "Why?"

To that, Bee just shrugs. "Look what happened to me."

———

He's there in the parking lot, like he's waiting for her. Damon Carrizo, smirk like a boomerang, eyes almost a dark bronze like drum cymbals.

"You get my flowers?" he asks, standing in her way as she heads through the parking lot. She veers past him, forces him to trot along like a dog looking for a treat. "The roses?"

"I did. Put 'em in a nice vase called *the trashcan in our kitchen.*"

"Oh, sick burn."

"It's right there in my name."

"You never gave me an answer about Homecoming."

"Then I guess you have your answer."

She keeps walking. He stays behind. He calls after: "You'll fall in love with me yet, Atlanta."

Her only response is a middle finger thrust upward. She doesn't look back as she serves it to him. The high school equivalent of walking away from an exploding building, all cool and shit.

———

Later that night, she's hanging out with Shane on her front porch. Whitey's rolling around on his back, writhing like a beetle who got turned upside down. Mama's gone again. Paul's nowhere to be found—though when he is around, he keeps mentioning the hunting class, which is coming up for them. An event she's kinda sorta dreading.

But for now, it's just the three of them: her, Shane, the pooch.

"You like my mustache?" Shane asks.

She's been eyeing that thing since she saw him that morning. "It's not really much of a mustache."

"I like it," he says, stroking what little facial hair is there with the length of his index finger. "I'm hoping Damita likes it."

"It looks less like a mustache and more like you went to town on a box of Thin Mints."

"Whatever." He sits up. She can tell he's a little irritated. He asks: "How's the thing with Bee going?" Way he asks is strange, though: he doesn't look at her when he says it.

"It ain't going nowhere yet." She tells him everything about Samantha, the party, the rich guy with the polo shirt and the tan beard that matched his tan face. "I don't even know why she wants to know. Not like she's gonna find some Father of the Year waiting for her at the end of this crooked road."

He shrugs. "Well, this is what happens."

Atlanta narrows her eyes. "Whaddya mean?"

"I just mean—I dunno. If you don't want to end up pregnant, don't go to a Mason High rich kid party and drink so much you pass out."

"I hear what you're saying." Atlanta sits up straight and stares out at the middle distance—same place he's looking. "But you know that's bullshit."

"Well, I dunno—"

"I get it, we like to say, you don't want your car broken into, don't leave it unlocked. You don't want to get robbed, don't walk down that alley. But what the victim did or didn't do doesn't change the fact that what happened to them is someone else's fault. Bee didn't ask for this. She made a mistake getting drunk, but she didn't deserve what came to her. You think I didn't hear that after I ended up in Emerald Lakes? People always asking me what I did to lead that sonofabitch on, like I was trying to seduce him. Hell, even if I was wearing something pretty—or skipping rope naked as a baby bird—that don't give him the right . . ." She feels her jaw clench. The words dam up behind her teeth. Deep breath. "That's done now. It's not her fault. Same as you getting your ass beat isn't your fault because you're brown."

"Yeah, I guess." He looks at his feet. "And I don't call myself brown."

"Mocha?"

"I prefer to think of myself as *cinnamon*."

"That'll make a nice stripper name," she says. They laugh. But then she gets serious again. "I just feel bad for Bee. Despite what she did to me. Now her future's gone all wonky." Atlanta fidgets, picks at a hangnail. "You ever think about what's coming down the pike?"

"Like what?"

"I mean like, what's next. After school."

"College."

"Yeah?"

He gives her a look like, duh, durr, of course. "Are you not going?"

"To college? No, I don't think so."

"We're all supposed to go to college."

She shrugs, feeling suddenly, weirdly isolated. "I guess I just . . . I can't figure why I would. It's not like I know what I want to be when I grow up, so it'd be a big waste of money anyhow. Money I do not currently possess, and I'm sure my mama doesn't possess."

"You could get a scholarship."

"With my grades?" She whistles. Whitey's head perks up and she boops him on the nose with the toe of her boot. "I'm not talking to you, lunkhead." She sighs. "With my grades, best I can expect is a diploma still warm because they didn't know if they should print one or not. You're the scholarship type—your 3.8 average, your AP calculus, AP English, AP underwater basket-weaving."

"There's always financial aid."

"More like, financial AIDS. I may have poop-ass grades but I'm no dum-dum. You get saddled with that kind of debt, you never pay it off."

"Community college, then."

"Enh" is all she says to that.

Shane looks like he's experiencing some kind of existential panic. Like he's talking to an alien being that makes him question his humanity, his world, his very place in the universe. "You have to think about your future."

"You know what?" she snaps. "I got this. I got my future all figured."

"How so?"

"Well, *since you asked*, you know how I've been helping people? You wanted to know what I'm doing with that money, right? I got a shoebox. Under my bed. I'm taking that money, and the day I graduate, I'm getting way the hell out of here. Gonna use it to buy a bus ticket or if I have the money, a train ticket. Then I'm going . . . somewhere. Somewhere nice and warm. Probably back down South. Florida, I'm thinking. It's cheaper down there in places."

"So you're just going to leave."

"That's what you're gonna do, Mister College."

"But . . . what are you going to do there? In Florida, I mean."

She shrugs. The question is like biting into a corn chip the wrong way—sticking in her mouth like a sharp stab. But she pretends it's no big thing. "Whatever I want. My life, I own it."

"Yeah, yeah, okay," he says, backing down. There's this great big abyss between them—stretching wider and wider as evening settles in over the corn. "I think, umm. I think some of us are going to the game and the dance next week. Like, you know, stag? No big deal."

"Jeez, why?"

He shrugs. "I dunno. Last year of school and everything. Seems like a thing to do. You could come. It'll be fun, we'll make fun of it—"

"You don't have to do everything before you die like you're collecting *Pokemon* cards—"

"I really prefer *Magic: the Gathering*—"

But she ignores him and keeps on rolling. "You don't have to jump out of a plane or swim with sharks just because they're there. You hear that sometimes like, *Gosh, Dan, why did you climb that mountain?* And Dan is like, *Well, Dave, because it was there.* That's the reason I use for *not* doing things. *Hey, Atlanta, why didn't you swim with the sharks?* Because they were there and that means they're probably gonna try to eat me."

"Sharks don't really eat people all that often. It's a myth."

"God, you never quit," she says. She feels hot under her neck, and a pressure at her temples. Anger, irrational anger, rises up inside her like a tornado juking left and right, flinging trailers and sucking up bovines to throw through barn walls. "You're always actin' smarter than me. But I was the one who saved your little behind from Virgil and Jonesy, let's remember."

"I know. I'm sorry."

"You know, just . . . never mind."

Whitey whines.

"I should probably go," Shane says.

"You should."

"I have homework."

"I bet."

"See you, Atlanta."

"Uh-huh."

She watches him go to his car. Listens to the pop of gravel. Watches the taillights head up the driveway like a demon walking in reverse. Thinks every ten seconds or so, *Yell to him, tell him you're sorry, tell him you don't know what's up or why you're mad or any of that, just get him back and it'll all be fine.*

But she doesn't. And he goes.

CHAPTER TEN

Spirit week.

Atlanta missed it last year. (Because . . . well.)

This year, she gets a faceful.

———

Monday is Wear Your Pajamas to School Day, and of course that comes with a whole list of prohibitions because otherwise you'll start seeing guys come in wearing boxers with their things hanging half out and you'll see girls wearing skimpy frilly nighties from Victoria's Secret. Some kids do it—the popular kids, the student council kids, those in the middle who think they're maybe cooler than they are or have better social credit than they do. Mostly it's fuzzy footy pajamas and flannel pants even though it's still almost eighty degrees here in late September.

Atlanta wears what she wears. White T-shirt underneath her Army Navy store jacket. Jeans. Boots. End of story. (It fits the theme, too, because she's been known to sleep in this very outfit.)

She spies Shane throughout the day—glimpsed here and there through the crowds or way down the hall. At lunch she sits with everybody *but* Shane, who told everyone he has some kind of yearbook stuff to take care of. Kyle's on yearbook, too (and the AV club and the literary mag and he's also a theater monkey, because Kyle apparently never sleeps and can multitask like a meth addict), and he says he's not sure what's going on there. And in classic Kyle style, he adds: "I think Shane is mad at you."

Yeah, yeah, she says, that's probably right on. She tells them she didn't even get a ride from him, that she left a message early (too early, probably) on his phone saying her mother was going to take her in and he didn't have to worry about picking her up. (A lie, that. She ended up making the hour-long walk to school.)

And of course they're all like, *Are you going to the game later this week, are you going to the dance,* and she's like, *No, jeez, shut up about it.*

———

Tuesday is Tacky Tuesday.

Haw haw haw haw, wear your tackiest clothing, they say. Mismatched colors and funny wigs and clowny bow ties.

Atlanta feels like an alien.

And Shane still isn't talking to her.

Her feet are tired from walking to and from school.

———

Wednesday is Disney Day, except of course they can't just call it that. No, some yahoo had the idea of calling it WeDisneyDay, probably thinking they were clever. And that clever, not-clever person probably had a gaggle of social servants and sycophants orbiting them like pieces of trash around an ugly planet, and they probably said, *Yes, yes, you're so clever*, and so the name was born.

Atlanta never really understood the Disney thing all that much. Even now some girls her age are chest-deep in it. They sing *Frozen* songs in the hallway. They wear Mickey Mouse backpacks like they're still eight years old.

One of the theater chicks, Mara Darrow, wears a Tinker Bell costume today.

A *sexy* Tinker Bell costume, because apparently that's a thing.

Shane's at lunch. He's polite. She's polite. It's tense. Everybody else seems tense, too. It's weird.

Whatever.

She still feels like an alien.

———

Thursday? That's Spirit Day. Because at night is the game, and mid-day, just after lunch, is the pep rally.

The pep rally (Atlanta's own little mental joke about it is, *Pep, Really?*) is a thing to behold, as long as you don't mind beholding really awkward, clumsy things. The sports situation here at William Mason High is backward from how it was at her last school: there, football was king. Here, it's kind of a half-breed kissing cousin. They acknowledge it. They *have* a team (though no field of their own). But the football players are routinely terrible. You go out for football because you're a half-assed athlete. You want real sports, you either join:

(a) wrestling

or

(b) baseball.

Football being what it is (a limping game-leg of a sport here) means the pep rally is almost perfectly mediocre. (Another little mental joke: instead of pep rally it's a *poop* rally, because that's about how much energy is going on here.)

The cheerleaders are a sad thing. It's not that they're not all slim supermodels—frankly, Atlanta likes that this squad runs the gamut of body types, from short to tall to thin to plump. It's that they have the gymnastic ability of a headless chicken and all the pep of a sleeping cow. They come out with some bass-banging club hit, but it's like watching a pack of grandmas dance.

Atlanta sits with Josie at the pep rally. It's the one happy moment she has in the week. The two of them snark and laugh and—without pointing and being total douches about it—have a pretty good time. Atlanta says her *Pep, Really* and *Poop Rally* jokes, and Josie chimes in with her own zingers, too: "Looks like that one's having a seizure," or, "This is like watching a dump truck crash into a busload of orphans, I mean, it's just sad," and they have a good laugh. And Atlanta then tells the cheesiest cheerleader joke she knows:

Q: Why did the ghost become a cheerleader?

A: Because she wanted to show off her school spirit!

Har, har, har. It's not funny, not at all, but that's what makes it funny, and in that theme, Josie then goes ahead and tells an antijoke:

Q: What did the cheerleader say when she answered the phone?

A: Hello, I am a cheerleader.

And it's funny because it's not funny, because it's dumb as paint, stupid as a cardboard box, and it makes them laugh so hard they're almost crying.

In front of them is sitting this pig-nosed kid, this junior named Keith Scarborough. He turns around, red-cheeked and beaming, eyes pinched like cat hineys, and he tells his own cheerleader joke:

Q: What do you call a cheerleader with pigtails?

And they don't ask *what*, they just stare at him like, *Who invited you to this party, skid mark?*

But he doesn't give a hot wet fart about who invited him, so he answers his own question and goes for the punch line anyway:

A: A blowjob with handlebars.

And he guffaws like it's the best thing anybody has ever said ever.

Josie raps him hard on the top of his head with her knuckles. Not hard enough to, like, be really violent, but hard enough to make him yelp and rub his skull. He asks her why she did that and she says, "Because you're being gross and fuck you, that's why."

He turns around, grousing like a guttering engine.

"Boys suck sometimes," Josie says.

Atlanta and Josie slap hands.

Another high five. It seems to be their thing.

———

It's toward the end of the day, and Atlanta's still feeling so good from hanging out with Josie that she accidentally bumps into someone in the hallway. A boy: blond hair with a conservative part, blue button-down shirt, a plain face. She'd think he was some kind of Jehovah's Witness or something, except that the sides of his head are shaved and—

"Hey, Atlanta," he says, and she recognizes that voice.

"Ecky," she says, then quickly corrects herself. "Joey! Joey."

He gives her a small, curt nod, then keeps on walking.

She catches him by the elbow. He flinches at being grabbed—she knows that flinch so well she instantly feels bad for touching him like that. Atlanta holds up both palms in surrender. "Hey. You . . ." She swallows hard. "You look different."

He—she?—shrugs. "This is me, now."

"No makeup. No anything?"

"I'm done with all of that. It was dumb." But the way he says it, there's this haunted look in his eye. As if his brain is a broken toy and now he's the child trying to hide what happened, pretending it's all okay, don't worry about it. "I'm a boy. Like everyone says."

She's about to say more, but then he pulls away, keeps walking. A fish joining the school in the stream.

———

She walks home. Past the little cluster of Mennonite houses where they build the sheds. Past the closed-down bait shop. Past the fields of soybeans and corn and down the road toward home. The sky is gray and thunder threatens the edges of the world, but even with the promise of rain for the game tonight and even for all the things there are to see, her mind wanders. To Joey Eckhart and to the way he looks now. Part of her thinks, *He was just putting on makeup and girly clothes sometimes because he was acting out, like some kinda defense mechanism.* But then she thinks, *No, that wasn't it at all, was it?* Now *he's putting on an outfit, now he's hiding it all.*

How long will he be able to take it? The abuse. And the non-abuse, the almost-abuse, too. The side looks, the whispers, the laughs and sniggers, the general *disgust.* She gets it. Atlanta's felt those things. First day back to school from Emerald Lakes almost killed her.

And that's her question for people like Joey: how long will it take before something pushes him over the edge? How long before he either becomes so comfortable with who he is that he's bulletproof to it forever, or—more likely—how long before he just decides to end it all?

Atlanta realizes then:

Sometimes, suicide doesn't mean you have a gun in your mouth or a bottle of pills dissolving in your belly.

Sometimes suicide is killing who you are to become someone you're not.

———

The rain never comes. The thunder lingers at the margins, like a lion kept in its cage. Close, but not too close. All the while, Atlanta sits around the house. She checks her shoe box, thinks about cleaning her squirrel gun but then remembers she doesn't *have* the gun because *Holger* has the gun—and oh yeah, the hunter safety course starts this weekend, too. Though before that happens she has to go to the dance and Samantha's party tomorrow night, ugh, ugh, *ugh.*

She throws the stick for Whitey.

Eats cold SpaghettiOs out of a can.

Looks at her Ambien and thinks, *Maybe I'll pop one now and just take an early trip to snooze-land.* Like an old person. Maybe she should watch *Jeopardy* or *Wheel of Fortune* first just to make the transition complete.

Thoughts of Joey stick with her like a ghost, or a bad smell. Shane, too.

Shane.

Shoot.

Atlanta looks at the clock. Sees the game is gonna start soon. Out the window: evening is bleeding in like an oil leak, and still no rain, still no storm.

Shane said he'd be there, at the game.

Atlanta grabs her bag, her jacket, gives Whitey a kiss—

Then she calls Josie to come pick her ass up.

———

Truth is, she's never watched a football game. Basketball's pretty all right and she loves fishing and thinks pro wrestling is aces, but football has never really caught on with her. She doesn't understand it, for one thing. Basketball's easy: take the round bouncy thing and get it in the other team's receptacle. Fishing makes sense, too: hook, bait, wait, fish. Football makes fishing look like NASCAR, and she doesn't much care for NASCAR either (oh, hey, look, a bunch of white dudes driving left for about *a thousand hours*). She watches football and it makes no sense: two teams slowly pushing against each other. One of Mama's boyfriends was a superfan and said, "It's like watching war." And she said, "War is boring." Then he threw M&Ms at her head because he was a motherfucker.

So now, the William Mason High Cockbirds—apparently somebody thought that was a good name for a team (at least the baseball team is called the Meteors)—are out there on the gridiron of another team's field, battling the North County Whitetails in a clumsy, muddy match to see who can solicit the most yawns. Atlanta and Josie wander the chain-link fence by the field as the folks in the bleachers and along the sides hoot and cheer and shake their pennants in the nighttime air—air that has gone surprisingly cool given the heat of the day.

Josie points: "There."

Sure enough: Shane stands over toward the snack bar. He's with Kyle, Steven, and another of their yearbook crew, Shelly Bogner (whose dad runs the weird little produce place in the middle of town). They're not looking at the game. Atlanta makes a beeline toward them, Josie following after. When she gets closer, she sees what they have in their hands—other kids might be passing around a phone with some YouTube video on it, or a joint, or some porn. Shane and the other two are passing around *Magic: The Gathering* cards. She catches a glimpse of a dragon and some kinda swamp-man before they see her.

"Atlanta," Shane says, half-surprised, half-disappointed. "You're here."

"Damn right I'm here." She hears the anger in her voice—and knows it's real, but also knows it's not what he thinks. She's angry at herself. At *this situation.*

"We were just leaving," Shane says.

"No we weren't," Kyle blurts, incredulous.

Atlanta grabs Shane by the elbow. "Hey, c'mere. We need to talk."

"Ow," he says.

"Sorry." But she doesn't let go, and drags him behind the snack bar. Near a trashcan that smells like old milk and a stack of empty cardboard boxes from a local restaurant supply place.

He starts to say something, but she boops his nose.

"No. Shh. Me talky first."

"Oh . . . okay."

Deep breath. "I am a big giant assy-faced butt-mouthed shit-heel," she says. "I was mad. *Am* mad. At you. For no good reason at all. It's like: oh, man, this sucks to admit, but I got *nothing*. Nothing at all. No future. Nothing much to look forward to. No plans, no dreams, not lickety-shit. And soon, that future I can't see and don't have is gonna be right up on me like a tractor trailer tailgating my ass, and won't be any way I can avoid it. When that time comes, you'll be gone. Because you have a future. And you should. You're a smart dude and the world is your enchilada."

"I think that's racist?"

She boops his nose again, harder this time. "Hey, shut up! I'm trying to spill my guts here. You going away scares me, because once you're gone, it's me and my dog. And . . . that's it. And then with you wanting to do things like go to football games and Homecoming dances . . ." She puffs out her cheeks, exhales. "It's like you're already leaving. Earlier than scheduled. It sucks when all your friends wanna do something you don't wanna do. It makes you feel alone. It makes *me* feel alone. But that's dumb. I'm dumb. I should be happy for where you're going and should want to try new things with you instead of being . . . scared. Because you're my best friend and I know I treat you like you're my sidekick—"

He flings his arms around her. She makes a sound—*grrk*. "You're my best friend, too. And I *am* your sidekick. I'm totally cool with that."

"No, you're not—ow, you know, you're stronger than you look—" She feels her blood pressure rise. Has to tell herself: *This is Shane. He's hugging you. This is what affection feels like. Calm down.*

But it's like he can read her mind. "Sorry." He lets go. "My turn."

"Your turn what?"

"To confess."

"Oh, that doesn't sound good."

"I'm pretty jelly."

"Jelly? I don't know what that means, jelly."

"Jealous."

She squints. "Then just say *jealous*, not jelly. You're a big boy, smart as a whip, you can use actual words, not made-up words."

"*Jelly* isn't a made-up word. You put it on your toast."

"Yeah, I know. Never mind, can we get to the confession, please?"

"I'm *jealous*." He enunciates that word. "Of Bee. And Josie."

"Josie I maybe get. She's part of the crowd. Part of us. But Bee?" She snerks. "*Bee?* Really?"

"She's back in your life. You guys were superclose."

"*Were.* That's the important part of that sentence. Then when I needed her most, she disappeared. Used me like a stepladder to more popular friends."

He kicks a stone. "I just figure we don't have much time left—like you said, this is our last year, and I didn't want anybody messing that up."

"She's not gonna mess it up. Neither's Josie."

"Promise?"

"Of course."

She hugs him, this time. It feels better. Because she controls it.

He says suddenly: "Does this mean you're going to the dance tomorrow?"

"Oh, god," she says. A sound rises in the back of her throat—the sound of an angry dog. It feels a bit like jumping out of a plane but: "Yeah, fine."

"Woo hoo!" he says. "You're awesome."

"You're my little tamale."

"You're also still kinda a little bit racist."

She holds up her thumb and forefinger about an inch apart. "Just a little. By the way, thanks for shaving that thing off your lip."

"It was not impressive."

"Nope."

———

"Turquoise taffeta swing dress," Josie says.

Atlanta stares at someone else looking back at her in the mirror. When she moves her hips, the stranger in the mirror does, too—and the sea-green dress sways and swishes with her.

Her hair, blown out and given shape—it swooshes and swoops.

Nails painted green.

Lips a kind of . . . she doesn't know what kind of yellow that is. It's metallic, but not quite gold. Bronze, almost. The whole package is . . .

"What's that word?" Atlanta asks. "When you get an antique with, like, this blue-green color on it. Like mold, but not mold."

"Oh!" Josie snaps her fingers. "Uhh. Uhh. Patina! Is it *pa*-tin-uh, or pa-*teen*-uh?"

"Jeez, I sure don't know," Atlanta says. "But that's it. I feel like that."

"Ergh," Josie says. "Sorry."

"No!" Atlanta protests. "No. I . . . kinda like it. This dress is a bit of all right."

Yesterday, in the car ride home after the game, Josie asked Atlanta if she was really going to the dance. When Atlanta said, *Ugh, yeah,* Josie asked if she had a dress to wear. And, of course she didn't. Atlanta hasn't worn a dress since that junior high choral concert she was forced to attend. (She sang in that concert, just a small voice amidst the chorus singing words she mostly forgot. Her mother was supposed to make it to that show but didn't. Was on a date with the coke dealer dude from Virginia.) So: no to the dress.

Josie offered to help. And so, here they are.

"You like it, then?"

"I don't feel like myself."

"That sounds like a bad thing."

Atlanta smiles. "No, no, it's actually pretty dang cool."

———

That, it turns out, is the theme of the night.

She and Josie walk in through the front door, and immediately the throng of people takes her breath away. And not in a good way. All those bodies in the half dark as shitty music from ten years ago plays. Her immediate feeling is to do what comes natural: be a wallflower. Cling to the wall like an ant trying not to drown in a water glass he wandered into. Stay at the margins and do her time and nobody can say she wasn't brave. Except, that isn't brave, is it? She'll go up against a barn full of neo-Nazis or stroll into a dog fight like she's the biggest, baddest pit bull on the farm, but a school dance is dang near making her pee.

She tells herself: *Be brave.*

And then it hits her: *You don't have to be you.*

You can pretend to be someone else.

Just for now. Just for tonight.

Not like Joey Eckhart. Not like someone pressured into it. But like someone at a costume ball—way a kid gains power over monsters by dressing like one.

Deep breath.

Hold it. And—

Jump.

Right over the edge.

Josie pulls her into the crowd and she doesn't resist. It's like a hard dive into a cold swimming pool—it hits her, takes the air right out of her lungs, but then suddenly the water is warm, and besides, this isn't happening to her. It's happening to a girl with big teased-up hair in a patina-colored rockabilly dress.

It works. They find Shane and the others: Steven, Eddie, Kyle. Eddie's got this thin little black tie like the flat blade of a machete; Kyle's got a baggy button-down and, for reasons unknown, some kinda *Star Trek* pin on his shirt; Steven's rocking a T-shirt made to look like a tuxedo shirt; and Shane, well, Shane's about as impeccable as he can get—a full-on black suit, white shirt, black bow tie, and hair slicked back into a shellacked helmet that makes it look like LEGO hair.

(He's like a teenage version of Gomez from *The Addams Family*. Atlanta used to love that show. Nick at Nite, boy howdy.)

They laugh and dance. Atlanta doesn't know how to dance, but neither do the other people she's with, far as she can tell. Actually, looking around, she's not sure any of these people really know how to dance—everybody's just kinda moving like they're snakes on fire, like they're possessed by clumsy devils, like the music is in them and they just don't care how they look.

She envies it at first, and then just claims it as her own, and soon she's flailing and head-banging and doing her own dumb thing.

It feels nice to be someone else.

It's funny, too—she doesn't see many of the elites around here. Not too many richie-riches. No Mandy, no Samantha. No Barford twins. She spies Moose Barnes dancing with Megan Luscas, but he seems drunk and loud (of course, he always seems that way). He tries to dance with Atlanta at one point, coming up on her with those big meaty paws, but she gives him the same look a rattle-snake gives a nosy dog and then he turns back around and he's donezo, gonezo, good-bye. Still, he's the only one, and the absence of the popular crowd makes her happy. That's one of those things you always see in movies: the popular kids go to the dances and they're always kings and queens of the dance floor. But here, none of that's true. They're so popular, they won't slum it here. Maybe they're already at Samantha's party. Maybe she doesn't even care.

She manages to slow-dance with Steven, and then Shane. With both she has to keep her distance—arms locked like she's some kinda prude, some 1950s housewife who has to keep twelve inches between her and her partner at all times. And sure, it mostly feels like her skin is about to crawl its way right off her skeleton, but that feeling breaks apart, too. And the dance is nice. Swaying like a couple of old boozers at a bar after last call.

Then she sees someone. She tells Shane, "Hey, hold on," and breaks away from him to cut through the crowd.

A half minute later, she comes back, dragging Damita with her.

"You two need to dance," Atlanta says.

Damita shrugs. "I can be into that."

Shane beams.

Moments later, they're dancing. A whole lot closer than Atlanta could ever get. Which makes her happy, and sad, too.

The night zips along, time gobbled down by an uncaring clock. There's a roller-coaster feeling to it all—she's given up some control. And it feels righteous.

Comes a point, though, where her armpits are itching something fierce. *Stupid powder roll-on deodorant.* It's hot in here, too hot all of a sudden, and that's enough to crack the mirror and chip the façade. A little bit of the bona fide Atlanta starts to peek through, and she tells the others: "I'm gonna go get some air." They all nod and keep moving. Shane asks her if she wants him to go with her, but she gives him an eye roll and says, "I can take care of myself, Lafluco."

———

She's outside at the back of the school, not far from the parking lot. Summer has finally loosened its grip—like the night before, the air now is cool, so cool she can see her breath. But it feels good after being in the furnace that is the high school Homecoming dance.

Jeez, she thinks. *Can you believe it, Atlanta?*

Her? At a dance? Enjoying herself?

She looks up at the moon just to make sure it hasn't gone bloodred or cracked open and hatched like some kind of world-ending egg.

It hasn't. It's still there, full and fat. Pregnant with a bunch of smaller moons, maybe. (And here she thinks of Bee. *Maybe I should've invited her.* But Bee wouldn't have said yes. Plus, this was for Shane. If he really is "jelly," then no reason to go poking that bear.)

She's about to turn around, go back inside, when—

Pop.

A sound coming from the back of the parking lot.

A sound like—what? Glass breaking? Maybe. A windshield.

A voice carries. Angry. Then laughing, braying, even. She knows that kind of laugh. It's the laugh of tormentors having fun doing what they were made to do.

So she does what *she* was made to do, which is keep on walking toward the danger and not away from it. Her feet—each in an oxblood boot, the one accessory she was able to bring to the rock-abilly-Josie-lipstick-lesbian makeover party—carry her down the steps and sidewalk like she's walking the gangplank on a pirate's ship.

Her boots crunch on loose asphalt.

She doesn't bother trying to be quiet.

But it hits her suddenly:

She's naked.

Not, like, *naked*-naked. But she's got nothing. Her shotgun is at the police station. Her bear mace and telescoping baton are both in her room, at home.

Most she has is this little clutch purse. Josie's, not hers.

Meaning: not naked, but *worse* than naked. *Vulnerable.*

From not far away, she hears the *whap* and *oof* of someone taking a punch.

Atlanta kneels down, opens the clutch purse. Starts scooping up rocks and bits of broken parking lot. With the flat of her hand, she bulldozes them right into the clutch. When it's full, she snaps it shut, lifts it up.

Heavy. Good.

With the little purse back over her shoulder, she keeps walking.

A voice goes: "Shh, shh, someone's coming. Shut up. Shut up!"

Atlanta thinks she knows that voice.

And when she rounds the bend, looking down one of the aisles of the lot, she sees that Mitchell Erickson and Charlie Russo have someone pressed up against a Jeep Wrangler. Charlie's got a baseball bat. Under the yellow streetlights, broken glass glitters like fake-ass diamonds.

Charlie makes a hissing sound—*hsst!*—to alert Mitchell.

Mitchell, who turns and sees her.

He makes a sound that, if she's being honest, tickles her to death: it's this frustrated, exasperated, straight-up pissed-off grunt of rage. "Atlanta Burns."

"As I live and breathe."

"That can be fixed," Charlie says.

She clings to the clutch purse.

Mitchell pulls away from whoever he's got pinned up—

And now she sees who it is.

Damon Carrizo.

He gives her a boozy, beat-ass smile, his white teeth pink with blood. Hair stringy, sweaty, stuck to his forehead. "Hey, Atlanta," he says, his words mushy. He spits a line of blood. "You should probably go. It's okay."

"It looks pretty far from okay."

Mitchell says: "You know what you're like? A bad cold. Just when you think you've kicked it, here it comes again to bring you down."

"Achoo," she says, sneering.

Charlie steps away from the pickup. He twirls the bat.

"You should go," Charlie says. "Like D-Bag here says. Right, D-Bag?"

"Cuntrag is right," Damon says, wincing. Mitchell pumps a fist into his stomach. Damon doubles over, a string of spit dangling from his lower lip.

"Back away," Atlanta says.

Mitchell turns. Sniffs. Cracks his knuckles. "You think you're untouchable now, huh? Think you got my father by the nuts just because you got some, what, some recording? Maybe he's on your leash, but I'm not." He steps forward. Charlie has now taken to thwacking the bat against his own open hand.

Charlie says: "Whaddya gonna do to us?"

"Maybe I got something special here in my purse."

"In that thing?" Charlie asks. "I doubt it."

"Maybe I'll run," she says. "Get help."

Mitchell says: "Not your style. Besides, we'd catch you."

A high-pitched whine rises in her ears. Her hand holding the clutch shakes. Her vision goes dark on each side and it feels like someone's put a vice over her skull—a crushing pressure at each temple.

All she says is "Bring it on."

Charlie licks his lips, steps toward her—Mitchell's got a scared look on his face because he knows what's coming. Charlie should, too, but he's dumb where Mitchell is smart. Soon as Russo steps up and brings the bat back—maybe just to threaten her, maybe not to hit her, but she can't take that risk.

Like a rattlesnake, she strikes fast.

She whips the purse off her shoulder and clocks him in the face with it. His head snaps back. The bat rattles against the ground and the clutch pops open, stones raining down. Blood streams down Charlie Russo's face and out through his fingers. He yelps and sputters, staggering back.

Mitchell's eyes go wide. Then narrow to slits. He's angry. Angry enough to do something. His body coils up and she thinks, *Shit, the purse is broken, the stones are gone*—the bat's just lying there, maybe she could get it—

A scuff of stone—a roar.

Damon tackles Mitchell from behind. The two tumble to the ground, punching and kicking. Throwing elbows. Rolling around like it's some kind of courting dance or mating ritual.

Atlanta picks up the bat, bangs it against the ground.

"Everybody up," she barks, putting some iron in her voice. "Unless you want me to start breaking legs."

The two of them pull apart. Mitchell sits back on his ass, panting. Damon's like a jungle cat, on all fours, ready to pounce.

"This isn't your business, Atlanta," Mitchell says.

Damon rolls his eyes. "It's not *our* business either, dumb-ass."

Mitchell shoots him a look.

Charlie Russo, for his part, stays on the ground, clutching his face. Whining and spitting.

"Carrizo," she says, "get up. Erickson, just stay there for a while."

She twirls the bat.

"You'll get what's coming to you, Atlanta Burns," Mitchell says.

"Uh-huh. Here's what's coming to you, hoss." She flips him the
bird.

"Thanks," Damon says, just to her.

"That your truck with the busted glass?" He nods. "Then let's
get outta here."

———

They stand against an old fence rail about a mile away from the
school. Behind them, the moon shines on a duck pond. Technically,
they're trespassing, but whoever owns this property has a house
way, way back off the road. It's quiet here but for the complaints of
crickets and other night bugs. Atlanta wings a pebble toward the
pond. *Ploop.*

"So, what was that all about?" she asks.

"Ah, nothing."

"It ain't nothing. Those two charm school rejects don't come at
you unless they got a reason. They play who they are pretty close
to the vest. Won't be any good to get suspended from the baseball
team. So: why you?"

"Their fathers aren't a fan of my father," he says.

"No kidding? Orly Erickson isn't much of a fan of my mom,
either. Or me. Or my dog. Well. Kinda my dog."

He picks up a stone, tosses it overhand into the water.

"You didn't have to save me," he says.

"Please. They would've broken your kneecaps or worse."

He hesitates. Like he doesn't want to admit it. "Maybe. I
could've called the cops, though."

"Using a mouth full of broken teeth, or fingers busted up like
bent coat hangers, sure." She leans over, bumps her elbow into his.

"And here's a little tip: the cops in this town may be in Mitchell's pocket, sooooo."

"Fine, okay, thank you for saving my butt."

"Yeah, well."

"You wanna make out?"

The word "Sure" escapes her lips, and next thing she knows, those very lips—the treacherous turncoats that they are—are mashed up against his, and they lean up against one of the fence posts. Teeth on teeth, tongues sliding against tongues. Maybe it's the way the night has gone, maybe it's the dress, maybe it's getting a few nights of sleep thanks to the Ambien, but for a good five minutes she forgets who the hell she is. The kissing is nice, like a warm bed on a cold day with sheets to get tangled up and lost in, and the sides of her mouth feel hot and chafed but in a good way, and then his hand drifts to just under her shirt and—

Bang.

The gunshot sound in the deep of her ear. The gunsmoke stink, eggy and violent. She staggers back, feeling hot, too hot, not turned on but rather like she's burning up—tossed in a furnace and gone to char. Damon stands there, mouth slack, eyes wide, and she thinks for a half second that the gunshot was a real thing and not just a thing her mind made up.

Her breathing comes in short gasps. Panting like a sick dog. Nausea rises up inside her, like a crocodile lifting its head out of grim, swampy waters.

"What the hell?" he asks. "Are you okay?"

He reaches for her, but she pulls away.

"Yeah," she lies. "I'm fine."

"I thought . . . I thought we were having a good time."

"We were. It was great." She knows she doesn't sound convincing even though she means it. The sulfur stink of expended gunpowder still hangs in the air. It's not real. She knows that. But it still smells like Satan's bad breath just the same, and she just can't shake it. "Maybe I ought to go?"

"I was . . . you know, before I was got jumped, I was about to get in my truck and head out to Samantha Whatever-her-last-name-is's party. Maybe you and I . . ."

Shit! The party.

"I'm . . . supposed to go to that, yeah." Suddenly she wishes they were all invited. Maybe she can crash it, bring everyone.

"Really?"

"Uh-huh."

"I'll drive you."

"It's okay, I can walk."

"I won't let you walk."

She sticks out her chin. "You'll let me do whatever I want."

"Sorry, I just mean—c'mon. It's a long walk, yeah? All the way up to Gallows Hill? Let me drive you, please?"

She has a lot of fight in her, but not for this.

Without another word, she gets in his truck.

CHAPTER ELEVEN

Last she saw Samantha's house, it was during the day. At night, with a party going on inside, it takes on a whole new dimension. Cars parked up and down the drive and on the lawn. Lights flashing inside. Bodies moving behind most of the windows. A dull *douche-douche-douche* beat coming out. Some girls out back yell *woo!* and some guys yell *yeaaaaaah!* and then: applause.

Atlanta walks up to the front door with Damon at her side.

She thinks: *Pretend like you're in the army. This is a mission. Get in. Secure the intel. And get the heck out before they know you were here.*

Damon says: "You ready for this?"

"Sure," she says. Another lie.

"At least you don't look like someone kicked your ass."

"I'm guessing that's your way of passing me a compliment."

He shrugs.

They go inside.

———

The music sucks. Some kind of club banger beat. Rock or country, okay, she could do that, but this is like a horse kick to her heart and a key stuck into her eardrum. Everyone else seems to like it, though: wall-to-wall students dancing, running, drinking, singing, laughing, making out, feeling each other up, playing video games. She catches a whiff of weed coming from somewhere. Hears a blender running over the sound of the music.

Damon's saying something, but she's cutting that bait and already moving through the crowd. She has to stick her elbows out to make sure nobody gets too close—a lanky dude and some tease-hair brat are making out while moving around like maybe they're trying to find the stairs or a bedroom or something, and Atlanta has to give the guy a hard elbow in the kidneys to get them out of her way.

But so far, nobody notices her.

A lot of faces she recognizes, but just as many she doesn't. Kids from other schools, maybe. Some of them look older. College? Bloomsburg, maybe, or the Penn State satellite campus. Whatever. They don't matter.

And she doesn't matter to them, either.

She's invisible to them, her irrelevance providing a perfect camouflage.

But then, like the gopher in a Whack-a-Mole game, Mandy Newhouse pops up right in front of her. "At-*lan*-tuh" is the way she says her name, and then she's shouting, "We got Atlanta Burns in the house!" And half the room cheers and half the room shrugs with total indifference.

"I need Samantha," Atlanta says, and realizes her voice is swallowed by the dragon's roar of the crowd. She yells it again: "I said I need Saman—"

"She's around!" Mandy yells back. "I'll find her! But first—"

She thrusts a plastic cup in Atlanta's hand. Something purple inside it sloshes, something that looks like grape juice. But the smell rising off it won't just strip the wallpaper from the walls, it'd probably burn the whole house down.

The cup already has Atlanta's name on it. Misspelled, of course: *Atalanta.*

"Hunch punch!" Mandy says, then laughs like it's a joke. "Drink up!"

Atlanta shrugs, thinks, *What the hell.*

She might need a little liquid ass-kick to help her get through this. Mandy ducks through the crowd and Atlanta tips the cup to her lips—

But suddenly, a hand darts out, grabs it away from her. Damon. She's already protesting—"Hey!"—but it's too late. He pivots fast and gives the drink to some girl passing by: a baby-cheeked chick with strawberry hair and eyes as blank as windows. Babycheeks squeaks: "Sweet, thanks!" and keeps on motoring.

"Asshole," Atlanta says.

"Trust me, you don't wanna drink random drinks at parties," he says. He winks and pulls out a little flask. With one thumb he spins the cap off—which dangles from it, still connected by a leather strap. "I bring my own."

"So I should trust *you*?" she asks, dubious.

"I'm trustworthy," he says, grinning like the fox that just crapped out a bucketful of chicken bones.

She takes it, gives it a sniff.

A high-octane whiff of burned sugar.

She takes a sip. Her eyes water. "The heck is this?"

"Some of my dad's whiskey. Bourbon. *Good* bourbon."

Atlanta wouldn't know good bourbon if it came in a gold cup, but it's a drink, and at this point she's pretty sure she needs it.

She takes another sip. It burns. But it's kinda good, too.

"Works for me," she says, and then ducks back through the crowd.

He wants to follow her, it's his business.

———

Atlanta wanders for a while, trying to scout out Samantha. After a while she parks herself in the corner of the living room, keeping a watch out. The blue glow from the back patio and pool shines in, shimmering like light cast through scattered sapphires.

She tries to keep an eye on everybody. Moose Barnes is across the room, leaning up against a baby grand piano—his hand tucked in the back of some blonde's loose jeans, him cupping her butt while she's got a hand slid down into one of his front pockets, maybe playing a little pocket pool, who knows. He gives Atlanta a look then he smirks at her. She scowls back.

Couple dudes are playing a game of quarters on a nearby table.

A couple chicks are dancing in a trio, stropping up against each other like cats who got into the catnip.

Some girl is crying, and a guy is trying to console her. *Probably just trying to get in her pants,* Atlanta thinks.

Next thing she knows, though, her little *hide and stand vigil* plan is ruined by Petra Bright and Susie Schwartz when the two of them come up on her like they're connected at the hip (those two always were). They start nattering at her about *Oh, man, it's good to see you again,* and *It's nice that you're starting to really connect with people,* and *Isn't this party great wow this house wow that pool wow the cars out in the driveway* and then Petra leans in and says, "Did you hear about Bee?" and Suzie says, "How crazy is that?"

Atlanta bites back some of her crueler responses, and just says: "I *heard.* That's why I'm here. You seen Samantha around?"

Petra shrugs. "Kitchen, maybe?"

Susie concurs. "Yeah. Kitchen."

Atlanta puts both her hands together like she's praying, then uses it to wedge the two apart so she can head to the kitchen.

Along the way she passes Babycheeks, who now looks like a complete space-case—eyes unfocused, mouth in a crooked, boozy smile. Drunk out of her pumpkin, that one. A couple of frat types are leading her by the elbows, keeping her moving. A third comes up behind her and puts a blindfold on the girl's face. Atlanta worries for a second—but Babycheeks is giggling and seems into it, so that's her business. Atlanta makes a face and goes past and into the kitchen.

Of course, Samantha's not in the kitchen, either. Damon's there, though, flask in hand. He's talking to two guys, one girl. One of the guys she thinks is a wrestler: he's got a head and neck like a telephone pole stuck up out of a squat, beefy body. Next to him, the other guy, a tall length of rope with a soul patch and bad acne, is pouring out white powder onto a red dinner plate.

The girl, who Atlanta is pretty sure is on the softball team and is named . . . Tina? Toni? Tanya? . . . points to the plate and looks to

Damon. Like a caveman she asks: "Want?" But Damon just holds up the flask and says he's "covered."

Then the girl spins, sees Atlanta. "You want . . . whoa. You're Atlanta. Atlanta Burns," she says, and whistles.

"Like the city and what Sherman did to the city in 1864," Atlanta says.

"Who's Sherman?"

Atlanta shrugs. "My accountant. Also: my lover. Sherman. Sweet, sweet Sherman." The girl just nods knowingly, like that all makes sense somehow. People, Atlanta thinks, will pretend to understand what you're talking about just so they don't have to look embarrassed.

(Of course, Atlanta wouldn't know jack squat about the city of Atlanta getting burned, either, but when she lived down South, at least once a month some history buff or enthusiastic yokel had to tell her about Sherman setting fire to the whole damn city during the Civil War.)

"You want?" the girl says, holding up the plate.

Atlanta scrunches her nose and shakes her head.

Damon hands her the flask. That, she takes. Sips a nip.

It's starting to taste pretty good, this whiskey. She hangs out for a while, shoots the shit with everybody. But eventually she asks:

"You guys seen Samantha?"

Soul Patch, the skinny dude, says: "Upstairs." Then points upstairs as if Atlanta doesn't know what the word means.

He hoovers a line of coke up his nose. Then gags a little.

The wrestler dude says, "Amateur."

Atlanta nods and ducks out of the kitchen.

Moving through the crowd is like crawling through mud. Too slow. She didn't take any of the coke, but even still, she's feeling edgy, worked up. Atlanta eventually gets to one of the two sets of steps that go upstairs, and she pushes past the crowds. Upstairs she finds a hallway lined with doors—more doors in this one hallway than in her whole house, inside and out, she thinks. Bedrooms and bathrooms and probably an office or two.

Atlanta goes door to door. Lot of the doors are open. One's got a crowd doing drunken karaoke. Another's got a ring of stoners on the floor smoking from a hookah that looks not unlike an octopus. They invite her to join, but she keeps walking, because again, there's a mission: get in, get intel, get out.

The first closed door, she opens. There, just a mound of sheets with lots of thrusting and humping going on underneath. Looks like some kind of monster eating its kill. The sounds coming from within don't disagree with that assessment.

Atlanta moves on.

Another closed door.

Before she even grabs the knob—a voice from inside.

Samantha.

Finally.

She opens it to reveal three people in what looks like a guest bedroom.

Against the far wall is a set of patio doors leading out to a balcony overlooking what must be the pool area. Samantha stands in front of it with something in her hands—something wrapped up in a brown paper bag.

A man stands there, too, facing her. He doesn't go to Mason. He's older—maybe even older than college age. Got a bit of a gut. A button-down shirt with a flared collar, showing off some chest hair. Bit scruffy all over. Big arms, too.

And on the bed, a half-naked girl. Face down. Jeans pulled half down, shirt pushed half-up. Head hanging over the end of the bed, hair like strawberries cascading down to the floor—

Oh, god. It's her. It's Babycheeks.

A string of drool connecting her chin to the carpet.

Samantha's saying, "I know it's not her, I don't know—"

She stops. Sees Atlanta. The guy keeps on talking: "I'll take whoever, I guess, I just figure—" But then he follows her gaze.

There's a moment between everybody. Silence drawn and quartered.

"Speak of the devil, and the devil shall appear," Samantha says.

"That's her?" the man says.

Samantha smirks. "Hey, Atlanta. Come on in."

It takes Atlanta a second for her whiskey-fuzzed brain to catch up.

Babycheeks lying there.

I know it's not her.

Speak of the devil.

That's her?

The cup. Red cup. Purple drink. Hunch punch.

Atalanta.

They drugged that cup.

Damon warned her about that, but she didn't understand the warning . . .

Bee's voice in the back of her mind: *And everything was going good. But I got drunk. Real drunk, I guess. I . . . blacked out and . . .*

She thinks: *Run.*

But her feet stay planted. That girl on the bed, whoever she is, she's not all the way out, but she's down for the count. Anybody can do whatever they want to her. That man, right there. What'd he say? *I'll take whoever, I guess.*

She could run, call the cops. But how long will they take to get here?

What will happen to this girl before then?

Atlanta swallows hard, steps into the room.

"Close the door," Samantha says.

"I'm gonna help this girl up and go," Atlanta says. She doesn't close the door.

"Wait, wait, wait," the man says. "You don't have to leave."

Samantha says, "Atlanta, I know this freaks you out. But look." She holds up the paper bag. "There's money in here. Two grand. I'll give you half if you stay."

And there, a little itch at the back of Atlanta's neck: *You need money. You wanna bail on this town and set up a life of your own, you can't do it with slobbery dog kisses and empty shotgun shells.* But she gets the cost, and she says as much, too. "You want me to stay for him. You want me to . . . *do things* with him."

He smiles. A devil's look on his face. Hungry and lean. "That's right."

"Like I said . . ." Atlanta creeps farther into the room. "I'm gonna wake this girl up, and we're gonna go."

"Atlanta," Samantha says, exasperated. "This is real money. Dude, what's your name?" she asks to the guy.

Guy says, "I'm not telling her that."

"Ugh, whatever. Up your offer," Samantha says.

The man looks angry and confused. "What?"

"Throw in another thousand."

"Hey, we had a deal—"

"Situation is changed," Samantha says through gritted teeth. "Atlanta's now part of the bargaining table, and that means you gotta make her a real offer—"

"I'm not part of some fuckin' *auction*," Atlanta seethes.

Samantha clucks her tongue. "Atlanta. Just be cool. Okay? Be cool."

The man's hands bundle up into fists. "Be cool or I'm gonna make it cool. I didn't come here to pay for nothing."

And with that, he starts to move around the side of the bed. Slowly. Like he's a zookeeper approaching an escaped lion.

The desire in his eyes. Atlanta knows it. She's seen it before. He's a thirsty coyote who hasn't had a sip of water in a while.

He'll do what he has to, to get it.

And she'll do what she has to do to stop him.

That word goes through her head one last time—*run*—before she rejects it.

She doesn't need to assess the room much to know what to do next.

Her hand darts out, grabs a lamp off the bedside table. The man sees her moving and starts moving fast himself—coming at her hard.

Which is the wrong thing to do.

The plug pops out of the wall, the lamp cord lashing like a stingray's tail as she smashes the ceramic base of the lamp right against the man's forehead. It's like slamming a pie into somebody's face, but much harder, much meaner.

The ceramic shatters with a pop. The man cries out and drops to the ground, knocked cold—

Atlanta quick moves, and kicks the door shut. Just in case Samantha has backup out there.

Samantha curses, and heads to the *other* bedside table, fumbling for the drawer—whatever she's going for, Atlanta can't have that. She jumps up on the bed, lets the springs carry her forward—

She slams into Samantha as a stun gun spins out of the other girl's hand.

Samantha's head thumps against the wall.

Atlanta straight punches her in the jaw.

It hurts. Hurts like she wouldn't believe. Her hand throbs, pain shooting up through her wrist and all the way to her elbow.

Dang!

Samantha leers with a bloody mouth. "You dumb bitch. You're ruining a good thing. You could've been rich."

Atlanta paws at the wad of money inside the paper bag—now on the floor. "Already am. And what the hell do you need money for, anyway?"

"Mommy's new book is tanking. Her advances shrink with every new book coming." Her tongue snakes out of her mouth, tastes a line of blood running from her nose. Nearby, the dude groans. Samantha flits her gaze toward him like he might be her savior—but he stays down and out. "We're almost broke."

Poor baby. "Is this what you did to Bee?"

"Bee?" She barks a laugh. "Bee knew what she was getting into. Just not who was getting *into her*, if you know what I mean."

"Who? Who was it?"

"That did the deed? I dunno."

Atlanta smacks her.

"I said I don't know!" Samantha protests. "*Jesus.* It was different with her, all right? They . . . came, they picked her up. Took her somewhere. Brought her back and . . . dumped her on the lawn like she was garbage for the curb."

From behind her, the girl on the bed starts to moan.

"You, though," Samantha says. "You fetched big dollars."

"Who was it? Who picked her up? Bee. *Who picked up Bee?*"

"I dunno him. Some thug. Mahoney or something."

Atlanta still has more questions—but there's a pounding on the door.

From the other side, a voice: "Sam. Sammy. Everything cool?"

"Uh-oh," Samantha says with a smirk. "Cavalry's here."

Move fast. Atlanta's up. Back onto the bed. Bounding toward the door as Samantha is yelling: "Get in here!" The door starts to pop—

Bam. Atlanta jams her shoulder hard against it, slamming it shut. With quick fingers she bolts the lock. The door strains against its hinges. And of course when she turns back around, there's Samantha standing up, the lower half of her face a mask of blood—she staggers toward the bed.

Atlanta's like a Ping-Pong ball, from one side of the room to the next. She back-hands Samantha, grabs the stun gun, and jams it into the other girl's ribs.

Every part of Samantha goes rigid like a coatrack. She makes a sound like *ngh ngh ngh ngh*—part of her pink tongue sticks out from between clenched teeth.

Then she drops like a lung-shot deer, moaning and writhing on the floor.

From the other side of the door, the voice again:

"Sam, you okay? *Sam,* answer." Atlanta knows that voice. Moose Barnes. That prick is built like two refrigerators belted together. He'll have that door down in no time. Which means—

Atlanta gets under Babycheeks. Drapes that girl's arm over her shoulders, and hauls her up. *Thank heavens she's tiny,* Atlanta thinks. She gives the girl a jostle and a shake. "Wake up. Hey. You. Wake up."

She smacks the girl's face.

The door rattles as someone slams into it.

The girl's eyelids flutter. "Wuzza," she says, drool swinging from her chin.

"Can you swim?" Atlanta asks.

"Swih? Wuh?"

This is a bad idea.

But it's the only idea.

Atlanta moves—the girl's legs only barely keeping up—toward the patio doors. She pops them open. They head out onto the balcony and sure enough, it overlooks the pool below: crystal-blue waters. Music in the air. The beat going *doom doom doom doom.* Kids in the water. Horsing around. Feeling each other up.

Behind her: the door rocks open, splinters thrown wide.

Atlanta yells: "Watch out!"

She thinks: *Please don't drown, Babycheeks.*

And then she throws the girl over the edge.

Moose yells for her. She feels the floor shake with his footsteps bounding toward her like he's a loose T. rex trying to catch a goat.

Soon as Babycheeks hits the water, Atlanta bunches up Josie's very nice taffeta dress and jumps.

———

Water blue like Windex surrounds her—lights glow beneath her, the dark of night floats above. Feet churn water nearby, not far from her head. A flurry of bubbles like marbles tossed in zero gravity. The sound of a roar rising up—

Atlanta breaks the surface.

The roar is applause.

Clapping. Hooting. For she and Babycheeks—

Babycheeks, who has already come up for air, whose eyes are bugging out like a choked Chihuahua's, whose mouth is open in a silent, gasping scream.

Atlanta hazards a look up, straight up.

Moose Barnes stares down over the railing at her. He ducks back inside, fast. Which means he's probably coming for them.

"Gotta move," she sputters to Babycheeks, both of them blinking away stinging chlorine. They tread to the side of the pool. Hands appear to help them up. Everybody's congratulating them, laughing, slapping Atlanta on the back—each slap smacking wetly against what is likely a completely ruined dress.

First chance she gets to wear a dress in forever, and Atlanta ruins it.

Typical. And not at all surprising.

No time to ponder that now. "We have to go," she says to Babycheeks.

"Okay," Babycheeks manages to say—she's still high, but the fall and the pool water sharpened some of the softer edges. The girl's confused but aware.

They start to weave their way back to the party. People are talking to Atlanta, but she can barely hear them. The water in her ears makes everything sound like *wah womp wah* and she's not really paying much attention, anyway. She gets to the patio door, and already she sees a head slightly taller than the others coming down around the one staircase—it's Barnes.

Goddangit!

She wheels back around.

And there's Damon.

She's never been happier to see him.

"You need to get us out of here," she says.

His eyes, wide. Mouth slack. She forms her thumb into a weapon and jabs him hard in the ribs.

She hisses: "I *said*, we need to go."

He nods, and she points to the same exit she used last time she was here—the gate at the far end of the patio. They cut a sharp line, duck around the side of the house, and get to his truck. Tires peel asphalt, and they're gone.

———

They stop at the same place because comfort, however small, matters. Same fence rail, same duck pond. Nobody gets out of the truck, though. They sit there with the heater on because as it turns out, being sopping wet on a late-September night is a very good way to make your teeth chatter so hard they crack.

Babycheeks is back to the world of the living. She's maybe still a little foggy, but for the most part, she's alert.

On the way over, Atlanta told her what happened.

"They were gonna . . . rape me," Babycheeks says, those words coming out high-pitched, almost broken apart, as she strains not to cry.

"I figure so," Atlanta says.

But the girl's brow furrows. "You gave me your drink, though. That means . . . they wanted you."

Atlanta nods soberly.

Damon just stays quiet, staring over the edge of his steering wheel like all this is just too much for him to deal with.

"What do I do?" the girl asks. "Do I call the police?"

Damon, for the first time in several minutes, speaks: "Atlanta said the cops around here aren't that trustworthy."

"Not for me," Atlanta says. To the girl she says: "But you—maybe it's different. You come from money?"

"I . . . I dunno . . . I . . ."

"You do know. Big house? Nice car?"

A tiny shake of the head turns into a full-bore nod. Atlanta doesn't know what it is, whether the girl doesn't think she's rich or if she's just traumatized.

"White girl, got money," Atlanta says. "You'll be okay. We're gonna take you home. You get there, you tell your parents what happened. You call the police. You get that ball rolling. Okay?"

A small nod and a faraway look. "O . . . okay."

"You go to Mason?"

"N-n-no. I go to Briere. The, uhh, the ch-charter school in Bloomsburg."

"That's good, then. Hey, I'm gonna need your phone number—I'll check up on you. God, I'm dumb—what's your name?" *It sure ain't Babycheeks.*

"Skylar. Uh. Sky."

"All right, Sky. This is all gonna be fine. You're fine. You good?"

". . . I'm good."

"Then let's get you home."

———

After dropping her off—sure enough, she is rich, living in this old stone colonial house that looks like maybe George Washington hisownself took a dump in at some point—they head back to

Atlanta's place. Damon is still quiet. Like he can't process it all. She tells him: "You know, the thing happened to me, not to you. And yet you're all clenched up like cramped toes over there."

"It's just been a long night," he says, offering a small smile. "I'm glad you're okay."

"I'm glad I'm okay, too."

His hand reaches for hers on the seat, but she pulls it away.

Not now, dude, she thinks.

"What are you gonna do now?" he asks.

She shrugs. "I guess same thing I always do. Burn it all down and see what comes running out of the flames."

PART TWO: LICENSE TO HUNT

CHAPTER TWELVE

Morning comes and Atlanta jostles awake at the kitchen table.

Paul is standing there, staring at her, his mouth agape.

"What?" she says, and wonders for a moment why everything tastes like strawberries. But that answer is fast forthcoming.

Sitting there in front of her is an open container of store-brand strawberry ice cream. A whole quart of it. It's rolled over, onto its side. A pool of pink melty mess gathers beneath it, forming a skin. In her hand is a spoon. Her mouth is ringed with sticky sweet goo.

"Had yourself a little ice cream social last night?" Paul asks her.

"I . . ." She swallows hard. "I don't remember."

Then her stomach surges, and before she even knows what's happening, she's over at the sink, her stomach cinching up like a hangman's rope—

She doubles over and sends a hot pink strawberry geyser into the sink.

Paul's standing by her, looking worried. "Hey, listen, if you're sick or something—we can maybe put off the hunter safety class—"

That's today.

She glances at the clock.

In an hour.

"No," she says, almost puking again. *Gotta get my gun back.* She presses her fist to her lips and winces, choking it back. "I'm good. It's not a bug, it's just . . ." *Just what, Atlanta?* "I'm cool. Lemme just hop in the shower. Ten minutes, okay?"

———

On the drive over, Paul says: "You just had a hankering for strawberry ice cream last night, huh?"

"I guess."

"You don't remember?"

"Sure, I remember," she lies.

"Smart money says I know what this is. Listen, when I was your age I did all kinds of drugs—I smoked weed like I was some kind of marijuana chimney. I dropped acid a bunch of times, too, not enough to think I was a glass of orange juice about to spill, but enough to make me think the clouds were telling me my future and enough to make me think one time when I was biting my nails that I was actually eating off my own fingertips. Drugs are weird, and I don't blame you—"

She sets her jaw. "I'm not on drugs."

She means it as truth, at least to answer the way *he* means it.

But then, a reminder: the Ambien. She came home, rattled from the night. Couldn't sleep, of course. So she popped a pill before bed.

Can Ambien do that? *Shit.* Sleep-eating? And since she ended her night—or thought she ended it, anyway—in her own bed, that also means sleep-walking.

"Well, either way, hope the ice cream was good," he says, offering a dubious smile. "Where'd you buy it from?"

"Whaddya mean?"

"Looked like Giant brand."

"I didn't . . . I didn't buy it. It must've been in the freezer."

"There's ice cream in the freezer, and I bought it for your mother and I. Rum Raisin, which she said you don't like."

Atlanta feels like she's back in Emerald Lakes all of a sudden—like there's this whole tornado of crazy suddenly descending upon her.

They pull up a long drive through some pine trees. A sign for the Danville Gun Club is tucked back into the evergreens.

Atlanta stays silent, wondering what's going on with her.

The truck slows, stops, and as she moves to get out, she feels something crinkle in her pocket. Her hand goes there and she finds it.

A receipt. From the grocery store. Dated last night.

One thing purchased: a quart of strawberry ice cream.

In her head she adds to the list: *sleep-shopping.*

———

Atlanta hates school, so she knows she's gonna hate this hunter-trapper education thing.

They sit in a wood-paneled room with puke-green carpets underneath them. They've updated the decor since Paul's been here, but that means it looks like something out of the 1970s rather than the 1950s. The animal heads are all scruffy-looking. There's a mounted bobcat by the entrance that has cobwebs caught in its open mouth and between its mangy ears.

The guy who comes out to teach them isn't some manly, rough hunter—she expects someone like Orly Erickson with his big chest and his *let's go on safari* vibe, but what comes out is a pair of teachers. First is a scrawny fellow with all the muscle tone of an old Band-Aid: his name's Wayne Sleznick, and he looks more like an accountant than anything else. Someone who kills spreadsheets, not whitetail deer. Second person is a woman: a broad-shouldered lady, built like a pellet stove. Joanne Kinro. Local park ranger, apparently.

Atlanta thinks: *I'd sure like to take a nap,* but she's wide awake, almost like she's had a cup of coffee or something.

And the two teachers start talking and it takes about an hour of the class for Atlanta to realize that she's listening. Not just listening, but taking notes. Taking notes with interest, as it turns out—and this isn't the Ambien, either.

She actually likes the class.

Today's not about gun safety but about the hunt: they show different kinds of animal tracks and animal scat (translation: they look at pictures of rabbit, deer, bear, raccoon turds). They go over how to track an animal over distance, how to set traps, how to be mindful of animals. Why it's necessary to hunt (turns out, cars hitting whitetail deer are one of the bigger reasons for accidents in the state of PA, alongside drunken dirtbags who think they can drive while sloppy on Crown Royal). How it's important to conserve the wilderness and the animals in it—and how hunting is a part of conservation. Atlanta's not sure she *agrees* with all that, though some of it makes a certain kind of absurd sense.

Not one talk of guns.

The whole time, she falls into the class. Face forward, eyes up, brain engaged. For the two hours, she forgets all about who she is.

———

On the way home, Paul says, "That was fun. You have fun?"

She gives him a suspicious side-eye.

"It was all right," she says, guarded.

"Uh-huh." But he's watching her and wearing this cheeky grin. "It seems to me you took to it like a monkey to bananas."

"Do monkeys really even eat bananas or is that bullshit?"

He laughs. "C'mon, admit it. You liked it. You were all—" And here he does an impression of her. He leans forward against the steering wheel, eyes wide, and with one free hand pretends like he's diligently scribbling notes. "Right?"

"It was *fine*," she says, but her smile betrays her.

Stupid smile.

Stupid Paul.

Stupid hunter safety class.

———

Later, she's home. The day is cool so she pulls on her jacket, takes the long walk to Guy's place. Whitey trotting alongside of her, him chasing moths, grasshoppers, even leaping about while trying to catch the first few falling leaves of autumn. Along the way, she rings up Babycheeks—er, Skylar.

But there's no answer. Just goes to her voice mail.

Still midday. Maybe she's asleep. Or could be she's with the cops right now.

Then she texts Josie: *I fucked up your dress and I'm sorry. I'll pay for it.*

Then she texts Bee: *We need to talk. Tonight. My place. 8pm.*

At Guy's place, he's there heating up a microwave pizza and, unsurprisingly, cleaning. Got a bottle of glass cleaner and a feather duster out. It's not the first time she's called him out on it, and it won't be the last. "You missed a spot, Suzy Homemaker."

"Yo, hooker, don't be rude. I don't have no damn cleaning lady," he says. "Actually, my *abuela* cleaned houses for a living and she took my dopey ass along, put me to work. Cleaning makes me think of her. And hey, if that dog takes an epic dump in here, I swear—"

"Relax, he's trained." She plops down at his little kitchen table. Whitey lies at her feet. "Hey, lemme ask you some stuff."

"That's never good."

"Not really. First up: Ambien."

"What about it?"

"I had . . . something happen."

The look on his face tells her he knows exactly what's coming. He says as much, too: "Oh, snap. You had the thing happen. The sleepwalking thing."

"Not just sleepwalking, dude."

He raises his eyebrows. "Uh-oh."

"I woke up this morning and things were not as I left them. Last I remember, I went to sleep and popped one of those little pills, but apparently not long after—" She pulls out the receipt. "I walked my ass to the store, walked *through* the store, found strawberry ice cream, bought it, walked my ass *home*, and then binged on it with a spoon before . . . I guess passing out again, leaving the rest there to melt all over the table."

"That's messed up."

"You don't say, Doctor Obvious."

"It coulda been worse, though. I heard a story of one guy who took Ambien and woke up in the middle of shaving. Except *he* was shaving dry, and poor bastard had cut open his face." Guy splays his fingers out on his cheeks. "Blood everywhere. Like something out of a *horror flick*, man."

She wads up the receipt and pelts him in the forehead with it. "You knew about this? Goshdangit, dude! A heads-up woulda been nice."

"Sorry! Sorry. It's a side effect, not, like, the main event. Some peeps actually get high from Ambien on purpose—they say that if you pop the pill but then force yourself to stay awake, you get really gonzo."

"You might could've warned me."

"My bad, my bad." The microwave beeps. "You want some pizza?"

Her stomach growls—she hasn't eaten anything since apparently gargling a bunch of strawberry ice cream last night, most of which ended up in the kitchen sink. She takes him up on the offer. He slides the pizza—a personal-sized one—toward him and cuts the whole thing in half. One half on a plate to her. The other to him. It's cheap, nasty pizza. And it's hot and plasticky and good anyway.

"Lemme ask the second thing," she says around a mouthful of napalm-hot cheese, dough, sauce. Then a new sensation kicks in— not just temperature hot, but hot sauce hot, too. Like she's chewing on chili peppers. Eyes start to water. Nostrils flare like that of a cantankerous bull. She fans her mouth as she speaks: "What the hell, man? This is hot. Spicy hot."

"Oh, yeah, I slicked that thing good with some *pique*."

"Is *pique* a word that means 'battery acid'?"

He laughs and keeps eating. "You're tough, you can take it. Whatcha got, c'mon, c'mon, what's the other question?"

"You know anything about a . . ." She's trying to think how to even put it. "It's like a prostitution ring, but . . . the girls don't get a choice."

"Lot of hookers don't get the choice. Not streetwalkers, at least."

"This is something different." She tells him the story—or at least the parts of it that matter. As she tells it, his face goes cold and blank as a cemetery headstone. "Know anything like that?"

"I'm not into stuff like that."

"No, I just mean—you're a player in this area."

"I'm a player in the same way the guy who supplies bats to the Phillies is a player. I'm just a link in the chain, 'Lanta—a little link a long way down."

She takes another bite. The hot sauce makes her chest feel like a house fire. "Any new players in town? Wayman's gone and Orly's quiet. Maybe . . . someone saw an empty hole, decided to plug it." *Or maybe this is old business and has been going on a lot longer than you'd like to hope.*

He puffs out his cheeks while he thinks. "New customers, maybe, but no new players that I can see."

"New customers?"

"Yeah. I'm rolling in it right now with the guys from VLS."

"VLS? That supposed to mean something?"

"Vigilant Land Systems. They're like, uhh, you know fracking?"

"You wanna curse in front of me, it's okay. I got a mouth like a sewer."

He laughs. "No, bitch, I mean, like, fracking for oil. Or natural gas or whatever it is they go looking for down there." He must see the still-bewildered look on her face because he explains further: "I don't know how they do it, but I guess it's like drilling for oil except they get natural gas instead. This state's got a big-ass fracking boom going on right now, and they're puttin' in wells north of here by about fifteen miles. Some people don't like it because it shits up the water supply or something. But they say it's safe, so whatever." He grabs a napkin and wipes pizza grease on it. "They got a whole crew of guys and you know, they're the kinda guys you'd expect to find: most of them travel with the company. Hard-asses who make a lot of money. The company puts them up in a . . . Holiday Inn Express near the wells, I think."

"So what do they want?"

"The guys?" He laughs. "Drugs, man. Some of them want weed, some of them want meth. I don't have either, but I got pills that'll get 'em halfway there. Vikes and Xanax to calm down, Adderall to ramp up. Ambien to help 'em sleep after the Adderall ramps them up. They find a proper dealer, most of them will probably ditch me, but they do random drug tests and what I sell? It's legal." He clears his throat. "You know. Kinda."

"Doctor Guy, in the house."

"Got my degree in Getting-Your-Ass-Highology."

"So—nothing funky going on there?"

"Besides taking illegal pharmaceuticals and then probably violating Mother Earth to rob her of her precious resources? I hear they run a card game there—which ain't legal, but ain't weird, either."

So, what he's saying is: dead end. Buncha blue-collar joes won't have the kind of money it takes to pay big money for young, drugged-up girls. Mister Beardo from Samantha's place—or the Flared Collar guy—didn't look like they got their hands dirty working natural gas wells.

Dangit.

Text comes in from Bee:

See you at 8.

All right, then.

———

Josie calls her. Atlanta's on her way home, walking when the phone rings. She doesn't even say hi, she just picks up the phone and tells Josie just how sad she is, how mad she is at herself, how sorry she is about the dress and she'll buy another one, and Josie says, "Screw it, Atlanta. It was worth it to see you in the dress." Then she says she heard there was some kinda kerfuffle at Samantha's party and does Atlanta know anything about that? Something about a pool? Atlanta hems and haws, then asks: "Did you hear anything about cops breaking the party up?"

"No," Josie says. "The cops always seem to leave her parties alone." Then Josie gets quiet for a second. "You *were* there, weren't you?"

More hemming and hawing, but Atlanta finally nods, tells her that the kerfuffle at the party is how the dress got screwed up.

Josie laughs, then says it was more than worth the price of the dress.

Josie, Atlanta decides, is a good friend.

———

As night settles in, Paul and Arlene are in the house drinking, laughing, having a grand old time, and there's a little part of Atlanta that thinks: *I should join them.* She's starting to like Paul despite every cell in her intestinal lining telling her to do differently—and Mama, well, heck. Mama's got a proper job now. She's helping keep the lights on, keep the roof firmly over their heads.

It'd be nice to go in there. Join up.

Like a family.

That thought hits her like a space rock flung down from the heavens. Instantly, she twists up inside. Paul isn't her daddy. Hell, Mama's barely her mama—half the time, Atlanta's the one who has to be the parent here.

Besides, she's got this dark cloud over her head. Again she feels like things are moving out of her control: making that YouTube video and getting paid to help other freak-shows and underdogs, that made her feel like she was at the wheel, like she was the one driving this car. But recent events have made it clear just how fast the wheel can slip through her fingers—and just how fast the car can crash. Joey Eckhart. The incident at the junkyard. The man with the money at Samantha's house. Even the Ambien—waking up like she did, ice cream in her mouth?

Down the driveway—headlights.

Bee's little car comes bumping along.

Atlanta walks outside to meet her. Bee gets out and starts to do the whole small talk thing, *oh, hey, what's up, did you go to the dance*, but truth is, Atlanta doesn't have the stomach for it right now. She cuts through that overpolite knot with a big old machete:

"You're not telling me the whole truth," Atlanta says.

"I . . . I don't know what you mean."

"I had a little *talk* with Samantha Gwynn-Rudin."

Bee stands there in the half dark. "Oh."

"Yeah. *Oh.*"

They head to the fire pit—which right now sits dark and cold—and Atlanta hooks a chair with her foot and kicks it over to Bee.

"Atlanta, I—"

"This wasn't just you going to a party and getting too drunk to know better. This was you . . . throwing yourself on the slab."

"I . . ." But the words die like flower blooms under withering heat.

"You get paid?"

A nod. "Yeah."

"God, Bee. How much?"

She stares into her hands. "Fifteen hundred."

Atlanta bites her thumbnail. "That's not far from what you were gonna pay me to figure this out for you."

"I know."

"Why'd you need the money? You got a new car. You're not one of the richie-riches, but you're not like me."

"I got the car just before my dad lost his job. We're already behind on payments. They'll probably come repo the damn thing sooner than later." Her voice shakes a little. A faint tremor, like from an earthquake far away. "I wanna go to college, but my grades aren't good enough to get a scholarship. And financial aid is a bear, so I just thought . . . I just needed some money." Whatever tears seemed like they were about to come, they disappear as Bee grunts in rage and kicks a stick. Whitey thinks it's for him and he goes after it. "Not that any of it matters now, I guess."

"Why?"

"Because I'm pregnant! Jesus."

"Pregnant chicks still do stuff."

"Yeah, thanks, I'm sure my professors won't mind if I bring a screaming little rug rat to class. That'll go over well."

"Your parents can watch it." A moment then as Bee gives her this look, this grim, knowing look. Atlanta puzzles it out pretty quick: "It's a sore spot with them."

"Yeah."

"And you're counting on me to figure that out for you."

"That's right."

Atlanta buries her face in her hands. Her emotions on this are a pinwheel, the wind blowing one way, then the other. She's pissed at Bee for not telling her the whole story. She's sorry for Bee, because no matter what she thought she was getting into, something far worse happened—and it's not like Atlanta's any stranger to performing dubious tasks for fast cash. But then the wind howls the other way again as she's reminded of how Bee threw her into the fire then walked away.

"Walk me through it," Atlanta says. "You needed money. You asked Samantha to set you up?"

"Kinda. She started asking us. Said she had a thing going since end of last year and if any of us wanted to make a little extra money . . ."

"So you said you did. She told you the price. And then what?"

Bee taps her foot, seeming anxious and agitated having to go through this. "She told me to go to the party. It was like any other of her parties. They . . . handed me a drink, said I looked like I could use it. Loosen up and all that. I was really nervous. I'm not a virgin or anything, but I didn't know who was gonna pay, only that Samantha said she 'had somebody.' The drink tasted fine, rum and Coke, I think, but then . . . I remember people leading me through the party. Remember people laughing. Everything felt slippery, rubbery, like I was in one of those inflatable bounce castles. Then next thing I know, I was waking up on her front lawn. I'd been . . ." She makes a barely perceptible sound—a whimper, almost. "Something had happened."

"Samantha told me that someone came to pick you up. Someone named Mahoney. You know him?"

Bee wraps her arms around her middle. Shivers. Shakes her head. "No." Then she says: "Samantha told you all this? Out of the blue?"

"I had to smack her around a little."

A smile tugs at the corners of Bee's mouth. "Good."

Here, another gut punch to Atlanta's middle: for a little while, she actually thought Samantha, Mandy, and the others were interested in being her friend. Not that she liked them back, but it felt good to be wanted. Now she knows the truth: they just wanted to hurt her.

And get paid for it in the process.

"What happens now?" Bee asks.

"I guess come Monday, I put the screws to Samantha. I'll shake that tree hard as I can, see what comes falling out." She thinks but doesn't say: *And hopefully Babycheeks Skylar got the ball rolling with the police.* "What's your endgame? Because I honestly don't get it. Finding out the father—what's that gonna do for you? No good'll come from that. I say get rid of that baby. It's gonna be a boat anchor all your life, keeping you floating in this one spot: Maker's Bell for the rest of your life. Abortion's not a dirty word."

"I told you, no."

"So, why, then? Why look for the baby daddy?"

"Because once I find him, I'll get a paternity test and I'll make whoever it is pay me a whole lot more than fifteen hundred bucks.

I'll keep this baby in diapers and formula and gross mushy peas with that money."

"And what if you find him but he doesn't want to pay?"

Bee lifts her chin, narrows her eyes. "Then I'll kill him."

CHAPTER THIRTEEN

Ninety-nine times out of a hundred, Monday sucks. It sucks the shine off a bumper. It sucks a golf ball through a garden hose. It sucks like a black hole and bites like a snake. She tells her mother this sometimes, and Arlene, she always responds the same way: "You're like that fat cat, Garfield," and Atlanta says she still doesn't know who Garfield is, and then at some point Arlene tries to pull up Google on that ancient clamshell cell phone to show her, but it takes forever and by the time she either manages or gives up, Atlanta's already out the door and on the way to school.

Today, Atlanta's awake early.

Though to be more correct: she never went to bed.

(Atlanta hasn't slept in two nights, because bye-bye, Ambien.)

Giving up the Ambien was a hard row to hoe, because now she's left again without sleep. She figures, *Maybe I'll do a couple nights on, a couple nights off, see how that feels.* Last two nights, she mostly just lay there in bed, sweating and shaking at every tink, tap, creak, and groan of their old, off-kilter house settling. Every squeaking floorboard. It's bothering her so much she's been keeping Whitey in the room with her despite her mother's protests. And now, every time Whitey growls in his sleep, it just makes her heart jump faster. She'd settle down again, but then she'd hear another noise (real or imagined) and her temples, her neck, her wrists would feel suddenly like they were in a woodworker's vice.

Now, though, she's up and out of the house and she's not tired. She's gone so far past tired, she's come all the way around the world and back to *wired*.

Because today she's on a mission. Today, she's gonna hunt down Samantha. Confront her. Get another name. Get *something*. Kick her ass, maybe. Make some threats. Something, anything, to move the needle.

———

Samantha isn't at school.

Atlanta stalks her spots, doesn't find her. She spies her friends walking without her, goes through the reasons Samantha might not be here:

She's skipping. Her group seems to do that and not get caught. Or at least not catch any hell for it.

She's sick. Or probably—she's still a little beat-up from her last run-in with Atlanta. Samantha doesn't want to explain the cuts and bruises, and so she'll hide until they heal up.

She's arrested. This is Atlanta's one true shining hope—a golden ray of light whose brightness she basks in like a sleepy, content puppy. If Skylar Babycheeks called the police, said what happened, maybe they already swooped in, stuck her teen pimp ass in a squad car, and rolled her off to juvie.

At first, Atlanta really hopes that's what happened—but then a part of her realizes: everybody would already be talking about it, wouldn't they? Besides, if Samantha ends up in jail, that means juvie, and juvie's about thirty miles away. (Atlanta knows, because she thought she might be headed there after what she did to Arlene's boyfriend.) That means Atlanta will have a harder time figuring out who actually mixed up the baby batter inside Bee's belly.

Why are you helping her, anyway? Atlanta thinks. Bee abandoned her before and now, lied to her about what happened.

But then she reminds herself: It's not so simple as some dude came along and knocked her up. Someone had his way with her when she was passed out cold, or at least drugged up enough to be unaware what was happening to her.

Even thinking about that sets off sirens inside her head.

Her index finger reflexively twitches. Like it's pulling an imaginary trigger.

———

She sees Damon in the hall. It almost looks like he's dodging her. With a quick side step, she intersects his path and he stops short. "Atlanta," he says.

"Hey, Damon." She scrunches up her nose like a bunny sniffing for carrots. "You need a nickname. D. D-Mon. Demon. Carrizo, Carazzo, Hasenpfeffer Incorporated."

"What?"

"C'mon, you never watched *Laverne & Shirley*?"

"I don't know what that is."

"Nick at Nite, dude. A classic." She waves him off. "Whatever. Hey. Just wanna make sure everything's cool. We cool?"

"Cool as . . ." He swallows hard and it's like he's searching for a word. "Ice."

"You seem weird."

"It was a weird weekend."

"Okay."

He shrugs. "See ya," he says, and then he's gone.

She thinks: *What the hell, dude?* A week ago he was all in her face, and now he acts like she's covered in the Ebola virus.

Men can be such dipshits.

———

During lunch, Atlanta heads over to the Mandy Newhouse table, and plunks her butt down right next to her. Mandy gives her a sour once-over. The others at the table—the Barford twins, Petra, Suzie, but no sign of Moose Barnes.

"Oh, you," Mandy says.

"Hey, you," Atlanta says, quick swiping a fork from Mandy's tray. She tries to iron the Southern accent out of her voice, slap on a fakey-fakey, super-generic, rich-girl accent. "Gosh, wow, it's nice to see you again. Great party the other night, huh? Off. The. Chain. What was really great—"

"Atlanta, don't be weird."

Joshie Barford says, "It was *so awesome* how you cliff-jumped off the balcony and—"

Atlanta doesn't care to hear it and repeats herself: "*What was really great* was how you handed me a cup of *hunch punch* that had some kinda *date rape* drug in it. That was *high-larious.*"

At that, the table goes quiet.

Mandy doesn't get that memo. Her face twists like a squeezed lemon and she says: "Atlanta, don't make up lies to make me look bad, because—"

Under the table, Atlanta pushes the fork against Mandy's thigh.

"*Ow*," Mandy says.

"Yeah, *ow*. You wanna revise your statement, Miss Newhouse?"

"Suck my tits," Mandy says.

Atlanta presses the fork harder. Mandy winces.

"Fine!" Mandy says, breaking. "I didn't know what was in the cup. Okay? Samantha just said to give it to you, so I gave it to you. Don't kill the messenger."

"That's one helluva message," Atlanta seethes.

"Here's a real message for you," Mandy says, sneering. "You had a shot to run with the big dogs. You could've been cool. But you're not even fit to sniff our asses."

Atlanta thinks: *Stick her like a pig.*

But she holds off. The fork is a threat—actually stabbing her with a fork is probably not going to fix anything.

Still, though, the threat has to count, so she removes the fork from Mandy's thigh—and sticks it in her side, where the flesh is more tender.

Where more organs exist to perforate.

Mandy yelps.

"All your asses smell like some bad shit," Atlanta says. "And I wanna know what's going on. Where's Samantha?"

"I don't know," Mandy says through clenched teeth.

"Do I need to call someone?" Joshie Barford says.

Mandy gives a subtle shake of her head.

Atlanta asks: "Moose Barnes. Where's he?"

All around the table, a series of shrugs. Someone says he hasn't been in school, either.

"I have a message for *you*," Atlanta says, leaning in and whispering in Mandy's ear. "Whatever you rich bitches have going on, I'll find out what it is. You won't hurt good people on my watch. You've seen my video. You know what I can do. Don't mess with me, Mandy Newhouse."

Jason Barford jumps in and with a Scottish accent says: "I've got a particular set of skills—"

Atlanta bumps an elbow, knocks his Coke can over. It spills and fizzes into his lap—he leaps up, cursing.

She withdraws the fork and stands up.

"You see Samantha," Atlanta says, "you tell her I'm fixin' to have a talk."

Mandy nods. But then, as Atlanta is walking away, the girl calls after, loud enough so that the neighboring tables can hear:

"Hey, Atlanta, I hear you went to the Homecoming dance with Josie Dunderchek. I always pegged you for a dyke."

Behind her, all around her, come laughs.

Atlanta thinks: *Be cool.*

Stay calm.

Just walk away.

She picks up a lunch tray and hits Mandy Newhouse in the head with it.

———

Vice Principal Wilson stares at her. Little eyes set back in his big head. Eyeglasses so big they might as well be goggles.

"You hit another student," he says.

"I know." She realizes that's not much of a defense. "I didn't hit her hard."

"You broke the tray."

"They're pretty flimsy trays."

He sighs, taps a pen against his knuckles. "I know it's been hard for you," he says.

"I'm fine. It's fine. Everything's fine."

"Everything isn't fine. Not even for us adults. But for students, it's particularly hard. I get that. You're young and . . . confused. Lots of emotions. Driven by a cocktail of hormones. I try to be understanding. I do. But you represent an element of chaos and I . . . there has to be order here."

"Okay," she says, offering a half shrug.

He sighs again. Looks at the clock above them—some ancient, utilitarian thing from when the Beatles were still new—each tick and each tock so pronounced the sound is like the hammer of her gun pulled back and snapped forward. Backward and forward, backward and forward. Finally, he says:

"I can't tolerate violence."

"Looks like you can't tolerate not eating ice cream and ham sandwiches."

He stiffens, face jiggling as he purses his lips. "A fat joke. Really? I know they call me Planet Wilson. But from you? It betrays who you claim to be. I have a thyroid condition. And I take omeprazole for my heartburn, and one of the side effects is . . ." He frowns. "I don't have to justify myself to you."

It's like a cold slap to the face because he's right. "Man, I'm sorry, Mister Principal. I . . . haven't slept in two days. I'm a jerk. I didn't mean anything by it."

All she gets in return is him looking down at his hands. At his fingernails. At the pen. There's a moment where she can see she actually hurt him. Cut him with a knife no less real because it came from her mouth and not her hands.

I'm such a bitch.

"To clarify, we have a zero tolerance policy here at William Mason High. Particularly toward acts of violence."

"Oh." That strikes a vein of fear. "I don't know . . . I don't know what that means, but I promise you, I'm a good kid. All right, maybe not a *good* kid but I'm an okay kid, the *okayest*, and please, don't expel me—"

"I'm not going to expel you. I'm going to suspend you."

"What?"

"Three days' suspension. Tuesday, Wednesday, Thursday. You will come back on Friday, and Friday night is parent-teacher conference night, so you and your mother—who has never deigned to show her face here before—are mandated to come and discuss your academic behavior with your teachers. She should know that if you continue along this line you will not graduate."

"She might be working."

"Then she should find a way to get time off."

"That's awfully presumptive."

"It is what it is. You're dismissed."

She stands. Realizes that he's throwing her a bone. Maybe even trying to reach out, be friendly. And yet she can't muster a kind word in return.

As she heads toward the door, he says:

"It really does get better, you know."

She looks back. "If you say so."

CHAPTER FOURTEEN

Ambien that night puts her down like an old horse: she doesn't sleep so much as she falls into a six-foot grave and ceases to exist for a while. She's afraid to find out what happens this time, but come morning, she wakes up in her bed the same way she went to sleep: no shoes on, no ice cream in her mouth, no spoon in her hand.

Down in the kitchen, there's Paul—not a night now where he isn't staying over, which doesn't scare her as much as she thought it would, or maybe as much as it should. Something about it even feels comforting, which is itself uncomfortable—it makes Atlanta feel like she's dropping her guard.

Part of her thinks: *Maybe this is how normal people feel most times.*

Like, they trust other people. Don't figure on them being monsters.

Huh.

Paul is eating cereal. "Your mom's still in bed," he says.

"That's kinda her jam," Atlanta says. "Sleeping."

He looks at his watch. "Shouldn't you be getting to school?"

"Oh. Uhhh." She almost tells him that she got suspended. But now there's another weird feeling inside her—she doesn't want to say that because of what he'll think of her. *Wait, slow down, why do I care what he thinks of me?* She tries to shake it off. In her head she imagined three days of vacation—suspension always struck her as a pretty dumb punishment, like, why don't they make you go to *more* school, weekend school, night school, whatever—but now she's not so sure. So instead she goes through the motions: packing up her bag, grabbing a couple store-brand Pop Tarts from a box. "Good point. I'll see you later."

"You're not walking, are you?"

She told Shane last night not to pick her up. "Shane's my ride."

"He should've been here by now."

"Maybe he's running late."

"Smart money says you'll be late, then. Come on." He stands up, slips on his sneakers, grabs his keys from the table. "I'll drive you. I gotta go to work soon anyway."

"Paul, you really don't have to."

"I want to." He smiles. "Come on."

Well, here we go.

———

She lets him drive her, because what choice does she have? He takes her to school, and along the way she's pretty quiet. He tries to make conversation—tries to open her up about the hunter safety class coming up this weekend, but she tunes out most of the conversation. Which makes her feel bad because Atlanta likes the class and, despite her every mental muscle screaming otherwise, actually likes Paul, too.

He drops her off at the school platform and he says: "Have fun at school," which is maybe the dumbest thing anybody ever says to kids. She thinks she might have more fun at a gyno appointment.

So, as a response, she leans in through the passenger's-side window and says, "Have fun being a fireman."

And he gives her a bemused look. He chuckles: "The fireman thing isn't a job, Atlanta. It's a volunteer-only gig."

"Oh. I just thought—oh." She frowns. "Where do you work, then?"

"VLS."

"The fracking people?"

"How'd you know that?"

She shrugs. "I know things."

"I guess you do."

"Is it safe? Fracking? I hear things."

He waves it off. "All just to score political points. You hear it causes everything from groundwater pollution to . . . earthquakes, even, but none of that's true. Safe as a school bus ride."

"School buses are, like, superdangerous. Those things crash all the time, and the kids don't have any seat belts."

"Oh." He shrugs. "Safer than that, then."

But the way he says it, she's not sure he believes it.

"Have fun fracking," she says.

When he's gone, she hops off the school platform. The rest of the crowd heads toward the school, but Atlanta—she swims upstream. Goes another way.

She heads toward the parking lot.

———

She looks around, doesn't see what she's looking for. By now most of the kids have streamed in through the doors, and the parking lot has only the stragglers in it—those with heavy packs over their backs, keys jingling in their pockets as they bolt toward the school so they're not late for homeroom.

Atlanta hears someone coming up behind her.

It's Bee who announces herself. "Hey."

"Hey," Atlanta says. "You're rolling in here kinda late."

Bee shrugs. "Morning sickness."

"Oh, hey, really? I'm sorry."

Bee leans in, smiling. "Nah, not really," she says. "But they don't know the difference. One thing the preggo-sitch has gotten me is a standing doctor's note."

"Cool."

"What are you doing out here? Aren't *you* late?"

"Got suspended."

"No shit. Why?"

Sigh. "I sorta hit Mandy Newhouse with a lunch tray."

It takes a second for the wave to break over Bee's beaches, but when it does, she starts laughing—hard, then harder, then so hard Atlanta thinks she might fall down and puke all over herself. Bee wipes tears away and says, "That's basically the most amazing thing I've ever heard. Was it really satisfying?"

"Aw, man, you have no idea." They laugh. Then Atlanta says: "Hey, you up for a senior skip day?"

"Like I said, standing doctor's note. What's up?"

"Hop in the car. You drive, I'll talk."

———

When she finds out where they're going, Bee's face goes gray. "Really?"

"Uh-huh. I didn't see her car in the lot, which means she's still not at school. So, I figure, let's hit up her house, see if she's home. If not, then we'll just . . . I dunno, ding-dong-ditch or something."

The car winds its way through the maze of minimansions that comprises Gallows Hill.

"I'm gonna stay outside," Bee says, pulling up to the curb. She doesn't even pull the car up the driveway.

"You can't drive up?"

"Atlanta, please."

Oh. "Oh." Now she gets it. "I'm making you . . . I'm making you return to the scene. I'm sorry. I didn't think. Man, I'm such a dummy. I'm sorry, Bee."

"It's cool. I can hack it." But then Bee licks her lips and stares out. "I remember waking up over there." She points toward a manicured flower bed next to a rocky waterfall feature. "I woke up hearing that little stupid waterfall."

"We can go," Atlanta says.

"No. You're doing this for me. I'll wait here. You go on ahead. See you when you get back, okay?"

"Okay."

———

Ding-dong.

Nothing.

Ding-dong.

Foot tap. *Tap, tap, tap.*

She cracks her knuckles.

Chews her lip.

Rings it one last time:

Ding-dong.

Atlanta doesn't hear footsteps, doesn't hear voices, doesn't hear anything.

But Samantha's car is right there in the driveway.

Maybe, she thinks, *they went away.* Heaven knows the richie-riches can do that whenever they please. Just pick up and go. *Vacation homes.* The concept is hard for Atlanta to even understand. She's moved around a whole bunch and most of the folks she became friends with didn't get many vacations, and when they did, it meant packing up a tent or a small pop-up camper and hitting some KOA site to roast weenies and melt s'mores. Around here folks liked to go to the "Shore," which is really just another way of saying "New Jersey."

But these people here, they're different. They have their *home* house, and then they have, like, extra places. As if life is one big Monopoly game. Collecting houses like they're little plastic pieces on a game board.

People with houses to spare confuse the hell out of her.

Whatever. Nobody's home.

On a lark, she tries the doorknob—

The door drifts open.

Huh. How about that.

She steps into the peachy foyer. Her footsteps echo.

No sounds. No footsteps, no housekeeper, no television white noise, no running dishwasher or air conditioner or heater. Samantha's house is a dead space.

So Atlanta decides to poke around a little.

In the kitchen, she pops the big double-door stainless steel fridge. Inside are foods she's heard about but thought half of them were jokes: almond milk (*Ha ha ha you can't milk an almond,* she thinks); a kale-kombucha drink (it looks like something a swamp monster threw up); some kind of meat or fish wrapped up in a brown wrapping with a label on it that says BARRAMUNDI (okay, somebody's just making that word up).

In what appears to be one of several living rooms, she sees a coffee table with a small "fireplace" right in the middle of it—looks like two glass windows with an arched, shiny burner right in the middle. In another room they have a TV on the wall that might literally be the same size as Atlanta's own dining room table. You could take that TV off the wall, turn it over, and eat off it.

In the bathroom: towels embroidered with the word *Guest.* Towels so light and so fluffy she figures they must be made of something exotic, like koala or wombat or something. By the sink: a series of hand soaps and lotions, like she's in a fancy hotel or something. The toilet has a heated seat.

A heated seat.

If that's not just the tippy-top of Rich People Mountain, Atlanta doesn't know what is.

She's about to turn the light off in the bathroom when—

There.

A noise. A faint *tap, tap, tap.*

She listens, tries to pinpoint where it's coming from. The ceiling, she thinks. Which means it's coming from upstairs.

She knows the house well enough by now—and she goes up the same staircase as before, when she found Skylar in one of the bedrooms.

Up here, the *tap, tap, tap* becomes a different sound:

Drip, drip, drip.

Just a faucet gone leaky, she thinks. There, a humbling moment, a small connection between the rich and the poor: *We all get leaky faucets.*

Still, she figures, good time to poke around up here, too.

So she does. Heads in through bedroom doors. Each bedroom its own decor: all some shade of modern. All clean and spare and with bold colors and simple furniture. European, is how Atlanta imagines it, though she's not sure what that means or why she thinks it.

She's near now to the *drip, drip, drip* sound.

One door down.

She finds it cracked open and—

Even in the crack, she sees the human hand.

Draped over the edge of a soaking tub.

Someone's here, she thinks. At first she doesn't want to move, doesn't want to startle the person, and she turns to go and—

Whap.

Bangs her knee on the doorjamb.

She winces, rubs it.

In through the crack, the hand hasn't moved.

Hasn't *twitched*, even.

Oh, no.

No, no, no.

Atlanta knows not to do it, knows that her best course of action here is to turn tail and fly this coop quick as her little wings will carry her, and yet here she is, easing the door open with the flats of her knuckles.

Samantha Gwynn-Rudin is there in the tub.

Eyes staring out, empty as drinking glasses. Black marks banding her skin—face gone alternately pale and dark in striations. Her head is craned back over the porcelain lip of the full tub, her chin sticky with what at first Atlanta thinks is food but then realizes is what happens to food after you puke it up.

The tub is full. The faucet drips. And water drips over the edge on the floor. A puddle gathering on the white subway tile.

An empty pill bottle bobs in the water.

Other pill bottles lie scattered about the floor, too.

A few pills here and there. Blue, pink, white. Round, long, triangular.

Atlanta has to stifle the sound that tries to come up out of her.

"Okay," she says. "Okay. Samantha, oh, man." She tries to think: What now? What does she do? Call the police? How to explain this? Holger told her to stay out of trouble and now she's here, trespassing. With a dead girl in a tub, a dead girl who she rather publicly had a fight with recently.

Maybe she can call the cops from the house phone here. It'll seem anonymous. *But maybe I've left fingerprints around.*

If this is really a suicide, that won't matter.

But if they see it as anything but . . .

They ruled Chris Coyne's death a suicide, too.

But it wasn't. Not really.

And here Atlanta's prevailing thought is: *Chris, I miss you.* She misses him so bad it feels like she's a doll with her stuffing ripped out. Last month or two she's been able to keep that feeling tamped down, filled up, but here it comes roaring back. A tsunami wave about to overtake her.

Focus. Focus on the here and now.

Samantha was mixed up in something bad with . . . well, Atlanta doesn't know who, but she can dang well assume it's with some bad or worse people.

So, maybe the solution is to just leave. Someone will find the girl's body eventually. The parents. The housekeeper—er, Delfina the *house manager*. Calling the cops now won't make Samantha any less dead.

Atlanta backs out of the room slowly.

And downstairs, the sound of keys jangling, rattling.

Voices that start muffled and get louder.

Footsteps.

Someone's here.

Shit, shit, shit.

Quiet as she can muster, Atlanta darts back down the hallway, near to the staircase—just close enough so she can see over the railing.

Two people coming in. People she recognizes not from meeting them in person, but from the portrait downstairs. The mustached dad, the sharp-angled mother. Next to them sits a pair of roller suitcases, Gucci. He's crying. Blubbering and blowing his nose. The mother sighs, steps past him, says: "I'm resetting the alarm." And then punches a code into it. The alarm panel goes green.

The mother heads toward the curved staircase. Begins her ascent.

Right toward Atlanta.

She quick ducks into the first open door, trying to be quiet.

But the mother stops on the stairs, halting her climb.

"Richard?" the woman says. "Did you hear something?"

But the man blows his nose again: *honnnk.*

The woman makes a *hm* sound, then keeps coming up the steps.

Atlanta peeks around the edge of the door frame, sees Samantha's mother walking down the wall. Chin lifted, eyes forward. Such poise and grace. A kind of fierce and frosty determination.

The tall woman makes a beeline for the bathroom.

Atlanta peeks out.

Samantha's mother pauses at the doorway, staring in at her dead daughter. She stands like that, stock still, for ten seconds, then twenty, just staring, mouth pulled taut like a fishing line—

Her hand flies to her mouth. A strangled cry comes out. Her knees start to buckle, though she never goes all the way to the floor. The tears come, then. Loud, shrill sobs. Her whole body shaking.

It goes like that for a minute or so.

Then the woman clears her throat. Stands tall once again. She steps into the bathroom and now Atlanta hears *her* blowing her nose.

Back out in the hallway, Samantha's mother calls: "Richard? I need you to make the call. Richard?"

From downstairs, a bleated call: "I can't. I . . . not now. You do it."

"Jesus Christ," the woman hisses under her breath. "Fine! Where's the phone?" To which the man doesn't answer. Atlanta only hears him weeping.

And here, the woman looks down the hall—

Atlanta ducks back into the room.

Footfalls, coming closer.

"Phone, phone, where's the goddamn phone?"

Atlanta quick pivots, hides behind the half-open door of the room—

—just as the lights flip on.

Atlanta finds herself standing and hiding in what must be (or have been) Samantha's room: It's a teenager's room, but only barely. Walls purple like smashed grapes—if Atlanta had to compare the room to anything, it's what she figures a Wild West boudoir would look like. No art on the walls, though. No posters. Big bed, four tree-trunk-sized pillars anchoring the frame. Stereo. Makeup. Clothes on the floor. A bong on the drawer because, well, why not.

And next to the bong: the stun gun from the other night.

Samantha's mother steps into the room.

And, like before, stands there, staring. Another sob rolls through her and again, she quickly stifles it—amazing, if completely crazy, emotional control.

She clears her throat, then begins looking around the room for the phone. Lifts a pillow. Lifts the blankets. Begins toeing clothes away.

All the while, doing a circuit around the room.

Closer and closer to Atlanta.

Now, she's staring at the bong. The woman sighs.

Then she starts to turn toward Atlanta. The door starts to move, and the woman's head starts to turn—

Atlanta's hand darts out, grabs the stun gun.

The woman sees her.

Her eyes narrow. "Who are—"

Atlanta winces and sticks the stun gun right under the woman's armpit.

Those narrow eyes go big as moons.

Atlanta flings the stun gun to the ground and bolts. Down the steps so fast she trips over her own feet, starts to pitch forward—her hand darts out, catches the railing, and she regains her balance without losing momentum.

She hears someone yelling for her—a man. The father. Richard.

Shoulder out, she flings open the door.

There, at the end of the driveway, the road is empty.

Bee is gone.

And once again, Atlanta Burns finds herself running through the yards and houses of Gallows Hill—past tall privacy fences, across yards so manicured they've got those dark bands and light bands made from a perfect mowing effort.

She tumbles out onto a side street—

Brakes squeal.

It's Bee.

She gets in the hatchback. The car lurches forward like a rabbit with a bottle rocket tied to its tail.

CHAPTER FIFTEEN

They drive around for the rest of the day. They park in the dingy lot of an old emptied-out Giant grocery store on the edge of town. Atlanta tells Bee everything—there came a moment when she thought to protect Bee from all this, but it's Bee who got her into this. And she just can't stomach keeping it to herself.

And now Bee stares out over her steering wheel, watching the middle distance as if she's not sure how to feel or what to think.

"They saw you," Bee says.

"I think. Her mother definitely did. Her dad, I dunno."

"They'll tell the police."

Atlanta swallows hard. "That's just it. I don't know that they will. Somethin' real weird was going on there, Bee. They came in, already upset. Samantha's mother went upstairs all mechanical-like and headed right to the bathroom. *Right to it.* That woman *knew* her daughter was dead in a tub before she walked through the front door. Father knew it, too."

"Maybe Samantha called them before she did it. Told them what she was going to do—"

"Uh-uh, I don't buy it. That happens, and the first thing you do as a parent is call the police. And even if they didn't—let's say they didn't take her seriously—then still, you get home and you call Samantha's name, you go upstairs to check on her. That's not . . . not what these people did."

"What are you saying?"

"I'm saying somebody killed Samantha. And her parents were in on it."

"That's . . . insane, Atlanta."

"You don't know what this town is like. Heck, *I* don't even know. But I've seen a glimpse of what's hiding in the dirt. Lots of things squirming." She turns toward Bee. "You might be a target."

"What?"

"I don't see why they'd have any reason to come after you, but just in case. You got a tie into this. Samantha hooked you up. I don't know why anyone would wanna kill her—"

"We don't *know* that someone killed her!"

"Just be careful. Okay?"

"It'll be fine. I'll be fine." Way that Bee says it, it's like she's trying real hard to believe it. Like she's not a target. Or like Atlanta isn't one, either. (Atlanta figured by now she'd be used to that, but turns out, you never really get used to being a target.) Just saying the words aloud is akin to casting a magic spell. The equivalent of knocking on wood to make sure the universe doesn't spite you.

———

When the school day should be over, Bee takes Atlanta back to her house. She pulls up, and she and Atlanta just sit for a while, quiet as a couple of sneaky, scared-ass mice. Atlanta's about to speak when—

Wham.

Something slams into the car, makes the whole thing shake, makes her heart jump into her throat, makes a mad, panicked sound come out of Bee—

A white shape appears at the passenger's-side window.

Whitey's lumpy, misshapen head. His maw opens and he licks the glass like it's candy. Tongue dragging across it, leaving smeary streaks.

"Jesus Christ," Bee says. "I may have legit peed."

"I better go," Atlanta says.

"You be careful, too."

"Sure," she says. But what she thinks is: *I'm about a hundred miles past* careful, *Bee, and there's no turning around.*

———

She paces outside for a while. Shaking even still.

Then she makes a call.

Phone rings. And rings. And rings.

Eventually, a voice answers. A familiar voice.

Babycheeks. "Hello?"

"It's me," Atlanta says.

"Who?"

"The girl. From the party. You remember? *The party.*"

Silence on the other end. "Oh."

"You never called the police." An accusation. And on the other end: a small gasp and the sound of someone licking lips.

"I . . . I'm sorry."

"Don't be sorry," Atlanta hisses. "Just call them already." Babycheeks calls the cops, it'll bring them to Samantha's house—and maybe, just maybe, they'll catch something. Atlanta sure can't call them. She can't tie herself to this. Might as well tie herself to a car's bumper just as it's driving off a cliff.

"I can't. I told my parents what happened—"

"So?"

"They said I shouldn't call. That . . . that it wouldn't do me any good. That I got away safe and sound—"

"Yeah, thanks to *me*."

"I know. I know. But . . . I don't want that kind of attention."

"Please. Listen to me—"

"I have to go."

"Wait!"

But the girl hangs up. When Atlanta tries her back, the phone just rings and rings and rings.

———

Inside the house, the sound of sniffling, snuffling, nose-blowing.

A bright fear jumps inside Atlanta's chest like an ember leaping off a crackling campfire—she thinks: *Samantha's mother is here.*

How? How did she get here that fast? No car in the driveway.

Atlanta winces, not sure what to do. Go back outside to hide? Creep through the house? *No.* Creeping and hiding isn't her way. Not today. Not ever.

She puffs out her chest, sticks up her chin, walks into the living room where she hears the sound—

It's not Samantha's mother crying.

It's her own.

There sits Arlene, a tissue box in her lap. A battlefield of used tissues cast across the coffee table like dead enemy soldiers.

Atlanta's first thought is: *Paul left her.*

And she says as much, too. "Paul, huh?"

Arlene's face knots up like a twist tie—her brow darkens and her mouth scowls. "No, *Atlanta*. Not Paul." And here tears threaten to spill again. "Not Paul."

"Then what's going on?"

"That's no way to speak to your crying mother."

"Well—you know what? You cry a lot. And I don't know how to deal with it so why don't you just cut to the chase?"

"I got the mail today," Mama says. That's when Atlanta spies something next to Arlene on the couch, something she dismissed as unused tissues:

Two envelopes. Each torn open.

"I see that." Atlanta's chest tightens. "Quit with the suspense."

"First envelope? You got *suspended from school.*"

Uh-oh.

Atlanta plays it tough: "Yeah, so?"

"You got suspended from school and you didn't tell me."

"Is that what bothers you? That I didn't tell you? Fine, sorry I didn't say something but I didn't want to have to deal with—" she gestures at her mother with waggling fingers "—*this.*"

"It's not that you didn't tell me. It's . . . it's what you did. It says you *assaulted* another girl, Atlanta."

She rolls her eyes. "They put that in there because they like drama. They want it to seem like what I did matters when it really doesn't matter one bit."

"What did you do? Tell me." Another nose blow. "What was it?"

"I . . ." Atlanta licks her lips and realizes it maybe sounds worse than it was, but here goes: "I hit a girl with a lunch tray."

Her mother gasps.

"*Atlanta.* We do not do that. That's . . . that's prison behavior."

"School *is* prison, Mama. That's how it goes." She thinks: *All of us just sitting there day in and day out, doing our time, trying to get to the end of our sentences. And part of that means surviving alongside the other inmates. Maybe that means a little prison yard justice happens from time to time.*

"Other kids, they don't do these things."

Atlanta blasts out a laugh, but it's not a happy sound. "No, they don't, they just sit there and suffer in silence. They take their whuppin' from whatever sonofabitch wants to give it to them on that particular day."

"What made you so hard, Atlanta?"

"*You did.*" The words don't simply fall out of her—it's like they're launched forth, an arrow from a bow, a cannonball from a cannon's mouth, a fusillade of bunker buster bombs dropped from a very great height with the sincerest desire to *blow it all to hell.* "It hasn't even been a year since Emerald Lakes and what, you think I'm just fine? A-okay, okie-dokie, all squared away? Spoiler alert: I'm not fine."

And that launches Mama into a new wave of weeping.

Atlanta stands there, waits for it to subside, waits for Mama to speak—which she does, eventually, when she says: "You're right.

This is my fault. Dangit, I was trying to do better. And Paul, he's nice, he's genuinely nice."

Well, hell. Sometimes it's easier to attack than to back down, easier to kick and scream and bite than to say you were wrong. Easier to take the poison inside you and spit it into someone else's mouth.

But now, spitting up that poison has left an emptiness inside Atlanta.

Guilt fills the void.

Dangit.

Dangit!

She sighs, sits down, grabs her mother's hand, and holds it in her own. "You have been doing better." *I'm the one who isn't doing much better.* "And Paul is . . ." Saying it is like performing rectal dentistry on a rabid wolf, but here it goes: "Paul is really actually maybe kinda nice. I'm sorry I hit that girl. Okay?"

"Okay." *Sniff.* Then Arlene says, "Did the little bitch deserve it?"

"*So* deserved it."

Arlene pats her hand.

Then she gets the second envelope.

"Is this door number two?" Atlanta asks.

"It is."

On the outside: the name of a bank. Never a good sign. Just seeing a bank's name makes Atlanta's blood go rancid. She pulls the letter out.

One word stands out like the light of a freight train bearing down:

Mortgage.

It's déjà vu. A flashback. Sitting with her mother not even six months ago, getting a letter about a potential foreclosure. That, the result of Atlanta's meddling in the business of neo-Nazi money-man, Orly Erickson: mean, bloodthirsty chickens come home to roost.

Now: a different message, but no better.

The bank that had the mortgage sold it. To another bank.

And now that bank is invoking "balloon payments." Which at first blush sound a lot nicer than they are: balloons are fun, festive, floaty. Atlanta would love to pay in balloons. Latex squeaking, balloons thumping together. But that's not what it means. A quick read tells her that the payments are going up. Way, way up.

"We can't afford that," Mama says.

"It doesn't say anything about foreclosure." Though here Atlanta appends the unspoken words: *Not yet, anyway.*

"*We can't afford it.* Foreclosure is the end of this road." Mama's high-pitched voice tells Atlanta how hard she's trying to keep it together. "I'm gonna have to get another job. We may need to move anyway. Goddamn. We were doing so good, baby. I don't know what happened."

Atlanta's not sure, either. She has, or *had*, a deal with Orly Erickson—in return for her not sharing certain information on his pet police officer, Officer Petry, he interfaced with the bank to make sure their payments were kept low, and foreclosure was last night's bad dream.

Now, though, something's changed. The bank sold it.

Which means she'll need to make a call she doesn't want to make.

But that's a problem for later. In the meantime:

"Gimme a minute," Atlanta says.

And then she chokes back her pride, her selfishness, her future plans, and she heads upstairs to her room to fetch something.

———

It's gone.

It's gone, it's gone, it's gone.

That's not possible. That's just. Not. Possible!

The shoebox is there. The notebook is still inside it.

But all the money?

Poof. Like it never even existed. A ghost exorcised, gone to plasmic vapor.

She searches under the bed. Under the pillow. Around the room. Underwear drawer. Sock drawer. Closet. She tries not to make a sound, but the frustrated roar that comes up from her lungs cannot and will not be contained.

Atlanta kicks the shoe box back under the bed.

"Fuck!"

———

Downstairs, Arlene's piling up all the used tissues and sliding them into a plastic Walmart bag. She sees Atlanta come down. "You okay, baby?"

The tension in Atlanta's neck is like bridge cable—feels like that's the only thing stopping her head from going *pop* and hopping off her shoulders like a spooked frog. She wants to ask her mother about the money, wants to *accuse* her, but it doesn't add up. Mama's a lot of things, but duplicitous isn't really one of them. She's a bad liar. She's shit when it comes to keeping secrets.

So she doesn't ask. She puts on a brave face even though inside, she's a tornado ripping through barns and cow pastures and pretty houses.

"I'm good," she says.

"You find what you need upstairs?"

"Not yet," she says. "But I'll keep looking."

———

Paul isn't there for dinner. He's at work, so it's just Mama and Atlanta. Mama tried to get an extra shift at the Karlton, but it didn't happen. The two of them, mother and daughter, don't speak much—it's like the day's events have left them both gutted. Blown tires on the side of some highway. They don't even eat at the table, the two of them chowing down on canned spaghetti while sitting on the couch, watching bad TV. Some show about a bunch of doctors who are also detectives or something? Atlanta doesn't really get it.

Whitey just lies there on his back, farts a lot. Room killers, that gas. Smells like someone managed to get a rotten egg inside a balloon before setting the whole affair on fire. It's equal parts *devil stink*, *tire fire*, and *sour garbage*.

Eventually Atlanta heads up, leaving her mother behind.

Been a long day, so she takes out the Ambien.

Sure hope I don't have any wacky fun-time adventures tonight, she thinks.

She pops a pill, but even as she chases it with a glass of water, the thought strikes her like a bullet pinging off a bell—

The money.

From the shoe box.

What if—?

Could she have done something with it while on the damn pills?

Oh, hell.

She lies there, panicked, until sleep comes for her like a wolf.

———

And, proof of concept: she wakes up on the couch downstairs. There's the smell of sausage cooking. Eggs, too. Atlanta asks Mama how she got downstairs on the couch, and Mama laughs like it's some kind of joke. Tells her that Atlanta came back downstairs about an hour after heading up. Seemed kinda dopey, but they talked a little, watched more TV, and then Atlanta passed out on the couch and Arlene headed to bed. Nothing more complicated than that.

Even still: Atlanta doesn't remember one second of it.

Not coming down. Not talking or TV watching.

The pills gotta go.

CHAPTER SIXTEEN

For the next two days, she doesn't do much. It's not depression, at least she doesn't think so, but it sure is *something*. Mostly she sits around. Her deepest desire is to just sit here and do nothing, and everything will get better. Maybe all her problems will sort themselves out. It's easier than dealing with things. The loss of the money. The dead girl in the tub. The mortgage payments. She takes her temperature, but everything's normal. Even though she feels clammy and weird, even though her skin crawls and she feels like a vase on a table wobbling back and forth.

She's fine. Everything's fine.

Nothing's fine.

———

Night before she has to go back to school, she makes the call she doesn't want to make. Orly Erickson is in the phone book, so that's who she rings up.

A woman answers. His wife. Mitchell's mother.

"May I speak to Orly, please?"

The woman asks who's calling.

Atlanta answers: "It's June, from the office."

The rasp of something against the phone. A fumbling sound.

Then: "June from the office," Orly says.

"Hey there," Atlanta says.

"I know that guitar twang voice. Hello, *June*. How's Atlanta this time of the year? Temperature still hot down there? Like it's burning up, I bet."

"Ain't you clever. I won't keep you. I have a question for you."

"Hold on." Then, to his wife: "Hon, I gotta take this in the other room." Footsteps. A throat clearing. "I bet it's about your mother's mortgage."

She tenses up. "Bingo."

"Funny thing about that: I don't control the banks. When my friend at First United told me what was happening, I said, well, that's a shame that a whole different *financial entity* is scooping up these mortgages with a shovel, but I thought, my god, that's a thing that's just plain out of my hands. Act of God. Sorry, Atlanta. Adult business is strange sometimes."

"This is some kinda vendetta."

"Oh, but for what?"

"For me kicking your son's ass."

A bit of anger in his voice when he says: "Mitchell gets his ass kicked by you, he deserves it."

"What about when *you* kick his ass? He deserve it then?"

"Have a nice night—"

"Wait. I still got that tape."

"You do, but you want to know what I heard? I heard the police brought you in for something the other week. You're on their radar, especially after your little Internet video stunt. So, let's play this out. You release that tape, then what? You fire that gun, you won't be able to handle the kickback. It might—*might*—dent my armor, but you? It'll do more damage to you than me. So, you feel like your moral compass demands you let slip those dogs, by all means, do so."

"You asshole."

"Good luck paying that mortgage, little girl."

Click.

It takes every ounce of willpower she can muster not to throw the phone across the room.

———

Friday, she's back at school.

And classes are off for the day. Because today is a *grief day*, a day where the school comes together and deals with the subject of teenage suicide.

Pictures of Samantha Gwynn-Rudin hang everywhere.

Little vigils at different corners, in different hallways.

Various assemblies break out into smaller groups where everybody can share their thoughts. People who didn't know Samantha talk about how nice she was (a lie), how she made them better people (probably a lie), how she helped others aspire to something greater (what?). Atlanta sits through all of this with a sick feeling in her gut. She thinks as the day goes: *They didn't do this for Chris.*

At lunchtime she sits with her crowd and they all shoot the shit, and Atlanta pretends everything is fine and that Samantha wasn't murdered and that her parents weren't involved and that she doesn't feel like she's standing at the edge of an old well throwing pebbles down in it but never hearing them land in water or anywhere else. An endless pit like a hungry mouth waiting to swallow her up.

Moose Barnes still isn't back at school.

The rumor mill is hard at work, there: his parents are on vacation, he ran away, he was secretly "doing" Samantha and now he's so broken up he's depressed or in an institution or tried to kill himself, too, and *now* he's in an institution. Of course Atlanta wonders: *Is he dead, too?*

Nobody seems to have a straight answer.

Kyle says at the end of lunch: "See you guys at parent-teacher night."

And Atlanta shrugs and says: "I doubt it."

———

When she gets home, Mama is in the kitchen, all done up. Hair teased out, lipstick on, pink blouse swaying. Paul comes in, too—he's wearing a button-down shirt, jeans, nice shoes, if a little scuffed. Atlanta cocks an eyebrow: "Hot date?"

Arlene gives her a dubious look. "Baby, it's parent-teacher night."

"What?"

"That letter I got about your suspension said we had to go."

"Oh. Uh." Atlanta tries to wave it off. "You really don't have to. You guys go do something else. This isn't, like, mandatory. Go have fun or something. I'll be cool. Won't mean much to me."

Paul says, "Well, it means something to your mother that she's involved with you and knows what's going on."

"I haven't always been there," Mama says.

"No need to start now," Atlanta offers, and realizes that it sounds a whole lot snarkier than she meant it to. "I just mean—"

"Go get ready," Mama says. "We leave in thirty."

———

In those thirty minutes, Atlanta sequesters herself upstairs and grabs the cordless phone and the local phone book. She tries to find the phone number to Moose Barnes's house—but, of course, the book has eleven different Barneses.

Screw it, she calls all of them.

Or would—but it only takes to number five to get what she needs, because number five is his uncle's house. Jimmy Barnes. Guy who sounds like he doesn't smoke cigarettes so much as he gargles them.

He doesn't know much about his nephew except for the correct phone number to call, so she calls it up.

"Hello?" It's a woman's voice on the other end.

"I'm looking for Moose."

The woman, prickly sounding, says: "Mark isn't here."

Mark. His real name is Mark. She never even considered that "Moose" wasn't the name you'd find on his birth certificate.

"Is he . . . okay?"

"He's fine. He's away."

"Away?"

"Away." A pause. "As you know, he lost somebody close."

"I . . . of course." Samantha? Were they close?

"He's taking time away at our mountain house."

Ugh. "Oh. Sure. Just tell him I called."

"Who should I say is calling?"

Atlanta draws a sharp breath, then hangs up.

————

At the school, she, Mama, and Paul sit down with all the teachers. Mr. Lovegrove. Miss Prasse. Mr. Dinkins. Mrs. Wryzek. They all tell the same story: blah blah blah, they like Atlanta and think she's smart, but she has problems "focusing," barely turns in homework, and is hovering somewhere around a C or D average, and if she's not careful she could end up failing a class, which means repeating a class, which means *potentially* not graduating—

Mama, for her part, gets fighty with every one of them. "School isn't fun," she says. "It's like *prison*." Atlanta smiles a bit at that. "You make them sit here day in and day out while you teach them things they don't care about and then are surprised when somehow you don't magically change their minds—oh, and meanwhile all you're doing is teaching to somebody's *governmental standards* and this Common Core business isn't how *I* learned things in school . . ."

And the teachers nod and smile and take it on the chin.

Paul at one point pulls Arlene aside and says: "You know, these teachers are just trying their best, sweet-pea. My sister, you know, Katherine, she's a teacher in New Jersey, and it's a rough game. They don't get results, the school doesn't get funding, the teachers don't get tenure—"

"Don't start with me, Paul," Arlene says, putting a little venom on her tongue. "Atlanta's a good kid and deserves the best."

"Mama," Atlanta says, but Paul keeps talking:

"Arlene, I'm not starting with you now—"

"*Mama.*"

"Paul, you are not this girl's father, so maybe just be my arm candy and nod and smile when I talk—"

"*Arlene,*" Atlanta says. "*Paul.* Dang, you two. Listen, I got this, okay? Ain't the teachers' fault. I should do better. I'll try." Though even as she says it, it feels like a lie—just the thought of having to invest more in school, more time, more work, more everything, makes her feel tired. Ugh.

Last teacher of the day is Mrs. Strez.

And her report, thankfully, is glowing.

The teacher—an old biddy with eyeglasses big as the eyes on a praying mantis—says, "Atlanta has a poet's heart and a ditch digger's mouth." Arlene's about to protest, but Mrs. Strez continues: "She's a student like I was, and she's doing very well in this class. Could stand to turn in some more *homework*, of course." And there a wry smile because Mrs. Strez *still* hasn't docked her any points for not turning in her homework. Not yet. And at this point, maybe not ever.

It's a good end to the night, or so Atlanta thinks.

They come out into the hall where a lot of other parents and their kids have gathered. Some parents are happy, chatty, their kids beaming. Others are dragging their kids away by the elbow, disappointment hanging on their faces like hats on a rack peg. Mama's beaming. Paul looks lost—satisfied, maybe. But a little uncomfortable, too. Atlanta's studying him when suddenly he stares off, and his face brightens. Someone calls to him in a voice she recognizes:

"Paul. Hey there."

She follows Paul's gaze.

And there's the tan, bearded man. The one from Samantha's house. Then in a pink polo, now in a brown blazer with a cranberry button-down underneath.

He marches up to Paul. They shake hands.

Paul says: "Hey, Ty, how the hell are you?"

The man—Ty, apparently—turns toward Atlanta. His smile broadens. "Hey, now. I know this girl."

Arlene looks confused. "You do?" she asks.

Panic fires like a piston in Atlanta's chest.

"I don't think we've ever met," Atlanta says, already hearing how stiff, how fakey-fakey, her words sound. "I'm sure I don't—"

"No," the man says, "but my son talks about you a lot."

"Your son?" she asks.

And then Ty pivots just so.

About ten feet behind him is a big bleach-blonde woman in a straining yellow sundress. And next to her?

Damon Carrizo.

A hard wind blows this house of cards over.

"You're Damon's daddy," she says, trying to mask . . . whatever it is she's feeling right now. Fear, disappointment, anger, confusion. Some nasty-tasting cocktail of all that, shaken up and poured down her throat.

Paul clucks his tongue. "I'm sorry. Arlene, Atlanta, this is Ty Carrizo. He's the CFO over at VLS. He works up in the offices, obviously."

"But," Ty says, grinning ear to ear, "I love coming down to visit the boys working the wells and tanks. Vigilant brings about seventy-five percent of its workforce with us wherever we go, but the Keystone State here has really been a gem for us. And Paul, gosh, what can I say about Paul? A lot of the locals we hire, we bring them on for a season, maybe two, but this guy has long-term potential. He has a future with VLS if he wants it." Ty claps Paul on the shoulder hard. Paul looks genuinely chuffed about the whole thing, like a little boy winning a kiss from his mother.

Damon comes up, then, staring at this meeting between his father and Atlanta. Behind him, the woman who Atlanta figures is his mother wraps up a conversation with the PE teacher, shakes his hand, and wanders over.

Ty puts his arm around Damon, hugs him close. Damon looks embarrassed about it but doesn't pull away. He introduces the woman: "This is my wife, Sue." Handshakes and introductions all around. Then he gives his son a noogie: "My boy here's doing great. This is a fine school. How are your grades, Atlanta?"

She's about to answer and say something about *who cares*, but Arlene jumps in: "Her English teacher just *raved* about her. Said she had a poet's heart."

Ty laughs. "That is a wonderful thing. Not sure how that translates to the workforce and getting a job, but maybe we could all use a little poetry in our hearts." Then the man's face looks suddenly downcast. "That poor girl who killed herself probably didn't have enough of that in her life. Rest her weary soul."

Here, he watches Atlanta way a cat watches a can of tuna being opened.

She feels her palms go cold and damp. *Am I looking at the man who killed Samantha?* He was involved somehow. She's sure of it.

"I gotta go," Atlanta says. She clears her throat. "To the, ahh, bathroom."

Then she darts away to go dry heave in a girls' room stall.

CHAPTER SEVENTEEN

Next day, hunter safety class. Atlanta thinks she's going to be distracted, but it's Paul who's the distracted one. He seems off, somehow. Lost. He bites at the calluses along his thumb. Well, whatever. That's his business. She's suffering no such nonsense today, because today they get to learn about *guns*. How they work. How you clean them. How you store them.

(Though not, of course: *how you fire them*. No practice session.)

But they've got her attention. Her eyes are wide open. She's bright and awake and aware, in part because she didn't really sleep last night and she's at that point where she's gone so far over the hump she's gotten her second, or third, or fifteenth wind. She can almost feel the weight of the .410 against her shoulder. The cold metal of the trigger tucked in the softness of her finger. The satisfying click it makes when the hammer draws back and settles in, ready to go.

It hits her, then:

I want to shoot somebody.

Maybe even kill them.

That thought scares her so bad she almost gets up and runs out of the class.

Paul must sense something. "You okay?" he whispers as the teacher goes on about the various kinds of safeties you find on firearms.

"Are you?" she whispers back to him.

But he stays quiet, and so does she.

———

Back home, outside, she paces. Whitey paces with her, turning every time she turns, making every pivot, walking every ten-foot length. Sometimes she stops to pick up a stone and pitch it into the corn. Whitey barks and runs after it—never finds the stone she throws but always finds *some* stone, and whatever he brings, she tosses. Then they pace once more.

She can't put it all together.

She's got pieces of a puzzle scattered across her table, and she can't figure out how they go together. Bee. Samantha. Ty Carrizo. What about VLS? Doesn't seem to figure in—could be Ty is working on his own. A little voice asks if he could really be involved, but of course he is—she saw the look in his eyes. And he was there at Samantha's house. *Are you cool?* Handing her his card. No, that sonofabitch is in this somehow. She's just not sure where he fits.

Then it hits her. The puzzle doesn't come together because:

I'm still missing too many pieces.

That means it's time to start filling them in.

She's got a job here—*find the father of Bee's unborn bug.* That means she needs to start digging and pulling up roots to see what comes out of the dirt.

Okay. What name did Samantha say when Atlanta asked her who came and took Bee away from the party that night?

Think, think, think!

Wait. There it is.

I dunno him. Some thug. Mahoney or something.

Mahoney.

Good. A name. A start. A thread to pull.

She calls Guy. "Hey," she says.

"'Lanta, yo."

"Whatcha doing?"

"Trying to figure out how to fix my toilet."

"That sounds like fun."

"Yeah, it's like a nonstop party around this joint. What up?"

"I need a favor."

He audibly scoffs. "You always need favors."

"It's what makes me adorable."

"It's what makes you *annoying.* Especially since you always seem to drag me into some shit that ain't got nothin' to do with me. How about you do *me* a favor for once?"

"Fine. Tell me about your toilet."

"What?"

"The toilet." She enunciates each word now: "Tell. Me. About. Your. Toilet."

"It's where I dump."

She makes an *ugh* sound. "Man, c'mon, I mean tell me what the heck is wrong with it."

"It's running all the time and the tank won't fill."

"Fine. I'll fix your toilet if you help me with something."

"I think you owe me, like, fifteen fixed toilets, but let's hear what this *something* is first. Whatchoo got?"

"You know a guy named Mahoney?"

Silence on the other end.

She says: "Hello? Guy?"

A sigh. "Why are you asking about that?"

"About that, or about him? You saying you know him?"

"You don't wanna get involved with this. Whatever it is. You feel me?"

Her hand tightens around the phone. "I need this, Guy. Who is he? Where can I find him?"

Another long sigh. "You sure?"

"I'm sure."

He tells her.

And after that, she wishes he hadn't.

———

Four of them in the car. Shane's car. They're parked in the lot of a bar—the Wagon Wheel, up on Grainger Hill. It's still daylight: five o'clock. A couple Harleys sit parked out front. In the back corner of the gravel lot there's a beater Ford Explorer, and opposite that, a red seventies Camaro that shines like a spit-polished apple.

Atlanta taps her foot on the ground, her hand bracing against the dashboard even though they're not moving. The smell of French fries in the car is making her sick, but they're part of the deal, so she tries to just breathe in through her mouth.

"You're sure this guy is in here?" Shane says, hands wrapped tight around the steering wheel. "You don't have to do this."

She nods.

From the backseat, Josie leans forward. "Who is this douche again?"

"Just some low-rent thug," Atlanta lies.

Next to Josie, Steven says: "I don't think we're supposed to go into a bar."

"*We're* not," Atlanta says. "It's just me. I'm going in."

"Atlanta," Josie starts to say.

"No, I gotta do this. You guys just pull around back."

"You sure this is gonna work?" Shane asks.

"I'm sure." Another lie. To Steven: "Hand me the bag."

On the bag, the logo for one of the local Italian joints: DiSilvo's. One of the things she wasn't prepared for moving up north is just how many Italian restaurants they've got around. Even the smallest town has a half-dozen pizza-pasta joints within a ten-mile drive. Sometimes they're across the street from each other. Different immigrant families. Italians at the counter. Latinos in the kitchen.

The bag is heavy, grease soaking through the bottom, but it's holding together. She smells the fryer grease, the sauce of the meatball sub. Then Steven hands her the big Coke. Sixty-four ounces. She can barely carry it. It's like an oil drum of soda. Enough to kill a whole room full of diabetics.

Without saying another word, Atlanta pops the door and heads in.

———

The door creaks open. Light streams in. In it, dust motes duck and dive in a slow-motion dogfight. Music comes from a jukebox in the back: it's something from the eighties, hairband glam music. Poison, maybe, or Mötley Crüe.

Atlanta squints, steps in with the bag.

Two bikers sit at the bar. One's got bare arms and a bare chest underneath a black leather vest. Maybe fifty, sixty years old, hair dyed black as squid ink. The other one's shorter, chubbier, younger, like a pig that ran away from the farm, dressed up in denim and dark leather. He clearly took the term *riding a hog* all literal.

Far side of the room, an old, old man. *He drives the SUV,* she thinks. Fella's so old he probably chaperoned Jesus and Mary Magdalene's prom. Everything about him looks dried up, bleached out, like the roads in winter after the salt trucks blast them: pitted, crusty, chalky as a ghost.

Bartender behind the bar: shape of a human pyramid. Head like a gas can, torso like a shed, butt like a garbage truck parked in a too-small garage. Big bug-eyes and rubbery lips. That dude looks like he could tear Atlanta in half like she was a Kleenex tissue.

By now, everything's gone tunnel vision. The roar of blood pounds in her ears. Her wrists feel tight.

At the back, she sees him.

Mahoney. Owen Mahoney, to be exact.

"This prick," Guy said. *"He's not someone you wanna mess with,* 'Lanta. *He's been around for years. Doesn't work with one bunch but works with them all: the Death's Head Riders, the Romans, the Poles, some other one-percenter assholes. He's like the Swiss Army knife of white supremacist* cabrónes. *He does it all. Getaway driver. Leg-breaker. Killer. Did a stint up in Frackville, just got out a year ago or so—been keeping a lower profile ever since."* She asked Guy where he hung out. Guy hesitated. She said she'd leave Mahoney alone—a lie, so many lies now—and he said, *"Fine. He's got some kinda owner*

stake in the Wagon Wheel off of 29 in Grainger Hill. He hangs there most days and nights."

And here he is.

He's fuzzy, grungy, like a rangy pit bull with a bad case of mange, leaning back in a booth, feet up on the table, looking at his phone. A Yuengling sits in front of him.

Eyes start to turn toward the girl who just came through the door.

Atlanta hot-steps it right toward the back.

The bartender says: "Hey. You. You're not s'posed to be in here—"

But she keeps walking even as his protests get louder.

She closes in, and Mahoney doesn't move a muscle—but his gaze flicks from his phone to her. She gets right up to the table. The floor shakes behind her as the human mountain bartender grabs for her arm.

Mahoney hisses like a cat. "Hold up, Derek, shit." Then, to Atlanta: "What is it, Red? I'm busy."

"I brought you this," she says, holding up the bag. Her voice shakes. She can hear it shake. *Be cool, you idiot.*

Mahoney takes his boots off the table and leans forward. His eyes are these black circles—like thumbtacks stuck there, almost colorless. The skin around them is baggy and dark. He nods, and she puts down the bag.

He takes it, opens it, gives a sniff. "I didn't order food."

She pulls her arm out of the bartender's grip. "I was told to bring it," she says. "To you."

"To me."

"To you, yeah."

"Who told you that?"

She knew it might go this way so she pulls out the only name she thinks might matter here: "Mister Carrizo."

A smile curls up at the edges of his mouth. He looks her up and down, and then her heart leaps right into her throat and gets stuck there like a frog in a drinking glass—oh, god. That was the wrong thing to say.

Suddenly, it's not about the food.

It's about her.

"Carrizo knows how to treat a guy," he says. "I like people with money. Real money. Higher class of folks, you know?"

He thinks *she's* what Ty Carrizo sent over.

The meal: just an excuse.

But that's not it at all—she didn't want it to go this way. The meal *is* the deal. The meal is the one part that matters. *Shit, shit, shit.*

He stands up, grabs her wrist. "C'mon, Red. We can make this quick. You can earn your dole, then I can eat the—what is that? Chicken parm?"

"Meatball parm."

Owen Mahoney whistles with his chapped lips. "Oooh. All right. Let's go."

"Wait," she says, swallowing hard. Her wrist in his grip makes her feel like a rat in a trap. *I have to get out of here. This is all wrong.* "You should eat first. Build up a . . . build up your strength."

"My strength?" He sniffs. Gives a look to Derek the bartender: the big mountain jiggles with quiet laughter. "Red, I'm good. I don't like to eat beforehand. I don't wanna be all belchy when we do it."

"It's . . . it's okay, I don't mind."

"You're nervous. Oh, Red. This'll be over fast enough."

He starts to lead her away from the table.

She looks to the food, sitting there on the table—receding as
they move away from it, toward the back. The food is everything.
That's where she crushed up the Ambien. In the drink. In the sauce
of the sub. Even sprinkled on the damn fries. Enough of the stuff
to knock out a whole stable full of Clydesdale horses.

But none of that matters if he doesn't eat it.

She thinks: *Just run. Pull away. Run out the door.* Maybe he'll
still eat it anyway, not wanting to give up a free meal. She tries to
pull away, but his grip is strong like a vice. He laughs, keeps pulling. It's like something out of a nightmare, one of those bad dreams
where your feet are stuck in greasy mud and you can't pull them
out, can't get anywhere, and the thing that's chasing you is right
up on you, and ain't nothing you can do about it, not one dang
thing—

She thinks: *Just go with it.*

Go as far as you have to but not as far as he wants.

A plan starts coming together. A broken, jagged thing—like so
much of her life, a puzzle with too few pieces—but some are better
than none.

Mahoney pulls her down a brick-lined hallway.

They pass a door: Exit.

One last chance to run—but she doesn't take it. They keep
going. Toward a back room. Employees Only.

All parts of her are lit up like a murderer in an electric chair—
every molecule in her body frozen and screaming. But she tries to
hide it, tries to shove the fear down into a hole.

Through the door: a wood-paneled office, dimly lit. Industrial
metal desk. Porn up on the walls: just nasty, nasty business, women
doing things to men, other women—kind of stuff you can only
find in the strangest parts of the Internet. He directs her toward a

ratty green couch with car magazines on the cushions. He sweeps them away onto the floor, then kicks them underneath.

Nearby is another door—it's open. She sees a toilet and sink in there.

Already Atlanta's looking around the room for any kind of weapon: she's got her baton in her bag, but she may need something bigger, sharper, meaner. There's a stapler on the desk. A letter opener. A couple pint glasses.

Then it hits her.

She has a different weapon on her.

Same weapon she's been planning on using all along.

Owen Mahoney starts unbuttoning his pants—but she clears her throat, tells him to hold up. "Ty sent these over, too," she says, taking out the little baggy with pills in it. The Ambien are inside.

Little blue pills with As on them and the MGs printed on the back.

It strikes her, then: there's another pill looks similar. Pale blue. An A on them, too—different A, smaller A, but maybe he won't know, or won't look, or won't care. She says, "Oxy. Will make us feel good beforehand."

"Party girl," Mahoney says. "Great." He takes the baggy, shakes out one into his palm.

"Take three," she says. "Those are only tens." Meaning ten-milligram pills.

He nods, pops out two more. "You want three, too?"

"I took mine already," she says. "You know, uh, pharmaceutical courage and all that. You should, ahh, you should chew 'em up real good. Make 'em work faster."

He nods. "Good idea." Into his mouth they go. *Crunch.* Dry swallow. He moves toward her for a kiss—

She pulls away. "Can I freshen up a bit?"

"No," he says, then kisses her.

Revulsion runs through her. His tongue tastes like beer and chewing tobacco and pulverized pharmaceuticals.

She tries her damnedest not to throw up in his mouth.

She pulls away. "I gotta pee. Won't be a minute."

He holds her wrists so hard it hurts. "You can hold it."

She tries to play it funny, tries to be quick and smiley, though she can hear how scared she sounds even when she says: "You don't want me to piss all over this nice floor. Plus, it'll give us time for the Oxy to work."

He hesitates.

Then his grip loosens. "Toilet's there. Sink. Go on."

She tries not to run screaming into the dingy bathroom. Even still, she puts a spring in her heel and once she's in there, she closes the door—again slowly, softly, denying every urge to slam it, letting it click gently shut.

Then she locks it.

Tries not to cry.

Tries not to throw up.

She sits on the toilet.

The bathroom's dirty—black mold around the base of the toilet, the sink with a rime of grime on it. It smells okay, though: a chemical vanilla odor rises from an unlit, scented jar candle there on the sink next to a bare sliver of soap.

Wait—right.

Her hand darts out, spins the sink faucet, lets a little water trickle out. Hopes like hell it matches the sound of her tinkling.

Atlanta works to catch her breath. This is all going sideways. Slipping in the wrong direction like a car on an icy mountain road.

A knock on the door.

"Hey," comes Mahoney's voice. "Occurs to me that you look familiar."

"Nope," she says, working hard not to cry out. The fear sound that wants to come up out of her has to be strangled in its crib before it ever wakes up. "Don't figure."

"Something about you. Red hair. That accent."

"Nope. Wait. Wait. I . . . I've worked with Ty before. Maybe that's it."

"No, I don't think so."

Dangit.

She calls out: "Oh, man, I . . . I got bad news."

A grunt of disapproval on the other side. "Jesus, what?"

"I'm on the rag, mister. Aunt Flo's here."

Another grunt, then a laugh. "So? Your mouth and your ass ain't on their period, are they?"

Her stomach lurches.

"You gotta be done in there," he says. "Come on out now."

He rattles the knob.

She braces her foot against the door.

Rattle, rattle.

"Open up," he growls.

The door shakes now.

"I don't feel so well," she says.

"I don't feel like I give a shit," he barks back.

The door bangs.

She thinks: *What now, what to do, how do I get out of this?* Maybe puke on herself. He won't want to touch her then. More likely he won't care. He'll take what he thinks is his anyway. She should've never come in here.

Atlanta wants to kick herself.

Call the others. That's an option. Get them in here. They'll help.

But that'll put them in danger, too. She won't be able to stomach that—any of them get hurt, that'll weigh on her shoulders till she's six feet deep. (A day she fears now is coming far sooner than she'd like.)

"God*damnit*," Mahoney roars on the other side of the door.

There, on the sink. Only thing in here that counts as a weapon beyond the lid to the toilet tank—that'd be too heavy to use. She could get out the baton, but this room is so small, she won't have much room to swing it.

The candle. Glass jar. Fits in her palm okay.

She stands up, holding the jar tight in her right hand.

The door strains against its hinges.

He curses on the other side.

Then a moment of silence.

She thinks, *Maybe he's gone.*

Gone to do what? Get the others, maybe. Get a weapon.

But then the door pops open wide—she has to tuck in her knees so it doesn't hit them. And there he stands. Owen Mahoney, chest rising and falling, staring out at her, leering like a starving lion.

"You little tease," he says.

Those three words slur together.

His face changes—it's like he hears the sludgy drift in his own voice. And it bewilders him. His eyes narrow and he looks down at himself. At his hands. He moves his hands, watches them.

His words go wibbly-wobbly when he says: "Thah wuzn't Ocks . . . Ocks . . . eeeee." He swipes a paw at her, but she pins herself against the wall of the little bathroom. His clumsy bludgeon misses.

Atlanta gives him a hard shove.

He goes ass down, heels up.

Now, she thinks, *it's time to make a call.*

CHAPTER EIGHTEEN

"Is he dead? He's dead," Shane says, pacing back and forth.

"He's not dead," Atlanta says, pretending to be sure. But just in case, she checks his pulse. Mahoney's got life in there yet—but it's just a flutter, like holding a spider in the palm of your hand, a faint tickle. She wonders: *Is it* too *weak?* She needs him alive. He has information she wants. But if he dies, he dies. He's not a good person, and unjust men deserve unjust ends. And yet, if that's true, why does the thought of him dying fill her with panic? And sadness? *Don't die, don't die, don't die.*

Above their heads, leaves starting to lose their green shake and shudder as a pair of squirrels run free. The fading light of day comes at them from the side like a wolf on the hunt. Mahoney sits at the base of one tree, an old paper birch, with so much duct tape binding him up that he's practically a duct tape mummy.

Steven says, "What do we do?"

"We wait," Josie answers. A hard, firm thrust in her voice. Maybe a little fear, too, but for her first time exposed to all of this, she's tougher than Atlanta figured. And there Atlanta chides herself, because the reason she thought Josie wouldn't hack it was because she is a girl. Except Atlanta herself is tougher than most boys she knows. Shane's the one here who's gone the color of over-milked coffee.

"He'll wake up soon en—" Atlanta's about to say *enough*, but then Owen Mahoney takes a long, deep gasp. His eyelids peel back, and big, bold eyeballs stare out—pupils gone all black. They drift upward, suddenly, up past the lids. Only the whites show, and then he's back out.

Again Atlanta checks for a pulse.

"Is he—" Shane starts to say.

"*I'm checking,* jeez," Atlanta says, again feeling around for his pulse.

It's not there.

Oh, god, oh, god—

Wait! Wait. That flutter. That tickle. It's there. *It's there!*

She just missed it.

"Owen Mahoney is still among the living," she says.

"I didn't sign up for this," Shane says.

"You signed up by driving the car," Atlanta says. "It's not like I sold you a bucket of spit and said it was a milkshake. I told you how this was gonna go."

"It went differently," he says. He stops pacing, stares down at Mahoney. "What did you give him again?"

"Ambien."

Josie says: "My mom takes Ambien. It doesn't do . . . this."

"I gave him three pills," Atlanta says. "He thought they were three ten-milligram pills, but . . . they were thirty." She sighs. "One helluva horse kick."

"He could be out all night," Shane says.

"Try to wake him," Steven says.

"And then what?" Shane asks.

Atlanta sighs. "We have a talk with him. Find out what he knows about Bee and her . . . situation."

"What's that mean? Talk to him?"

"It means I ask politely, and then when he tells me to screw off, I keep asking, less and less politely each time."

Shane stiffens. "You're talking about torture."

"No, I'm talking about kicking his ass until answers come out like coins out of a Super Mario Brothers block. It's not . . . torture. Dang."

"It's close enough. This guy—you said he's just a low-rent thug."

"An *armed* low-rent thug," she says, pointing to the gun on the grass. A small .38 snubnose they pulled out of Mahoney's ankle holster. Serial numbers scratched off it. When she called the others, they came to the exit door at the back of the Wagon Wheel, and together they carted his limp body into the trunk of the Saturn. Josie had the good sense to look for a weapon as they were taping him up—and sure enough, the gun. "Besides," she adds, "he's not . . . exactly a low-rent thug. Thug, yes. Low-rent, not so much."

Everyone goggles.

Shane leans forward. "What do you mean? You lied to us?"

"This fancy gentleman right here is more than just a thug. He's like, a thug's thug. The Terminator of thugs. Hired by every hate group this side of Pittsburgh to do work for them. And not nice work, either, like landscaping or babysitting. He's a killer. Guy told me once that some plumber from somewhere—Scranton or Wilkes-Barre or something—owed some people money, people tied to a neo-Nazi group called the Aryan Vanguard or whatever. This man right here didn't go after the plumber. He went after the plumber's wife. Cut up her face, her breasts, her back. And now he just got out of jail. Not the first time he was there, either, okay? Owen Mahoney is *not* good people." *And,* she thinks but won't say aloud, *he was gonna take what he wanted from me no matter how much I protested.*

"So, he's . . . more than just some thug?" Shane's eyes are wide and his hands are shaking.

"Look. Guy told me he has . . . *artwork.*" She pulls down some of the tape, pulls up Owen's sleeve. The top half of a keystone shape with a pair of red lightning bolts inside it. "Some kinda Pennsylvania Nazi group." She points to Shane. "He'd whip your ass just for the color of your skin. I say that lets us whip his ass to find out some information. And if that means—"

Owen Mahoney gasps again.

His hand flops around at the end of his bound-up arm, and he grabs hold of the bottom of Atlanta's jacket. A sound comes out of his mouth: a moan that gets louder and louder, higher- and higher-pitched. She clips him in the cheek with her elbow and his hand springs open—

She scrambles away, hurries to her feet.

Owen Mahoney is awake.

His eyeballs, big and bold, rotate in their sockets. Then his stare falls to each of them in turn, clearly studying each one before his gaze *flicks* over to the next. Shane whispers: "He's memorizing our faces."

"I need to buy a lottery ticket," Mahoney blurts.

They all look at each other.

"What?" Atlanta asks.

"I *need* to buy a goddamn *lottery ticket.*"

"Is this code for something?" Josie asks.

"Get me *out* of this fuckin' bed and *get* me my car keys."

Oh, right. "It's the Ambien," Atlanta says. She neglects to mention the side effects of this particular zombie miracle drug. "He's . . . half-asleep, sorta. Sleepwalking. Or talking, anyway."

"Somniloquy," Shane says. *"Cool."* When everyone gives him that standard *Shane what the sweet hot hell are you talking about* look, he says: "The technical term for sleep-talking. What, don't any of you read books?"

Steven shakes his head, not realizing it was rhetorical. "I don't read."

"I swear to God," Mahoney says. "One of you better pull the car around right now. If you don't . . ." He bites down, teeth against teeth, and makes a hungry sound on the back of his throat.

Atlanta reaches in her bag, pulls out the baton.

With a snap of her wrist, it extends.

Josie gently grabs her wrist. "Hold on." Then she kneels down in front of Mahoney and says: "Hey, we'll get you the keys, but we have a question first."

"Lottery ticket," he says, petulant, like a child.

"Question first."

"What." A statement more than a question.

Josie looks to Atlanta, gives a head-tilt. "Ask him." Then she whispers: "Think of it like a truth serum."

CIA spy shit.

Could it be this easy?

Atlanta steps up, gripping the baton tighter. Realizes she's aching to use it—and so, she sets it down. "You've been doing some driving for Ty Carrizo."

"Yeah." Mahoney stares off at nothing. Like he's half in a trance.

"Driving girls. Young girls."

"Teenage pieces of ass."

She kneels down, feels around the grass for the baton—but she sees now that Josie picked it up. Josie offers a small, sympathetic smile.

That girl really is a good friend.

"Over the summer, you drove a girl away from Samantha Gwynn-Rudin's party. A pretty girl, long brown hair, white girl. Doped up."

"I've driven a lot of girls like that."

To hell with being a good friend. Atlanta snaps to Josie: "Gimme the baton."

"Atlanta," Josie cautions. "Think of the endgame here." She lowers her voice: "He's not gonna talk if you smash all his teeth down his throat."

She's got a point.

Deep breath. In, out. Atlanta says finally, "This girl, her name was Becky. Bee. She got pregnant and—"

"Ah, yeah, *her*," Mahoney says, nodding, his mushy lips twisting into some boozy, crooked smile. "The one got knocked up. We been watching her."

"Who's watching?"

"Me. Carrizo's people."

"Why?"

"See if she talks." His head drifts in lazy circles. "No cops so far."

"Who was the father?"

Without a beat: "Carrizo."

"Ty Carrizo is the father."

"We took her to his house. He helped her druggy ass walk inside. I picked her up, took her back to the other little bitch's house. Dumped her on the lawn."

"Carrizo is the father," she says.

He repeats it: "Carrizo is the father."

They all stand around, looking at each other, dumbfounded. It's not exactly surprising news, but something about the reality of it all—confirmed here and now, spoken aloud by this doped-up monster—hits them all collectively.

"Jesus," Josie says.

"Isn't that Damon's dad?" Steven asks. "The new kid?"

Shane says: "Guys. We should go."

"I want my goddamn lottery ticket," Mahoney says, belligerent.

"Do we just leave him here?" Josie asks.

"We don't have to," Atlanta says, cold as a Canada winter. "We let him go, he could talk. Or come back to haunt us."

"He has no way to know who we are," Shane says.

Atlanta purses her lips. "Redheaded firecracker with a Southern accent. I'm like Bigfoot up in these parts. He can find me."

"So what do we do?" Steven asks.

That question, heavy as a piano hanging above their heads, tied there with a fraying rope. Atlanta knows the answer, and she hates the answer—or, maybe, she hates that it's the only one she has. This is not who she is. But at the same time, she knows: Part of her wants this. Or at least understands it. Her mind wanders, suddenly. She tries to imagine how she'd do it. Choke him, maybe. Or use his own gun on him. Even the thought makes her queasy. But that's the answer, isn't it? Even though nobody is saying it out loud?

Then, Shane says: "We pull a Spider-Man."

"*Lottery ticket*," Mahoney growls.

Atlanta looks to Shane. "Now maybe isn't the time to play superhero."

"Now is *exactly* the time," he says. "Listen. If you watch *Arrow*, right, the character of Oliver Queen on the show—"

Josie interrupts: "I thought we were talking about Spider-Man."

"I know, DC versus Marvel, I'm crossing the streams, but hold on, I'll get there. So, season one of *Arrow*, Oliver Queen is like this scary vigilante. He totally kills people who get in his way. He's a murderer, and by season two, he realizes it—and that's when he changes how he does things. He goes from being a vigilante to being a real hero. So it's not about vengeance, but about justice."

"Still don't get the Spider-Man reference."

"Spider-Man is a hero. He doesn't kill. He finds the bad guys, he . . . he just *strings them up*. Leaves them dangling for the cops. So, we play Spider-Man."

Josie gets it. "We leave Mahoney dangling."

Atlanta whistles. "I dunno about this."

"You said he just got out of jail," Shane says.

"The gun," Steven offers. "He has a gun."

Shane snaps his fingers. "Bingo. Guy gets out of jail, he can't be found with a piece. That probably means he gets sent right back up the stream."

"Up the river," Atlanta corrects. "Not stream."

"The point remains."

It does remain.

And it's a good one, too.

She worries, of course. The cops aren't exactly trustworthy. But Holger seems to be. Which means somebody else on the force has to be, too.

"Fine," she says. "But I have one more question for him."

She takes his gun, sticks it back in his holster—has to pry up some of the tape to get to it. Then she grabs the duct tape from in the grass, and pulls a long strip of it off with a *vbbbbbbt*.

"Hey. Mahoney."

He stares at her. Or past her. "I know that voice. You little tease."

"You kill her?"

"Killed lots of hers."

"You kill Samantha Gwynn-Rudin?"

He laughs. "Nah. Word out there is Carrizo did her in. Or had her done."

"Fine," she says. Then she sticks the tape over his mouth.

There's a moment where she thinks: Wouldn't be anything to take the tape, put a little bit of it over his nose. Just a little. Maybe the others wouldn't even see. He wouldn't be able to breathe out of his mouth or his nose and this . . . killing, raping monster would die. He'd just die here and that'd be that.

But maybe Shane's right.

Maybe she needs to figure who she really is.

A hero or a vigilante.

Wrath or justice.

Maybe there's a line between those things. Maybe there isn't.

She puts down the tape. "Let's go make the call."

———

Pay phones are going extinct, dying off like honeybees, but up here in the deep wide-open middle-of-nowhere Pennsyltucky, there's still a few around, like the one outside of the Sawickis' kielbasa stand.

It's there that they make the anonymous tip.

Let the cops go pick up Mahoney. Find his gun. Send him away.

On the way back to Atlanta's house, nobody says much of anything.

To them, though, Atlanta says, "Thanks. You're a stand-up crew. You make me a better person."

And she leaves it at that.

CHAPTER NINETEEN

She's not yet ready to tell Bee.

It's been a hard day. Every part of her feels tired. And scared. And tense. And right now having to tell Bee what she learned is just too much.

Instead, she vegges for a while. Throws a ball for Whitey. Watches bad television. Eats garbage food: little microwave pizza bagels that are past their expiration date, but they're frozen, and even though they're rimed with a glittering crust of Arctic freezer burn she can't muster enough feeling to care. So she cooks them and they taste weird and she eats three and throws the rest away.

Eventually, Paul comes in. "Can I?" he asks, gesturing to the couch, and she says sure. He drops down next to her.

It hits her, then: She trusts him. Because her first thought as he sat wasn't what he was going to do to her. Not even after today.

"It's nice having you around," she says.

"It's nice being around," he answers.

"Mom at work?"

He says she is. "Have a good day?"

A part of her flirts with telling him the truth, but even she's not that crazy. She says: "Fine. Just hung around mostly. You go to work or something?"

"Oh. Ah. Yeah." Something strange in his voice. A hesitation—but why? Problems at work? Problems with Mom? She thinks to pick that scab but then decides she's out of gas. People are weird. She decides to just leave it at that.

At some point in the middle of them watching a real bad movie about a small town menaced by both a robotic shark and killer bees, Arlene comes home and sits down with them. Says work sucked, and Paul asks her how much she pulled in, and Arlene empties her pockets of bundles of ones, says that everyone was a shit tipper tonight. "I should go back to being a stripper."

Paul and Atlanta both give her a look, and she offers a genuine laugh: "Goldurn, y'all. I'm just playing. Look at your faces."

They all have a good laugh at that.

And eventually, Atlanta decides to go to bed.

———

No Ambien tonight.

Probably never again. She thinks about it. Right now, the nicest thing would be to pop one and flip the switch. Power down like the good guys did that robot shark—go dark for eight hours.

But waking up with ice cream was her first warning.

Then on the couch was her second.

Seeing what it did to Owen Mahoney was her third, and her last. And all along this is why she hasn't asked her mother about the money missing from her shoe box. Because she fears that's where it went: gone because she got goofy on sleeping pills. Gone with her mind and spent or buried or eaten on top of strawberry ice cream.

Thing is, Atlanta knows that once again she's been jabbing snakes with sticks, and if she's not careful, they're gonna slither out of the tall grass and take a bite. When they do, what happens if she's doped up? That thought gives her the shivers, like spiders dancing on the inside of her ears.

So, no Ambien.

Which means no sleep.

She goes through the motions. Turns out the lights. Lies there on the bed while Whitey snores like a John Deere tractor: *chug chug chug chug.* (And the dog snores plus the occasional bunker buster bomb gas attacks from the dog's ass-end make her wonder if she should put the pooch back in the garage.)

She tries to sleep.

Doesn't. Can't. Ugh.

Not sleeping is weird.

She enters into these periods where she's *almost* asleep. Like, it feels as if she just dreamt something—but it's hard to grab, hard to be sure if it's the real thing. And time has a way of walking away from her. She glances at the clock and each time she does, the read-out has advanced by an hour or more.

Sometimes her heart beats like she's a coke addict in a race car.

Sometimes she hears a ringing in her ears.

Or smells gunpowder.

Or funeral flowers.

Or hears Chris Coyne somewhere laughing, crying, blaming her.

Then there's the standard-issue scary shit. The constant fear that someone is in the house, here to kill her. Or Arlene. Or Whitey, or Paul. Masked men. Or a cop. Or now, a new name and new face in the darkness: Owen Mahoney.

Footsteps. Floorboards creaking. Pipes tinking. The arthritic bones of the old house settling together, clacking and bumping, because all the cartilage and fat has gone out of the place, no cushion, no softness. Everything cracking like the ice on a lake as you walk across it.

Then, Whitey starts to growl.

Real low. A thunderous rumble.

A sleep-growl, she thinks. It happens. Then he'll make these sleep-bark sounds, and they sound like *woob woob woob*. Like he's one of the three guys from that old black-and-white show where they all beat the hell out of each other.

But the growl never changes.

And she hears her door open.

And she hears footsteps.

It's all an illusion. She knows that.

It's happened how many times before? And each time she's jumped out, flipped on the light, only to startle the poor dog so hard he cuts a fart.

The dog's growl stops.

See. There. Everything's fine.

Another squeak. Another footstep.

Your brain is messing with you.

That, she always thinks.

Then comes the next expected thought, the same one that always lines up in the queue, in the same order.

What if this time you're wrong?

What if someone really is in here?

What if you don't look, and the one time you don't—you're dead?

A long, loud creak of the floorboards. Something sliding . . .

Suddenly—Whitey is flipping his shit. A furious barking, claws scrambling on the floorboards, and a man is yelling, crying out—

Atlanta scrambles, fumbling at the nightstand for the lamp there—

Click.

Bright light. Her eyes start to adjust—there's someone in here, oh, goddang, there's really someone here, and Whitey's standing there with his hackles up and his head low. Atlanta flings open her drawer, reaches for the bear mace—

"Wait! Wait, wait—"

It's Paul.

It's *Paul.*

She thinks: *He's here to hurt me.* He's like all the others. Here in her room to take advantage of a sleeping girl. He stands there in his underwear, one hand clutched in the other, blood squeezing through his fingers like juice from a crushed orange.

But already she backpedals. She trusts Paul. He's not a bad guy.

Then she gets it.

There, on the ground.

Her shoe box.

The lid, off.

"You," she says. "You took my money."

"Atlanta, it's not like that," he starts to say. Whitey snaps at him.

"Dog's a pretty good lie detector," she seethes.

"Get the dog away, please, call him off. My hand."

Then the door behind him flies open.

Arlene enters, a candlestick in her hands—so clearly she thought someone was breaking in, too. "What the . . ."

It happens almost in slow motion, the way Mama registers everything. Whitey. Paul. The bloody hand. Atlanta in her bed with the bear mace.

Mama goes into grizzly bear mode.

She starts whipping up on Paul with that candlestick. Cracking him across the shoulders and arms, shrieking. Calling him names. Him yelping that it's not what she thinks, not at all—Atlanta thinks to say something, thinks to interrupt, but she lets Mama think what she wants to think. That makes her a bad person, she's pretty sure, but she can't quite make herself do better.

Mama chases Paul down the steps with that candlestick. Him howling. Whitey chasing after, too. Snapping at his heels all the way.

The front door slams.

———

Atlanta sits in the kitchen while Arlene and Paul stand outside for twenty, thirty minutes, her yelling at him, him yelling back. Once in a while Atlanta thinks to step out there, but turns out, her mother's handling it just fine.

Which surprises her more than a little.

Mama of the past would've just rolled over. Asked questions. Tested Atlanta to see if it was her just being some silly, paranoid, dumb girl.

But this time, it's different. The woman went right to entering in launch codes and dropping the nuke. Way Mama looked at Paul, her eyes were columns of fire—tornadoes of flame ready to boil his blood, burn him up to a roasty-toasty char.

Eventually, Atlanta hears his truck pull away. Arlene never lets him come back in to get his stuff, so he has to drive off in his underwear.

Mama comes back in a few minutes after Paul drives away. She's still mad. Atlanta's maybe never seen her this mad—even when her last boyfriend did what he did, she came to it too late to realize, and the look on her face was one of horror more than anything else.

But it's not all anger. Her eyes are rimmed with pink, the whites shot through with blood. Cheeks puffy, a little wet.

Mama sits. A cloud of cigarette smell comes off her. "Well, shit," she says.

"Sorry," Atlanta says.

"Don't you *sorry* me, baby girl. This isn't on you. This is on him."

"You thought something was happening that wasn't."

Arlene sniffs, then shrugs. "He still lied to me. Gambling. Stealing your money. It's me that needs to say sorry to you. I keep bringing these men—"

"Mama, don't."

Mama stops there. But the feeling hangs between them.

"I liked him," Atlanta says eventually.

"I liked him, too."

Mama slides her hand across the table. Atlanta takes it. They both give each other's a little squeeze.

Whitey stands up, puts his paws on the table, because he wants to be a part of it, too, it seems.

CHAPTER TWENTY

It's Wednesday now, over four days since she and the others drugged and kidnapped Owen Mahoney.

She still hasn't told Bee.

Atlanta doesn't really know why. Maybe she just doesn't want to deal with it. Like, if she doesn't tell Bee, doesn't get that ball rolling, then it'll all just evaporate. Same way an injury sometimes heals, same way winter comes and winter goes and brings spring in its wake, same way shit happens but sometimes, most of the time even, shit washes off.

Maybe I can be a normal girl, Atlanta thinks. *Just once. Just for a little while.* Go to school. Dick around with her friends. Eat a bad lunch. Skip her homework. Complain about what Mrs. So-and-So said, or how Mr. Whoozit doesn't actually read the papers he grades. Bitch about her mother. Talk about a party someone went to. Or about getting a driver's license. Go home. Run around.

Facebook, Snapchat, Twitter. Text her, him, that other her, that other him. Emojis. Reality television. Stay up late. Sleep hard. Get up late. Lather, rinse, repeat.

But then Bee comes into the cafeteria that day with her arm in a sling and her face half-shadowed with a wine-dark bruise.

And Atlanta is reminded:

Normal isn't on the agenda.

———

It was a car accident, Bee tells her.

The two of them sit in the far corner of the caf, not at a table but on one of the ledges of the big windows looking out toward the parking lot.

"A real accident," Atlanta asks, "or an on-purpose accident?"

Bee hesitates.

That answers that.

"Who did this?" Atlanta asks.

"I . . . I don't know," Bee says, eyes watering. "It was yesterday morning and I was driving to school and, and . . . a white van, like a cargo van, came out of nowhere when I was crossing over Old Mill from Danville Pike, and soon as I got across he whipped up alongside me and pushed me off the road. Car skidded down the embankment. I hit a tree. Blacked out. When I awoke—" She sniffs, then fishes something out of her pocket. She slaps it down on the table, then smooths it out. It's a crumpled-up note that reads: **NO MORE QUESTIONS**. "This was under my wiper blade. Against the busted windshield."

"You okay?"

"Yes. No. I dunno." She looks down at the note. "My arm's broken. My face got . . . punched by the stupid air bag."

"How about the, uhh. The—" She points to Bee's stomach.

"The baby is fine."

"Oh. Good. I was worried, because . . ." But she doesn't know how to finish that, so she just lets the words go away like air out of an untied balloon.

"Are *you* okay? You don't . . . look so hot."

"I haven't slept."

"In how long?"

"Too long." She sighs. "Hour here, hour there, maybe." Atlanta knows it shows on her face. The lack of sleep is almost a living thing now. A sparking wire dancing across a cracked and blasted road. Doesn't help that, to compensate, she's gone back on the Adderall—helps her keep on keepin' on. She grabs Bee's hand—the one not stuck in a cast. "Come on. Let's get you home."

"I'm fine."

"You're not fine. No way you can be fine. I'm not fine." *Nobody our age is fine. Especially in this town.* "Besides, we need to talk."

Bee eyes her. "Okay."

"Let's go."

———

They leave the caf and they're about to head out to the parking lot when someone clears his throat behind them.

Wilson. The vice principal.

"Where are you ladies going?"

Atlanta turns. Feels herself teetering on an edge. "I don't see any ladies around here."

"Where are you supposed to be?" he asks.

"Anywhere but here," Atlanta answers.

"Atlanta, you're on thin ice."

"And yet, somehow I keep standing. You wanna come over here and crack the ice beneath my feet, be my guest. Meanwhile, let me read you today's news. This girl? Bee? Take a long look. See anything strange? Maybe the cast or the beat-up face? Girl was in a car accident, Mister Vice Principal, sir, and she is not feeling well. As such, I have decided I'm going to take her home. Unless you want her driving? That what you want? She gets into another accident, you think that'll sit well on your conscience? I reckon not. So, we're gonna go now. If you're fixin' to make an example of me for that, or you wanna suspend me or whatever, then more power to you. I could not give any less of a *damn*."

Bee gasps. The girl knows that's not a word Atlanta likes to say. She'll drop whatever f-bomb, c-word, b-word, s-h-i-t-word, but something about that one, *damn*, has never felt right coming off her tongue. But there it is.

Wilson doesn't say much else. All he mumbles is, "Go on, then."

So they go on, then.

———

In the parking lot, Bee says, "I didn't actually drive to school today."

Atlanta sighs. "You maybe could've told me that before we came out here. And before I did all that big, dramatic speechifying."

"Sorry."

"You want me to call somebody or are you okay to walk?"

"We can walk, if we take it slow."

They walk.

Atlanta lays it out.

"I know who . . ." She kicks a stone. "I know who knocked you up."

Bee stops walking. "Wh . . . what?"

"I found him."

A wind whistles. Autumn coming in. Shaking the trees.

"How? When?"

"This past weekend. I . . . got a lead on someone. A not-very-nice someone. This particular individual, he, ahh, he was the one who drove you. Away from Samantha's house and to . . ." Gosh, this is hard. So she just blurts it out: "It was Ty Carrizo."

Bee's eyes glisten. "I don't even know who that is."

Of course she doesn't. Shit.

"You know the new kid? Damon? It's his father. He runs or is a high muckity-muck at some fracking company just north of here."

Bee looks struck. Like she's just now stepping out of the wrecked car. She staggers over to the side of the road and sits down on the shoulder.

Atlanta hovers. Then sits with her.

"He's older, then," Bee says.

"Mm-hmm, yeah. Old enough to be our dad."

"Jesus. *Jesus.*" Bee suddenly stabs out with a heel. Kicks her shoe down again and again on the road, grunting in rage as she does so. Her sneaker pops off, spins into the road. Atlanta hops up, grabs it, hands it back. Bee starts to put it on but then freaks out once more, and cries out as she wings it across the road into the bushes. "God! Damnit! What the fuck was I thinking? Why did I let this happen? This is all me. I asked for this. I went to Samantha.

I *made this happen* and now here I am asking questions—" And she pauses her angry tears, the realization sinking deep like a knife in her gut. "That's it. That's why someone ran into me. I had you ask questions and now . . ."

She buries her face in her hands.

Atlanta pulls her close. Bee burrows into her side, sobbing.

———

Back at Bee's house, Atlanta says: "This isn't your fault."

"It is. It has to be. I opened the door. I let this in."

Gone now are the tears. Bee speaks and it's a cold monotone. Her words and emotions are no longer a thunderous storm but a steady, pissing rain.

"I thought the same thing—that it was my fault. But it's not."

"No, I invited it. It's different."

"It's not. You're a kid. This guy is an adult. He's the one who should know better."

"Yeah. Well."

They stand outside her house for a while. The air's got a real bite to it. October's rolling in tomorrow, and if the chill around them is any indication it's gonna be a month with sharp teeth and a jack-o'-lantern grin.

"So," Atlanta asks, "what do you want to do about it?"

"About what?"

"All of this. You said you wanted to know, and now you know. Ty Carrizo's your man. Time to figure out our next move."

Bee bites at a thumbnail. "There is no next move. This is it."

"Gotta be a next move. These people . . . they can't just get away with it. You said you might want to get money from him and we can try that—"

"They can get away with it, and they will, because that's how the world works. I don't have to be a grown-up to figure that out. The deck is stacked, Atlanta. Some people get a better deal than the rest of us. I'm not you. I can't fight this fight. I thought maybe it was just some guy and I could . . . make him be the father in more ways than just what he did to me. But this is different."

"Oh." She blinks. "You could go to the cops—"

"I can't tell my parents all this stuff. I can't drag them into it. It'll kill them." She stares down at her feet. "I'm gonna let this one go."

"But—"

"Please."

"All right. Yeah."

"You'll let it go?" Bee asks.

"I'll let it go."

"You *promise* you'll let this go."

"Pinky-swear." She sticks out her pinky. They twist their littlest digits together and give a quick shake.

PART THREE:
LIKE A HOUSE ON FIRE

CHAPTER TWENTY-ONE

Fear and anger are two cats tussling inside Atlanta's heart. Fear that Owen Mahoney is still out there, that he's going to come for her—and that he may have been the one who ran Bee off the road. But then, anger comes in all spitting and hissing, mean claws swiping—because what happened to Bee makes her *mad*. Mad enough to burn away any of the last resentment she had for her old friend.

Thing is, it doesn't matter which one wins out.

Fear or anger.

Because she made a promise. She pinky-swore not to follow this road any further. So she's going to have to just sit here. And let it go. Let fear and anger keep circling and biting one another.

She tells herself: *I'm a girl of my word.*

Promise is a promise.

That's what she tells herself, anyway.

———

That night, two sets of pills:

Ambien.

Adderall.

One for sleep. The other for its opposite. Which one to take?

Ambien, Adderall, Ambien, Adderall.

Hit the brakes, or press the gas.

Adderall will keep her alert, but she's already lying down at the edge of the cliff, the ground crumbling beneath her, the stone gone to scree. She's jittery but sleepy. Hyperaware but confused, too. It's hard to remember the right words, almost like she's drunk, or so far beyond drunk it doesn't even matter anymore.

No, Ambien will give her what she needs.

But that could come at a cost.

In the end, she just wants to sleep.

She tells Whitey: "I'm taking one of these. Don't let me leave this room. I start to get up and do anything funny, you wake me up."

The dog whines.

"Anybody comes in here, you kill 'em."

The dog pants.

"Good boy."

She pops the pill.

———

The Ambien is opposite of the Adderall, but this time, the result is just as clean: morning comes and what she experiences is less like waking up than it is just detaching one thing from the other. Like unclipping a backpack from around your waist, like popping off one shoe by using the toe of the other. One minute, everything is dark and nonexistent. The next: she's up and alive.

Rising from the dead.

Thankfully, in her own dang room.

Whitey snores as morning light pours in.

———

That one night of sleep wasn't quite enough to get her back to speed, and during classes she still feels sticky and gummy, like a piece of candy spit out onto the floor. But she's better, and she doesn't fall asleep, and she doesn't need Adderall to get through the day. So there's that.

Toward the end of the day, she sees Damon Carrizo in her pre-calc class.

She stares bullet holes through the back of his head.

Once the bell rings, he hurries down the hall, but she rushes after him. He gets stuck behind a crowd of jocks bouncing a ball—and some teacher who is yelling at them not to bounce the ball, so that now it's a whole plug in the hallway, an arterial clot. She comes up behind him. Puts a hand on his neck.

"Hey, *Damon.*"

He startles. "Christ. Atlanta. Hey."

"You been avoiding me?" she asks.

"No. I'm just—I'm just busy."

The baller jocks part, and Damon starts to step through the gap. But Atlanta isn't keen to throw this fish back yet. She jukes ahead of him, blocks his way.

"Your father's a real sonofabitch."

"No," he says. He sounds defensive but won't look her in the eyes.

"Do you know what he's been up to? His little side project?"

He sets his jaw. "You don't know him. He's a good guy. Most kids our age, they hate their parents. But I actually like mine. Okay? So I don't want to hear whatever you have to say. Just—just leave it."

Damon goes to move past her, and as he does, she hisses at him: "You tell him that I *know*."

He freezes. His head slowly turns. He's like a frog caught in a flashlight beam, eyes wide. "That you know *what*?"

"He *knows* what."

It's a bluff and not a bluff all at the same time. She has part of the story, but not all of it. You see one cockroach running across the floor, there's bound to be a whole metric roach-load of them behind the drywall, skittering around. Having cockroach babies.

"I'll . . . tell him."

"You do that."

"I'm sorry," he says, and it comes across as an earnest plea. Desperate, even, like he's hungry for her to believe him.

But then he's gone again, ducking back through the crowd.

She wonders. Maybe she shouldn't be doing this. Stirring up the mud. Bee asked her to leave it alone. But then Atlanta tells herself she's not stirring anything. His father probably doesn't care what she thinks. Damon definitely doesn't care. Everything's fine.

———

Night two with the Ambien. Just to get caught up.

She figures, best to be clean and clear.

Which means time to get some sleep. *More* sleep.

She feels so tired.

Darkness takes her.

———

When she comes home from school the next day, Whitey's outside waiting for her like always. Shane pulls up to drop her off.

"Whose car is that?" he asks.

There's a white BMW in the driveway. Dirty, though. Tires are muddy, grungy. A black spray like wet, crumbled asphalt streaks the cream-white paint of the otherwise impeccable car.

"I dunno."

"You want me to wait here? Or come in with you?"

She chuckles. "My little hero."

"Oh, man, shut up."

Atlanta pinches his blushing cheeks. "Thanks, Captain America, but I'm good. I can handle my business. And Whitey here has a pair of jaws that could pop a kickball."

"I'll wait here for a few minutes just in case."

She sighs. "Thanks."

Up to the front door. She peeks inside the window—

Her heart stops in her chest like a rock-smashed wristwatch.

Sitting at the kitchen nook table is Ty Carrizo. Across from him is Arlene.

Atlanta tries to shake off the nerves. Even though it feels like she's going too fast down a steep hill in someone else's car, she wills herself to open the door.

"Atlanta, hey," Mama says. "Mister Carrizo, you remember—"

"Miss Burns," he says, standing up and offering his hand.

Atlanta looks at it like it's a shark's mouth.

"Atlanta," Mama protests, then tries to laugh it off. Atlanta reluctantly takes his hand and he gives hers a deceptively hard squeeze. Her knuckles grind together. It hurts but she tries not to show it.

Whitey growls. Ty winces, lets go.

Mama says, "Sorry. She's not very well civilized, this one. Like I was at her age—a little wild, maybe."

"My son's the same way," he says, smiling warmly. He sits back down. "But he's becoming his own man. It's a helluva thing to see."

"Atlanta," Mama says, "Mister Carrizo—"

"Ty, please."

Mama laughs a little. "Ty is here to offer me a job."

"That's right," he says, clapping his hands together. "Your mama is going to join VLS next week doing some . . . general around-the-office duties. Filing and answering phones and whatnot. One of our ladies went on maternity leave, then came back for a month before she decided she just couldn't stay away from that sweet little baby of hers. So, a vacancy is open."

"It's going to be a big help," Mama says, beaming.

Atlanta shifts uncomfortably. "Oh. I bet."

———

She goes upstairs and nearly throws up.

Ty Carrizo. What is this? Some kinda threat, she wagers. Seems like there were little codes hidden in what he was saying, too—that thing about maternity leave and a sweet little baby. A reference to Bee? To his own child? Or just a random one-off thing?

Maybe none of it was a threat. Maybe it was . . . a legitimate job offer. Something engineered by Paul?

Atlanta's head spins.

When she finally hears his car door pop shut and she looks out the window to see him taking off—driving past Shane, who she completely forgot was out there, so she quick-texts him *evrythng cool go home thx*—she hurries downstairs.

"Mama," she says. "Do not take that job."

"What do you mean? It's a good thing," Arlene says, whisking around the kitchen, doing an odd spot of cleaning up. "It's money, honey. Real money."

"He's not a good dude. Something about him . . ."

"He's just fine. You're being paranoid."

Atlanta drops the hammer. "You really think you're a good judge of men?"

Arlene turns. Face sober. Sad or shocked, too, Atlanta can't tell. "Honey, I . . . we need this money. We're trapped. That mortgage of ours is going to go up, up, up, like an out-of-control hot-air balloon and we can't catch it. We'll lose this place, and then I don't know what happens."

"Mama—"

"That's the last I'll hear it of, Atlanta."

Whoa. Arlene laying down her parenting voice. She's been getting some practice with that one as of late.

It makes Atlanta mad.

But it makes her a little proud, too.

Ah, to hell with it. She storms upstairs, slams a door. A classic move.

———

A few more texts with Shane before bed:

Her: *sorry bout earlier*

Shane: *It's cool, don't worry about it.*

(He always texts grammatically correct with full punctuation.)

Her: *stupid ty carrizzo carizzo carrizo however you spellit*

Shane: *You still going to let it go?*

Her: *i guess dont wanna go kicking over anthills*

Her: *this was prolly a threat and maybe i should learn to listen*

Shane: *That's not like you.*

Her: *turning over a new leaf*

Shane: *Good luck with that.*

(She sends him a string of poop emojis in response.)

Shane: *You're gross.*

Her: *you're gross*

Her: *hey didyou check out Mahoney*

Shane: *I did. Didn't take much to find it. News blotter item said* he was arrested with an unlicensed weapon. He's back in prison.

Her: *whew good*

Shane: *You sure you're letting it go?*

Her: *TOTALLY*

Shane: *If you say so.*

Shane: *Goodnight, Atlanta.*

Her: *gnite short stuff*

(He sends her a selfie of him frowning at her.)

(She laughs via laugh emoji and an added LOL.)

———

An Ambien sits in the palm of her hand.

It's getting colder in the house as the wind bangs the shutters, but Whitey lies across her feet. Her own personal canine heater.

"Do I take this?" she asks him.

He makes a sound like *murrowwwwph*.

"That's not helpful."

Already he's snoring.

Good times.

Taking the Ambien has been okay the last couple days. And she's not real keen on the idea of having yet another sleepless night, going into the weekend—and here she reminds herself that tomorrow is her last class for the hunter safety course, and Paul won't be there, which means she doesn't have an adult to go with her and *well, shit*. With all that's been going on, that didn't even occur to her. Dangit, dangit, dangit.

"I don't want to stay awake all night," she says to the dog, or maybe to nobody, or maybe to the whole universe and whatever god does or does not exist to govern over it. "I'm tired of being tired, Whitey."

The dog rolls over, still snoozing.

She decides to take a lesson from Whitey.

She dry-swallows the pill and heads to bed.

Everything's going to be okay, she tells herself.

She's wrong.

CHAPTER TWENTY-TWO

Everything is warped and greasy. Like being drawn up out of a swimming pool filled with motor oil. Something shakes her. A sound, distant but close. Loud but quiet. Every fiber of her being wants to stay down there in the dark, sinking into the oil—

Her arm whips back and forth.

Whitey is growling.

Chris Coyne whispers in her ear: *Atlanta! Get up, girl!*

She draws a deep breath and comes out of her Ambien sleep-coma.

Whitey has her arm in his mouth. A soft bite. He's snarling, shaking her like a doggy toy. She tries to say something, tries to protest—but it comes out mucky and slurry, all *wuzza you dooza*, like her tongue and her brain aren't yet in sync. And now that she's awake, Whitey steps back, ass up, head down, barking at her— deep, panicked, fast barks.

She smells something, then. Something smoky. Like someone's lit the fireplace downstairs, but nobody's ever lit that fireplace long as she's lived here.

Underneath her door, she sees a line of glowing light.

Whitey noses her hard in the side.

It hits her.

The house is on fire.

Whitey tugs on her. The message is clear: *let's go let's go let's go*.

Atlanta's up. She searches around for socks, shoes, but again Whitey is insistent—he's behind her, taking that big shovelhead of his and pushing her toward the door, barking all the while.

She flings open her bedroom door. The fire hasn't reached the upstairs—but downstairs, everything is bright, the color of a volcano's innards, and plumes of black smoke choke the stairway and are already filling the upstairs.

Atlanta coughs, eyes watering. Breathing in the stuff feels like she's breathing in a forest fire, her lungs seared like an overcooked steak.

Mama.

She goes down the hallway. Whitey's trying to pull her the other way, but she tells him: "Gotta find Mama!" and then he ruffs and hurries behind her.

Atlanta ducks low, trying to stay away from the smoke, her eyes watering so much now that it's hard to see, her nose burning, her mouth tasting like a campfire. She throws open Arlene's door and—

There. Through the black haze, she sees Mama lying there, still as a mummy in its tomb and *Oh god, smoke inhalation,* she thinks, *you can die from that,* and she hurries in and reaches for her mother and—

Pillows. Just a few pillows lying scattered. Arlene Burns isn't here.

She calls for her mother. Nothing. She hurries, checks the bathroom. Not there, either. She doubles over, hacking.

Atlanta turns, back to the hall. Whitey at her side, his hackles up.

At the top of the steps, it's too much. The smoke is a dragon shoving its head up the hallway: dark, serpentine, malevolent. And by now she can hear the fire, too, the beastly rumble, the devilish roar.

Can't get out that way.

The roof. She can get out from her window.

Once Whitey is back in the bedroom with her, she slams the door and shoves a blanket against the bottom crack of it. Suddenly all the obsessive fire training they do at school—elementary and up—makes scary sense. She's going through all the thoughts, *doorknobs get hot, smoke can kill you, stop-drop-roll.*

But then the room is filled with a red light, and she thinks, *The fire is here.* It's come up through the vents, maybe, or it's already at her door. The light is like Satan's own: crimson and sinister, the color of Hell's furnace, but then the red becomes white and then back to red.

It's coming from the window.

Strobe light.

She tries to open the window, but it won't budge—*dummy, it's locked.* So she unlocks it and it *still* won't budge. Because of humidity or crappy paint or some other scientific principle she should've studied in class, and right now she thinks her best bet is to kick it out—she braces herself, gets low, pushes hard—

It unsticks with a pop and opens.

She pushes out the screen. It clatters across the shingles.

To Whitey, she opens her arms. "C'mon. C'mon!"

He whines.

"Don't make me bark at you," she says, and now she can hear a fire siren—the warped banshee wail. Whitey readies himself, then jumps into her arms and *god-dang he's heavy* but she *oofs* and helps him get out the window. His claws scrabble on the roof, but he doesn't go tumbling off the edge at least.

She clambers out after him.

And now what?

She can jump. Ten feet down. Might twist her ankle, but probably won't be any worse than that. Whitey, though. Can he make that jump?

Will he?

And then, from the far side of the roof, looking toward the Cat Lady's house and way across the now-dead, now-brittle corn:

The lights from a fire truck get brighter.

A ladder truck pulls up, siren still blaring.

She hears yelling. The ladder extends.

Whitey growls, his fur bristling so much you could use him to clean your boots. She puts a steadying hand on his haunches.

"It's okay," she says. "It's okay."

CHAPTER TWENTY-THREE

This is a first, she thinks. After all the things that have happened in her life, sitting in the back of an ambulance is a new experience. And not one she had on her bucket list (not that Atlanta has much of a bucket list). The ambulance hasn't gone anywhere, and the doors are open and Atlanta's legs dangle out (the rest of her is swaddled in a green blanket), and it gives her a good view of the house.

The bottom floor is blackened. Some of the windows are blown out. Char marks like demon fingers run along the back door, like the fire was trapped inside and its whole plan was to burn its way out.

Smoke still drifts. Everything stinks of it.

It's midnight now. Atlanta's been out here for an hour or so. Mama's here—showed up just after the fire trucks, as EMTs were ushering Atlanta toward the ambulance. Mama said she was working a later shift at Karlton, though a little voice in Atlanta's mind tells her the Karlton isn't open that late, not even on a Friday night like this one.

The EMTs were wishy-washy about sending Atlanta to the hospital. Said they could do more tests there, though her lack of proximity to the source of the fire itself probably left her with no "thermal damage," which she figures means *burns*, which is of course her last name, and then she repeats her whole name to herself again and again: *Atlanta Burns, Atlanta burns, Atlanta Burns, Atlanta Burns burns.* An absurd mental exercise. Maybe the universe's idea of a joke.

Or maybe not the universe.

Maybe someone else.

Maybe someone did this.

Either way, Atlanta told the EMTs she was fine. They even checked out Whitey for her, but he seems okay, too—all the while he sits as close to Atlanta as he can, head up, one good ear cocked. Vigilant as a statue.

She leans over the edge of the ambulance to scratch his ears. "You saved my ass," she says.

He licks her hand.

And here comes Paul, pulling away from a few other guys— they still have the hose trained on the side of the house. No more fire but still some smoke. Given the way the wind keeps kicking up, she guesses they're just trying to be sure.

"Hey, Atlanta," he says.

"Hey, Paul."

"Your house . . ."

"One of your fire friends, Bill somebody—"

"Schuster, Bill Schuster."

"He said the house is in rough shape, but it didn't burn all the way down."

Paul pulls out a cigarette, lights it. "Yeah. First floor's in rough shape. But it's a farmhouse so the bones are still there. And the second floor—there it's mostly smoke and soot. They don't know what caused it. Could've been squirrels chewing wires or faulty knob-and-tube or . . . you know, who knows." He offers a wan grin. "I'm sorry about your house."

"You should be sorry about my money."

He hesitates. "I am. I really am. I, uhhh." He laughs, but it's a nervous sound. "I'm in deep with some people."

"You're a gambling addict."

"Yeah." He looks surprised. "How'd you know?"

"I didn't. But you kinda put out signals. Figured it was that or drugs, and you didn't seem . . . druggy."

"I thought I would be able to take the money under your bed and . . . it wasn't enough to pay back the people I owe but—"

"Lemme guess: you gambled the money in the hopes of getting more money, but instead you lost it because that's how gambling works. I bet this is something that's going on at VLS? Where you work?" Her brain recalls Guy telling her there was a poker game there.

He gives a shameful nod.

She asks him, "How'd you even know that money was under my bed?"

"Your mother found it cleaning up one day."

"You mean snooping. Mama doesn't clean much of anything."

He shrugs. "Maybe."

"Well. Great."

"I'm gonna pay you back."

"Sure you are. Moon's also made of cheese, I hear."

"Atlanta—"

"We're good here. Thanks for what you did tonight. I'll see you."

He nods, gives another anxious smile, then heads back to be with the other fire guys, or maybe to talk to Mama, she doesn't know. Atlanta tries not to cough, but that just makes her cough all the harder. She feels like getting up, walking around, so she does. Takes a look at the charred husk of the house. A house set ablaze. *Could've been squirrels chewing wires or faulty knob-and-tube.* Uh-uh.

Someone did this to her.

Same someone who ran Bee off the road.

This has Ty Carrizo's soot-black fingerprints all over it.

She sniffs. So, that's that, then.

Atlanta wanders over to her mother, waits for Arlene to stop talking to one of the fire guys—a chubby fella with a mustache like a horseshoe. (Paul's over by one of the trucks—he's keeping his distance, still. But he's watching like a hawk. Question is: a protective one, or one that's a predator?)

Once she's done she turns to Atlanta, gives her daughter a big hug. "Baby, I am so sorry I wasn't here."

"It's fine. I get it." She doesn't get it, not yet, but right now it's not high on the list. "Glad you're okay."

"I'm glad you're okay, too." Arlene pulls away, gives her daughter the once-over. "You sure you don't need to go to the hospital?"

"I'm sure. I'm sticking around."

Mama gives a sly grin. "Could be that we'll get an insurance check out of all this. That's something, at least. For once the system might work for *us.*"

"That'll be real nice." *If it actually happens.* "I need you tomorrow."

"Why, baby?"

"I have my last hunter safety course."

"Honey, sweetie, just let that go, they'll understand—"

"I need this. I want this. And that means you gotta be my adult."

Mama pauses. Then finally, she smiles and nods. "Sure, you got it, baby."

"Thanks."

She'll finish her class. Then she'll get her gun back.

Because it's time to break that pinky swear.

CHAPTER TWENTY-FOUR

They don't want her to take the last class. Not with her mother. Wayne Sleznik stands there, frittering about, wearing a disappointed mask as he says, "Atlanta, I am sorry, but we prefer to maintain continuity in your teaching. And your mother, Elaine—"

"Arlene," Mama corrects with a rubber-band snap.

"*Arlene* doesn't have a hunting license. The goal is that you leave the class with your sponsor and get to talk about what you learned here—"

"It's because she's a woman," Atlanta says. "Isn't it?"

Arlene steps up. "Is it because I'm a woman?"

"No, no, no," he says, waving his hands about and offering an uncomfortable *heh-heh-heh* laugh. "My other teacher as you'll see is Joanne Kinro—" Here he points to the park ranger across the room who's pouring coffee into a paper cup from a thermos. The ranger looks up with a grumpy glare.

"Let's go, Mama," Atlanta says.

But Mama, she's not done. She starts to cry.

It's subtle at first. Just a high-pitched sound coming from the back of her throat. Then a little shake to her shoulders. She starts to crumple up like the snot-slick tissue she'll inevitably end up with, and then she starts blubbering about how their house just burned down and her husband is dead and their dog got shot in the head and all her little girl wants to do is learn how to hunt—her father's dying wish, *I'll tell you what.*

Thing is, Mama doesn't cry like that. Atlanta knows what it's like. This crying jag is fake as a three-dollar bill, and she's sure that Sleznik here will see right through it like it's a squeaky-clean window—

But he waves his hands again. "Okay, okay, okay. You can stay."

Mama whimpers: "We can stay?"

"You can stay," he repeats again.

She throws her arms around him. Blubbers gratitude.

Then, as she pulls Atlanta over to take their seats, she sniffles one last time and whispers: "Babydoll, if there's one thing that ruins a man's composure, it's seeing a lady lose hers."

Atlanta wears a grin like a boomerang.

————

The class today is about the strategies of hunting, about setting traps. Tracking your prey. Capturing your prey. Taking the shot at your prey. Scents and lures and blood trails.

Needless to say, Atlanta pays real good attention.

————

On the way home, Atlanta pulls a little of her hair over to her nose. Still smells like smoke. In her lap sits the certificate of completion for her hunter safety course. That and a little paperwork signed by Sleznik and Kinro. All she has to do is mail this in to get her first hunting license.

She figures she won't need it. Animals have enough problems without her chasing them around the woods with a gun.

People, though. People can be a real problem.

And now she can get her gun.

Mama yawns. "Baby, I'm tired. I got us a motel room for the night and it's gettin' to be check-in time, but that's gonna kill our bank account lickety-quick. We'll need to figure out where we're staying tomorrow night. And fast."

"I'll call around." Atlanta rubs her eyes. She's tired, too. No, that's not it. Not just tired—but *weary*. She's a scarecrow with a broken pole holding her up, the weight of wind and weather pushing her closer and closer to the ground. "Hey, thanks for taking me today. I know you probably had things to do."

"I had a shift. At the Karlton. But this seemed more important." Arlene offers a small smile. "We don't spend much time together anymore."

"No, I reckon we don't."

"After . . . after everything, I know we don't always get along so hot."

"No kid my age gets along with her parents, it's fine." *Except Damon and Ty Carrizo,* she reminds herself. "We'll . . . get through it. Fences mended, bridges put back up over the rushing river, all that."

"I love you, baby."

Atlanta rolls her eyes. "Yeah, I love you, too." She quick points ahead: "Here, here, take a right here."

She feels Arlene give her a look.

But the car makes the turn.

———

Boom.

Atlanta slaps the certificate down on Holger's desk. Holger looks at it, then to Atlanta, then back to it. She plucks a pair of reading glasses from her front pocket, brings the two halves of the spectacles together (*click*) as she puts them on.

"This is legit," Holger says, sounding surprised.

"It's legit as hell," Atlanta says. "Now, if you please? My shotgun."

Holger pops the glasses off, leans forward. "First I want to say: I'm sorry about your house."

"Thank you."

"They're doing what they call an *origin and cause* investigation. Seeing why the fire started and all that." Holger lowers her voice, says: "Do you think someone did this, Atlanta? On purpose?"

"No," she says without hesitation. It's a lie, of course. She doesn't want to put anything out there for Holger to grab on to. Especially with what Atlanta's planning. No need to give herself any kind of out-loud motive. "It was an old house with wiring that I think George Washington himself installed by hand. I guess stuff like that just burns down sometimes."

Holger pauses, then nods. "Fair enough. Let's get you that gun."

———

Holger brings the gun out to the car. She's carrying it in a long fabric case and tells Atlanta, "This case has been sitting back there for a good while. I suspected you could use it. Besides, I don't think I should just hand you a gun."

Atlanta takes the case. She wants to unzip it, bring out her little squirrel gun with all the eagerness some people might possess when they pick a puppy up from a long stay at the kennel. But she holds off because, well, *weird*.

Holger leans into the driver's-side window. "Ms. Burns," she says.

"Arlene," Mama says, looking uncomfortable.

"Of course. I'm turning this weapon over to your daughter, Arlene. She's underage, but if I remand it to the both of you, and given that she now has the hunter safety certificate, it's all aboveboard. You understand?"

Mama offers a small, confused laugh. "Sure, okay."

Now Holger stands up, looks at Atlanta. "Do you understand, Atlanta?"

"I do."

"This means I trust you."

"Okay."

"That means don't prove me wrong."

"I said okay."

"What I said is true: something happens, your mother will share the responsibility. The criminal responsib—"

"I get it," Atlanta snaps. Then tries to cover it up with a smile. "Detective, it's fine. You have nothing to worry about." She almost adds *pinky-swear*, but figures that might be a little too sassy. And she's already broken too many of those anyway.

———

The motel they're staying at is called the Pole Barn Inn. Atlanta hoped that the name was as far as it went, but nope—turns out, the whole place has kind of a *barny-farmy* aesthetic going on. Outside is red like a barn. Amish hexes inside the motel office. Paintings of barns and farmhouses and silos everywhere.

Mama's out getting them dinner—cheap Chinese food from Hunan Palace down off of 80, where the General Tso's tastes like spicy candy and the lo mein is the greasiest, greatest lo mein ever made.

Atlanta's about to make a call—

—when her cell rings.

UNKNOWN number.

Huh. Okay.

She bites her lip, answers the phone.

A recorded message plays, which at first she thinks must be some kind of telemarketer hoo-haw: "*This is a call from the State Correctional Institution Frackville. Please press '1' to accept the charges, or press '2' or hang up to reject them.*"

Atlanta hesitates. Phone hovers over her ear.

Then she holds it tight and presses:

1.

CHAPTER TWENTY-FIVE

Sunday. A day later.

It's three of them in the car this time, Shane driving, Josie in the front (she said with some irony: "I know it's your thing, Atlanta, but I'm calling shotgun"). Plus, Atlanta owes Josie now, since she and Mama are done with the motel and she'll be crashing at Josie's at least for the next week to ten days until . . . someone figures something out.

Ahead, the prison. Past one gate where Atlanta has to give her name. Then another gate. Two sets of chain-link fences, each coiled with barbed wire. Four small towers with guards standing up there—each armed with what looks like a high-powered black rifle. The prison itself isn't much to look at: a flat, blocky box with fenced-in areas dividing it up all around. In the distance she sees what must be some kind of exercise yard; prisoners in lemon-yellow jumpsuits and jackets are jogging, lifting weights, or otherwise standing around in little clusters.

Mostly black guys by the look of it. A few bald white dudes, too. One of them has a swastika across his entire bald head, big enough that she can see it even from here. A bold, if terrifying, fashion choice.

Being here freaks her out.

Something about the place makes her think she could go inside and the metal doors will close behind her. They'll lock. She'll never come back out.

Absurd, because it's not like she's the FBI's most wanted. Nobody cares about her. (Which is, she figures, a firm advantage.) Still. Whole place makes her feel claustrophobic. Even looking at it makes her feel trapped, somehow.

"You sure you want to do this?" Shane asks. "I don't think he's going to be very happy to see you."

"He invited me," Atlanta says. "So, I'll pop my head up like a gopher at the hole, see what's shaking."

Josie gives her a scared smile. "Be safe."

"It's jail," Atlanta says. "What's the worst that can happen? They gonna riot while I'm in there?"

———

Dang, what if they riot?

She's sitting alone in a little room with five tables, each of those with a bunch of green stools. The door out is wooden with wire-mesh safety glass in it. Once in a while a shape passes by: someone's head. The guard, she thinks—a pornstached dude with mean, beady little eyes.

Eventually, the door unlocks—Atlanta didn't even realize it *was* locked, which is probably good because just the thought of it is giving her a panic attack right now—and the beady-eyed guard comes in.

Followed by Ellis Wayman, the Mountain Man.

The man who is a mountain.

She'd forgotten how big he is. His hair is shorter now, close cropped. But that big bushy beard hangs there like the root system of a briar thicket growing down deep into the dirt. He's gray as the steel wool she sometimes uses to clean her gun. He takes a seat at the table, hands shackled in front of him.

"We good?" the guard asks.

"Yeah," Wayman says. "Thanks, Lardner."

"You got it, Mountain Man."

Then the guard heads to the door and starts to leave the room.

Leaving Atlanta alone with Ellis Wayman.

She calls after: "No, wait, where are you—"

But it's too late. Door closes.

And locks with a click.

It hits her: this really is a trap. All along she's been thinking she needed to pay attention to Ty Carrizo, maybe even to Orly Erickson, but she thought Ellis Wayman was a checker piece that she'd knocked clean off the board. Now here he is. Sharing a locked room with her.

"I swear, you do anything I'll scream," she says, standing up, fists by her side. "You get near me, I'll kick, I'll punch, I'll bite. I'll make you eat that beard."

"Relax," he grumps. "Siddown. I'm not gonna hurt you. I got sway, but no matter how much I got, no way they're gonna let me murder a teenage girl in the prison. I harm one strand of hair on your fire-red head, they'd expel every last guard on duty. And worse, they'd boot my ass in a hole so deep and so dark I'd wish they just sent me to Guantanamo."

She doesn't sit, though. She stands, staring. "Why invite me here?"

"Better question is, why accept the invite?"

"I . . . I don't know."

"You do know. You owe me. Maybe you don't realize it consciously, but you know it in your heart."

She barks a laugh. "I don't owe you poop squat, Mister Wayman. Respectfully, what happened to you was the grave you dug."

"Maybe so, but you pushed me into it. Things were good. I had everything I wanted. The Farm wasn't really a well-oiled machine, but like an old, classic Massey Ferguson tractor, it kept chugging along and never failed me. Then you showed up. Took my dog. Shut everything down. Got me and—shoot, how many others?— sent here or across the state." He blows air out from his lips and his mustache lifts up like Marilyn Monroe's skirt in that old movie. "You did a number on me and my operation. And now you're doing it all over again."

"I don't follow you."

"You got a habit of stepping in shit, is what I'm saying to you. And then you . . ." He waggles his fingers like he's playing an invisible piano. "Track that shit all over the damn place, don't you? I'm talking about Ty Carrizo."

"I . . . I don't know—"

"You gonna sit, or what?"

She sits. At a different table. One over. Out of reach.

Ellis watches her do it, then chuckles to himself.

"I don't know how you know anything about that," she says.

"I didn't, up until very recently. Funny thing. A fella came in here, a fella I know but don't much care for, name of Owen Mahoney. Mahoney told a *pretty wild story*. Said some teenage piece of ass with firebrand hair doped him up and then called the police on him. Said he remembered little bits here and there. Her asking him about a specific set of operations run by a man named Ty Carrizo."

"I don't know any Owen Mahoney."

Wayman gives her a look that says, *Really, we're gonna play it that way?* Dubious as all get-out. "Uh-huh. Sure. Fine. Let me tell my story, then, and see if any of it *pings* your radar. So, Mahoney thinks maybe Ty Carrizo set him up. Carrizo, after all, like that bastard Erickson, he plays at being legit. Which is sneaky, snaky business. Because me? I always was what I was, no fooling around, no fancy foot moves to make people think differently. Mahoney starts asking around, and that's how word gets to me. And I do a little *shaking of the bushes* myself and, turns out, some shit has been going down, hasn't it? A little prostitution ring. A dead girl. A *pregnant* girl."

"And a house fire."

"You don't say?"

"I do say. My house burned down the other night."

"That's the thing, isn't it? *You* seem to be at the heart of all this."

"What's your point?"

He leans forward, resting his bearded chin in the cradle of his chains. "That is the question, isn't it? Here's something: you hamstrung my operation and the people in it. But I'm not done yet. I still got some juice. Carrizo, I don't like him. He's trying to steal what juice I have left. That's a no-no."

"You ran girls, too?"

"Little bit, though no teenagers. We kept it all aboveboard. But it's not just that. It's everything. I won't get into all the gory details, but I want him gone."

She hesitates, thinks, *Maybe we're being recorded.* A strange thought, but there it is. "I won't be a part of that."

"No," he says with a big smile. "You've got clean hands. A moral heart. You'd never put yourself in the eye of the hurricane. Hell, girl, you *are* the eye of the hurricane. But let's just make believe for a half a second that I knew about Ty Carrizo. About how, say, he was running a banquet this Friday night, a banquet that plays host to all manner of bigwigs. Couple state senators. Some lobbyists. Plus, all the higher-ups at his company, a lot of whose hands are nowhere near as clean, whose hearts are nowhere near as *saintly* as yours. And what if I were to tell you that after this banquet ends, Ty Carrizo will do what he always does after such events, which is bring out the young girls, the drugs, the cards for a high-stakes poker game."

"Why are you telling me this?"

His smile drops. His lip sneers. "Because even though I'm in here, I have reach, but not enough. Because I want my competition's legs cut out from under him. Carrizo doesn't belong here. He's somebody else from somewhere else. I'm Pennsylvania born and bred. I care about this place." He snorts up a snot into his throat. Chews it a little. "Besides, his business is a dirty one even without the crime. Fracking is naughty shit. Buddy of mine over in Tioga County was able to set his damn tap water on fire. That should tell you how safe it is."

"But why *me*? You got . . . juice, whatever that means. Go have your guys on the outside—am I using that slang right? The outside? Have them do it."

"They can't. They won't. And I don't wanna risk them getting scooped up by the competition. A tough little girl like you, though. They'll never see you coming. I didn't." He drops all expression now. His face, cold as an autopsy table. "I like you. And you owe me. And you need this."

"Let's say I do. How do I do it?"

"You'll figure something out. But the way I see it is, go with the classic. Use the same play as last time. Same one that brought *me* down."

———

On the car ride home—"home" for Atlanta now meaning Josie's place—Shane asks, "Everything go okay in there?"

Atlanta nods, staring out the window, watching trees pass.

"Yeah." *No. I'm scared. Scared of what's coming.* "Yeah," she repeats.

CHAPTER TWENTY-SIX

A few days later, Atlanta's got her hand deep in a toilet tank. Popping in the new—well, she doesn't know what they call it. The flappy bit that opens when you flush, snaps shut when it's done. The whatchahoozit. The thingamabibble.

She finishes popping that on, makes sure it forms a tight seal.

Door to the trailer ratchets open. She hears Guy come in with a few bags from Walmart. She leans her head out of the bathroom, blowing a jet of air to divert a strand of hair from her eyes. "You get what I need?"

"You fix my shitter?"

"Your toilet's fixed, yeah."

"Then I got what you need, 'Lanta."

———

She walks home with a new brick of .410 ammo under her arm and Guy's warning in her ear: *Whatever you're thinking of doing, girly, you might wanna think of doing something else. Go be a kid. Forget this stuff. The world's full of bad people doing bad things and you can't stop it. You feel me?*

She "feels" him.

She gets it.

She doesn't even disagree.

It's good, sound advice.

And she's still not going to take it.

———

Way she sees it is this:

Some heinous business is going down. They're doing things to girls. It's not just about running some sex trade—Atlanta figures any girl who sells her body is probably getting scammed, but that's her body and not Atlanta's business. This, though? It isn't that. It's girls *forced* into it. Young girls.

And she was almost forced into it, too.

Now her . . . ex-friend, current friend, whatever friend, Bee, has a baby in her belly. And Samantha Gwynn-Rudin is dead.

It didn't end with Samantha, either. It started there but keeps going.

She remembers having to clear out a bunch of briar that had ringed their last house down South—out there with a machete, cutting it apart till a neighbor told her that wouldn't fix it. What you see on the surface isn't all of it, she said. Stuff grows up, forms a big-ass root system underneath. Then it spreads. Both underneath the ground, with shoots and runners, and aboveground, too—any time one of those long, thorny briar fingers got *too* long, it drooped over like a sad man, worked its tip into the dirt, and started a whole new root system. All part of one plant.

So, you wanna kill it, the neighbor said, you either hafta hose it all down with weed killer, or you gotta dig up all the roots. Rip 'em out.

This problem is like that. It isn't just one thing. It isn't just the girls, though that's a big part of it. It's that Ty Carrizo is out there. The man's a blight. He's got a whole root system working underneath his feet while people think he's a shiny, productive, brand-new member of the community.

Time to rip out those roots.

———

Josie's house is nice. Not richie-rich nice, but suburb nice. Sits at the end of a cul-de-sac. Got a snazzy pair of red maples out front. It's all pretty standard, pretty boring, a pair of sensible shoes instead of a pair of Doc Marten boots, a line drive instead of a home run, a golden retriever instead of a pet Komodo dragon.

Her parents, too, are nice, if so distracted that Atlanta's not a hundred percent sure they're not secretly ferrets piloting people costumes. They zip around here, there, back to here. Josie's mother is an executive assistant at some small pharma company about an hour south. Her father is a sales rep for audiovisual systems—screens and speakers and the like. He's on the road a lot.

Right now, the core group—Atlanta, Shane, Josie (duh), and Steven—sit in Josie's room, which is about as far from *pretty standard* as you can get—a mishmash of punk and ska band posters and hand-painted, hand-embroidered roller skates ("I wanna do derby someday," Josie says with an almost scary fire in her eyes). A buncha weird antiques, too: some art deco stuff, a lamp that looks like a cowboy boot, a purple dresser whose entire top is a topography of melted candle wax in motley colors.

Shane says: "I don't think this is a good idea, Atlanta."

"I know it ain't," she says. "But they ran Bee off the road. Tried to burn my house down. Killed Samantha. I don't know that they won't stop coming."

Steven says, "You're sure it was them who set your house on fire?"

"Who else?" Atlanta shrugs. "The timing's a little weird, otherwise."

Nods all around.

Downstairs, a doorbell.

Atlanta stands up. "She's here. Hold on."

She heads downstairs, answers the door, comes back up.

This time, with Bee in tow.

Bee, arm in a sling. The bruises on her face are now more the ghosts of bruises—dark purple gone to sickly yellow, fading into her skin.

"Bee, the group. Group, the Bee." She names everyone as Bee takes a seat on the floor. Shane shakes her hand like it's a business meeting.

"Welcome to the Pennsylvania Trade Commission," he says, affecting a stuffy white-guy voice. "You will be a valued, uh, added member of our team."

Bee gives a quizzical smirk, and Josie says: "He's just being weird."

"He's good at weird," Atlanta says.

"I am Groot," Shane says.

"See?"

Bee smiles, apparently nervous. "So. Um. Hey."

"You're pregnant," Josie says with awkward awe.

"I guess."

"Can you feel it moving around?"

"Not really. Sometimes I get a little flutter but I think it's just, like, indigestion or something."

"Do you know if it's a boy or a girl?"

Bee laughs an anxious laugh. "Wow, twenty questions. I don't. I think they're supposed to tell me at twenty weeks if they can get a good ultrasound. Right now, it's just a little . . . peapod. God, bigger than that, I guess. An apple?"

Suddenly, Shane blurts out: "Atlanta's going to cause trouble with the Carrizos."

Atlanta stares at him, cross. "Dude. What, because Kyle's not here now you're gonna be the one who can't keep his trap shut?" To Bee, she says: "That's why I brought you here. I wanted you to know what I was doing so . . . none of it surprises you in case there's any blowback."

"We don't want her to do it," Shane says.

"This is kind of an intervention," Josie says.

Atlanta cocks an eyebrow. "What now?"

They all turn toward her.

Shane says: "Atlanta, you have to stop this. We're your friends and you have to . . . not be you. Or something."

"That's *so* not it," Josie says, and gives him an arm punch. "For someone so articulate you can't articulate crap. Atlanta, we're just worried. I'm only now getting to know you, but I think you're cool as hell, and if you get hurt or get dead . . ."

"Think about Chris," Shane says.

"I *am* thinking about Chris," Atlanta snaps. "I'm thinking about him, and you, and Bee, and all of us. I know I shouldn't go around stirring up the mud, but who else is gonna? The cops? Not likely. Teachers? Uh, nope. Our parents? Not that I can see. Everyone else is content to keep their head down so it doesn't get shot off, but, man, shit sucks out there. And it sucks because we got monsters, human monsters, who wanna do us harm, and nobody has the salt to do something about it. But I'm all salt. I'm a salt and vinegar potato chip."

Steven says: "We care about you."

She sighs. "That's sweet. It is. I just . . ." She looks to Bee. Sees Bee giving her a look. A kind of plucky, know-it-all face. "Oh, don't give me that. I know what you're going to say. You agree with these knuckleheads."

"Nope," Bee says. "I don't."

They all stare like she's betrayed each of them personally.

She shrugs. "I'm changing my mind. Someone drove into me, could've killed me, killed my baby. Someone burned down her house. Killed Samantha. They're doing things to girls that turns my stomach and should be turning yours. Besides. I've known Atlanta longer than all of you—" And here Shane makes an annoyed face. "And once she has her mind set, nothing we do will change it. She's like a dog chasing a car." She shrugs. "Only thing we can do is either get out of her way, or give her a hand. Otherwise, we're just yelling at clouds."

Atlanta grins. "Thanks, Bee."

"Is there a plan?"

Atlanta nods. "Yep."

"Good. So what do you need from us?"

———

That night, she lies in the sleeping bag—a pretty cozy one, truth be told—next to Josie's bed.

"You tell your parents?" Atlanta says abruptly.

"You mean, did I come out to them yet?"

"Yeah."

"Nooooo. Hah. No way. Not yet. Maybe never."

"That sucks."

"I love them both dearly, but they're pretty . . . conservative."

"Sorry."

"Maybe one day."

"Yeah." More time passes. "I sometimes think I could be gay."

"Really?"

"I mean, no, not really, but, like, I'm into fishing and I used to watch baseball and racing, and I'm kind of a tomboy, in case you haven't noticed. Even in elementary school I had some guys make fun of me, calling me lezzie."

"Those kinds of people will always find a way to make fun of you. I used to have guys make fun of the way that I chewed food."

"That's dumb."

"Hella dumb." Josie rolls over. Atlanta can feel her peering down at her through the darkness. "Everybody's a little gay, I think."

"You're more than a little gay, though, right?"

"I'm a lot gay. And I've always known. Even when I didn't want to admit it, I've always known."

"I don't know what I like or who I am. I mean, I like guys, but not that much." She chuckles. "I think that's because most of them seem to be shitheads."

"They kinda do."

"You don't think of me in a gay way, do you?"

"What?"

"I just mean—I always wondered, do you look at straight girls and think, oh, wow, look at her?"

"Not really. I dunno. I want people who would want me." She sighs. "Pretty is pretty, though, so I appreciate pretty. But I don't want straight girls. I don't think. Seems weird. I might as well be attracted to a lawn chair."

"I'm starting to think *lawn chair* is the way to go."

They laugh.

Then they're quiet again for a while. Atlanta wonders if she's about to fall asleep. She's still awake, but it's not like it was in the old farmhouse—it's not anxiety, really. Mostly just thoughts running laps in her head. Here she feels . . . safe. Why, she doesn't really know.

Suddenly, Josie says: "You going to be okay through all of this?"

"Maybe."

"That's not a real comforting answer."

"Life doesn't offer up a lot of those."

"No, I guess not. Good night."

"'Night."

———

She startles him without meaning to. Atlanta's standing behind one of the fire engines, just kicking stones, when Paul comes around the corner.

"Jesus!" he says. He clutches his chest like he's having a heart attack, then he laughs. "Atlanta."

"Paul," she says, her voice as dark and cold as a river in winter.

"What's up? Everything okay with your mom and you? You guys have a place to stay? Because you always know—"

"I've got a place and Mama's staying with a friend from the Karlton."

"Oh. That's good."

She sees the disappointment on his face. Not her problem.

"Hey, can we talk somewhere?" she asks. "Little more private?"

He nods, says, "Sure. Follow me."

———

Behind the firehouse, about a hundred yards out, is a small asphalt lot—burn marks all over it, black like the Devil's footprints. A ring of stones in the middle for a firepit. A small standing con-crete-block structure that's meant, she guesses, to simulate a house. A training area, by the look of it.

He sits down on the ring of stones. In the ring, the ashen remains of old logs. Paul asks her what's up, and she tells him. As she talks, he looks more and more uncomfortable.

"I can't do that," he says finally. "I can't help you."

"I don't need much. I just need you to get me in."

"Atlanta, this is . . . I don't know what this is all about, but I can't just sneak you into that banquet. I don't even work that site. I work the wells. You're talking about a different location."

She says, "I know where it is and what it looks like. I had Shane look into it. They're doing a kind of Oktoberfest thing there, in the parking lot of the office building. But that's also where they have the garage and a lot for the tanker trucks, and they keep most of the gas there, right?"

"In big tanks, yeah. These clusters of four tanks a pop. Drive from the wells across the tricounty area, fill up the tanks, then other trucks pull from the tanks to do fill-ups or send the gas to neighboring states."

"So, they'd still let you on site."

"They would. But—"

"You ever get the sense that something shady is going on there?"

He doesn't say anything. Which says a whole lot.

Atlanta keeps on him. "I'm telling you this knowing that you've already broken my trust, and I'm making my own bet here that it means you won't break that trust again. Because you do that, this bridge we're rebuilding will go up in a column of howling flames. You digging up what I'm burying?"

"I don't know what you think is going on there—"

"They're hurting girls. Young girls. Using them for sex. Plus they got the gambling thing going, and I know some of the guys buy pills, and from what I hear, there may be more going on, too. I don't know how far it goes, but I know some very important people are going to be there. Senators and other business folks and even some of Penn State's muckity-mucks."

"So call the cops."

"I need something solid first."

"And that's where I come in."

She pleads: "Just get me on site. That's it. Then you can wash your hands of it. And here, I'm gonna make another bet: I'll *bet* that who you're in hock to is someone there, maybe even Ty Carrizo himself. Am I right?"

Once again, Paul's silence speaks volumes.

"You let me handle this, maybe that debt disappears when he goes to prison. That means you're off that hook."

A moment of relief shines in his eyes, but it's over quick. "Then I'm out of a job."

"Not necessarily. Carrizo's just the CFO, yeah? That's not, like, the head of the company, right?"

"No. That'd be the CEO, Bill Lockhart. And there's a whole board, too."

"So. You in?"

He pops his lips, drums his fingers on the ring of stones. "Who's to say I won't rat you out to the cops? I could call them, tell them about this conversation."

"You could. And maybe you will. But like I said, then that bridge between us, narrow and broken as it is, will be forever done. And you won't get much out of it. You'll still have your debt. But the status quo is powerful, I guess."

Paul winces. The face of a man making an uncomfortable decision.

"You're good at this. Whatever this is," he says.

"So, you in?"

"I'm in," he says.

PART FOUR: FRACK YOU

CHAPTER TWENTY-SEVEN

The truck bounces beneath her. Paul's pickup must have a bunch of old Dixie cups for suspension, because it's not absorbing a single one of the shocks from the potholes on the road. Every hit sends a vibration up her spine like someone just kicked her dead square on her tailbone.

She hides in the back under a blanket.

Next to her: the .410 shotgun. Paul doesn't know it's back here with her—he's on her side for now, but if she showed him there's a gun in play, she knows that would change. She had to sneak it into the back of his truck before she rang his doorbell that morning. But now it's here, and she is, too.

Pockets full of little green shotshells.

Eventually the truck slows down. Paul knocks on the back window, which is the sign: they're here. Not in the facility yet, but at the front gate.

Front gate means a big metal bar that raises or lowers. A guard booth.

She peels back the blanket, listens. The old guard is saying to Paul, "I don't see you on the list. You don't usually work here, do you?"

Paul says, "No, I usually work the Mahoning well."

"I'm gonna have to call this one in—"

Shit.

"Hold up, hold up," Paul says with a nervous laugh. "Confession time: I'm filling in for somebody. You know Dave Filbert?" Before the guard can answer, Paul adds, "Dave tied one on last night real good and he's not here for work, but he's already got two demerits and a third means his ass is grass and VLS is the lawn mower. You call that in, Dave's done for. And I might be, too."

Silence.

It isn't working.

Atlanta tries to come up with a new plan. Hopefully they at least let Paul's truck in through the gate, and when they . . . detain him or whatever happens, she'll sneak out the back and keep everything on track—

The old guard laughs, a cigar-smoke chuckle.

"Okay. I'll just write *Dave Filbert* in here. Kosher?"

"As a Jewish deli."

Another knock on the window.

And the truck pushes on in to the facility.

———

Atlanta peers over the edge of the pickup truck bed as it drives on through. The office building is ahead—and sure enough, in the parking lot they're setting up for the banquet, with tables and tents and strung-up lights (though it's day now, so none of them are on). From a catering truck, people are bringing out burners and Crock-Pots. A little stage is already set up with a couple speakers. A few standing radiant heaters (that look like some of the robots in *Star Wars*) sit off to the side.

If Shane's map is right, it's a quarter-mile drive down the gravel road to the tanks, the garage, and the truck lot.

They wanted to come, of course—Shane and the others. Wanted to be in on it, go along on her misadventure. But she told them no good would come of them all getting hurt. Besides, sneaking one girl in here is pretty easy. Sneaking a whole crew of idiots? Not easy at all. That means it's just her, and that means *they* have the job of giving her information, being her eyes, her ears, and above all else, her brain.

Most of this is Shane's plan, to be honest.

Bless his little well-groomed ass.

He said it'd be smarter to sneak in during the day than closer to night—night rolls around and everyone will be on eggshells, thinking about impressing senators and keeping that security straight. Daytime, it's easy.

Just another workday.

Good.

Paul pulls the truck down the road. She keeps her eyes peeled, ducks anytime a tanker or other car passes on the left.

Soon as they get close to what she thinks must be the garage, she sees her opportunity, the one Shane circled on the blurry diagram he printed out—satellite photo from Google Maps. The truck has to round the bend behind the garage, and there Paul slows—she hops out over the side, and sees the perfect cover. Stacks of tires and wooden pallets. Shotgun in hand, she gives a tap on Paul's truck. As she goes to duck behind the tires—

—Paul's brake lights come on.

He sees her. In the side mirror.

His mouth is wide. His eyes, squinting.

He whips his head around, probably to check if it's just a trick of his eyes or if she's really carrying a shotgun—

Nope, nope, she's really carrying a shotgun. She can see the look on his face when he realizes it. She shrugs, gives a wave, then shoos him on his way.

Don't mess this up, Paul.

Don't you dare.

He starts to reverse the truck, and she drags a finger across her throat which is maybe a more threatening gesture than she intends it to be. She means it as, *You come any closer, you're gonna kill the whole deal,* but it probably comes across like, *I'll kill you.*

Either way, he stops.

Truck idling.

Looks like he curses silently, then pulls ahead.

Whew.

Atlanta's in.

———

The plan is this:

Atlanta remains hidden. Hidden for hours, in fact, until five p.m. Normally, this facility is never shut down—the trucks move twenty-four hours a day, seven days a week. But today is different. Today is the banquet. Can't have loud tanker trucks driving past the stage, making people smell their exhaust as they eat their knockwurst or chili or whatever else they're serving down there. Paul said that today, the trucks stop running at five, and they don't pick back up until midnight.

Hiding isn't too hard. She ducks in through an open door in the back. The garage isn't busy. Already it seems like they're winding down for the day. One truck up on the rack, and nobody's even working on it.

Atlanta finds a corner of the garage, hides behind an old rack of what look like propane tanks, the kind you might use for a gas grill (though she's reminded of how her daddy always said that a gas grill was no grill at all, and it was charcoal briquettes or nothing if you wanted a good burger, dog, or steak).

And there, she waits.

Time passes like dripping honey. Steady. But slow, too slow.

Her mind wanders there in the dark behind the tanks. She misses her daddy. Worries for Mama. Worries for herself, too. And here she starts to think the same way she guesses lots of folks do when they're in an anxious position—she starts chewing on her future. Not much of a future at all now. Her money's gone. Her grades are so bad she might as well flush 'em. Dang, even if she had the money—what was she thinking? She'd hop on a bus and head out to a life somewhere? Bagging at Walmart? Promoted to checkout girl? No harm, no foul to those who wanna do that or don't have much choice, but she never really saw herself wearing that little vest and running cat food or diapers over a scanner.

And it's then it hits her:

She needs a future.

If she makes it out of here, she's gotta figure that out, and pronto. Time is ticking. The wick on this high school candle is about to burn out. It's now or never. She flips through the mental scrapbook, tries to figure out what the heck she'd even wanna do with her life, but so far, that scrapbook is just a series of blank pages. Photo corners with no photos.

A future unwrit, but unimagined, too.

Dang, dang, double-dang.

She checks her phone. Four p.m.

Been here two hours already.

Only one hour left—

The sound of an engine. Not a truck engine. Car. Someone yells out: "Bring it to bay three, over here—no, not there, here."

A car pulls into the third garage bay door. One closest to Atlanta.

It's a little orange hatchback.

Bee's car.

Dread runs through her like a scouring force.

One guy gets out of her car from the driver's side. A grungy-looking dude with ratty long hair and bad skin. He meets a stubby fireplug of a man—older, balding, cleanly shaven. "What's this?" the fireplug asks.

Grungy guy says, "I dunno. They told me to move it down here."

"Put the keys on the pegs, then."

Why is Bee's car here?

It's one of two things, Atlanta figures—

First, they went and got her. Why, she can't imagine. But maybe someone brought her here. For reasons that aren't yet clear.

Second, she came here all on her own. Couldn't stop herself. Which would mean she's pulling an Atlanta—stepping right into it. Putting herself in the middle because she just can't help herself.

Either way, it's not good. It means she's here, somewhere.

And not down here, either. But probably back up toward the office.

Atlanta figures she's going to have to head that direction. Which means crossing wide-open space, because there's not a lot between the office building and this secondary backlot area. Someone will see her.

She always knew having to cross that distance was probable—she just figured she'd do it once the sun set. Easier to sneak along—and bring a shotgun—if it's dark. Now, though, it's light. And Bee's presence complicates things.

That means she has to move now. Not later.

After Grungy Guy puts the keys on the peg, Atlanta thinks to sneak over and grab them—then drive Bee's car back up. Two problems there: First, she can't drive. She'll probably be able to figure it out, but still. The other problem is it'll make noise, draw attention. Can't have that. Not yet, anyway.

But then a second idea pops into her head.

It could work. Means a sacrifice, though.

Atlanta looks around, sees another small stack of cardboard pallets over in the corner. Quiet as a mouse in a cathouse she creeps over and hides her shotgun just behind it. She loads it first, though. *Just in case.*

Then, once it's hidden, she heads out back again. Waits for a few minutes until—

—the next tanker truck is passing by.

Soon as it passes, she quick hurries after it, and jumps. She catches the back metal handle off the ass-end of the truck, and for a second her foot drags along the gravel as she struggles to pull herself up.

Somehow, though, she manages. Stands up on the back and hitches a ride up to the office lot.

———

Trickier, now. She's in the thick of it. Once she hops off the back of the tanker, she's gotta move fast—people are everywhere. Caterers setting up food, workers unfolding chairs, waitstaff gathering in little pockets, going over how to handle food and drinks and clearing plates.

There's a handful of generators running—humming along, not too loud, and so Atlanta darts over and hides behind one of those. That puts her about fifty yards from most of the action. Far away, but not far enough.

She feels naked without her gun.

At least she still has a pair of binoculars. Steven's idea. Steven doesn't have a lot of actual ideas, but when he does, they seem to be good ones.

These aren't much—just little fold-up ones. Atlanta pops them out, takes a glance, peering out at those gathering and getting ready, and—

There.

Ty Carrizo.

Smile as big as a barn door. With him are a couple other guys in sensible suits. They're standing around, directing some of the workers—pointing here, pointing there, looking at something on a clipboard.

He starts winding his way through, overseeing everything.

Someone comes up. His wife.

And his son. Damon.

You little dick, she thinks. *Daddy's boy.*

Damon shakes hands with the other men in suits. The wife stands back, silent as a judge, smiling like an Avon lady. Damon heads off with his mother, and the men all keep walking together. They're coming up on a cluster of servers standing there and—

No, no, no, no.

This doesn't make sense, doesn't track at all, and here Atlanta feels like maybe this whole thing has slipped a gear because now, *now* this is turning into a straight-up grade-A certifiable nightmare.

Her mother stands among the servers.

Mama, what are you doing here?!

She's dressed like the other servers: black pants, white blouse, little black bow tie. She's nodding and smiling, and then she shakes Ty's hand like she's grateful as anything. Atlanta feels like she's on a kids' carousel that's spinning fast, too fast, faster than she can handle.

You need to get out of here.

Just go home.

She could call the police. But on what evidence? They'd laugh her off the phone. Best-case scenario they'd send, what, one squad car? She needs the cavalry. Which means she needs some kind of evidence. She could *lie,* say something that might bring the whole department here, but if she can't point them to something—they'll come, disrupt the event, and go home red-faced and empty-handed.

Okay, she tells herself. This is fine. Not at all fine, really, but fine as it's ever gonna get. Plan is still the plan. It just means finding Bee first. Then track down the girls, or drugs, or something, *anything.*

Nobody's down by the garage or the tanks.

And they're not keeping Bee or any other girls in plain sight here. Why would they? That means—

Office building.

Gotta get in there. Shane said that was always a probable place she'd have to go, so—again, he found a building directory online from when this wasn't VLS but belonged to Indian Motorcycles. He was able to get a rough layout for her. His take was, if they're keeping anybody anywhere, it's the top floor. Executive offices. Best place to make everyone—lobbyists, senators, whatever bigwig shitbirds are flying into this nasty tree—comfortable.

Atlanta darts around the margins of the lot, trying to act casual, like she belongs here. She waits till Ty is going the other direction and then she moves.

Behind a few catering trucks. Behind another truck unloading crates of liquor and cans of A-Treat soda.

"Atlanta?"

The voice stops her in her tracks.

Damon.

She turns. Licks her lips. Fake smiles. "Hey, Damon."

"Wh . . . what are you doing here?"

"My mama, she's working the wait staff. I dropped her off."

"Oh." He's there in his button-down shirt and thin tie. Looking handsome, honestly. She wonders, *Is he like his father?* A littler monster made from the bigger one? Is he ignorant of it yet? What does *his* future hold? Will he be just like his old man or will he be the wheel that bucks the rut? "I didn't know you had your license."

"I do but only one car between us," she lies. "So."

"So."

"Well, I'm gonna go," she says.

"Yeah, all right." He squints. "You could stay."

"Huh?"

"You could come, sit with me at my table. Free dinner. Maybe we could sneak some drinks. Nobody will know." He laughs. "Or care."

"I'm . . . I'm good."

"Sorry about . . . lately," he says. Her eyes dart around the side of the truck. Ty Carrizo is making his way back toward this direction. *Hurry this up.*

"It's cool." Even though it's so not.

"I just, uhh. We got close and the thing at the party. Freaked me out. And what you said about my dad—"

"I was on the rag. You know us ladies on our Moon Times. We just get . . . we're like honey badgers. Speaking of that, I gotta pee. Is there a . . ."

Ty is roaming closer, talking to a woman dressed like a server.

"Porta-Johns are over there."

She loud-whispers: "They're totally gross. Is there a better one?"

He grins. "Yeah. It's cool. Just walk in. Bathroom right by the front desk. I don't know if anybody's in there, but it's fine."

"You won't tell?"

"I won't tell."

Ty calls over, "Damon, come here, son."

Atlanta quick pivots around the backside of the truck, breath held in her chest, waiting for that shoe to drop, for the sword to fall, for the earth to split open and swallow her, but . . . Damon calls after, says, "All right, Dad, hold on."

Nobody comes for her.

Nobody saw her.

She skirts the edge of the lot, smiling to a few servers.

Then she's in the front door of the office building.

Marble floors. A fountain against the wall—water cascading down over three big metal letters: **V L S**.

All around, kiosks with information like it's a car lot salesroom: information about *hydraulic gas fracturing*, how it works, how it's safe, how it's good for America. Flags and bald eagles and whatnot. Doesn't say anything about filling the air with plumes of fire and poison smoke or tap water catching fire.

No time to worry about their propaganda.

She actually does use the bathroom because, well, bathroom. Plus, while in there, she texts Shane to let him know she got in.

Then, while nobody's here, she ducks into the elevator.

Atlanta heads to the fifth floor. Top of the building.

———

Best way she can describe this floor: dudely. It's like how when you go into Walmart or Target and you smell all the smelly candles, there's always one candle that's clearly marketed toward *men*. It's called *sandlewood* or *oiled leather*, and the candle itself is nearly always black or dark brown, and it smells like a fake cowboy's cologne. All hat, no horse.

This floor is that. Dark woods and leather chairs and man scent.

Pretty simple layout—whole thing is in a long rectangle. Door after door, each marked with executive names. As you go from one end to the other the offices get nicer and bigger. She sees a conference room, a break room, and on both tables she sees bottles of good liquor. Dozens of them. Little baggies, too, some with white powder, others with pills.

That could be it. Could be enough to call the cops.

But what about Bee? What about the girls?

She envisions a scenario where the cops show up, and Bee?

Bee just disappears.

Or ends up dead—another teenage "suicide."

Atlanta has to keep looking. Just in case—since she remembers what happened last time she tried this plan at Wayman's dogfight—she checks her phone. Full battery. Strong signal. She quick leans in, pops off a shot with the phone's camera of all the drugs.

That's something, at least.

She keeps on poking through offices.

There, at the end. One more office.

Name on the door: CARRIZO, T.

She tries the handle.

Locked.

Well, well, well.

No window, so she can't peer in. The handle isn't much to look at—just a standard doorknob. She takes a look around and sees a potted plant on a metal stand—a small pedestal, same brushed-nickel color of the letters in the fountain downstairs. A little hint of the industrial here in this wood-and-leather kingdom.

Atlanta sets the plant off to the side, picks up the stand.

Got some heft to it.

She goes to the door, lifts it—

—and with a grunt, brings it down on the doorknob.

The knob rattles. But otherwise: nothing.

Dang!

She does it again, harder this time—

—and the knob pulls away from the door. Not all the way.

But one more hit—*wham*—and the knob hops off like a bunny rabbit, rolling away. The door drifts open without a sound.

"Bee," Atlanta says.

She sits at Carrizo's desk, eyes puffy from crying. Mouth bound up not just with a swatch of duct tape but a whole binding of it—over her mouth, around the back of her head and neck, and back again a few times. Her hands are behind her.

"Mmmph," she pleads.

Then her eyes go wide.

Atlanta knows what's coming. A shadow falls over her—

She moves fast, throws a hard elbow backward. It connects with someone's head, and a man grunts—

—just as something jabs Atlanta right under the arm.

Everything goes full-tilt boogie. Her bones lock. Muscles go from gooey fish guts to hard concrete. She can feel her teeth.

And next thing she knows, she's shaking on the ground, mewling like a half-dead kitten. Standing above her, with a bloody nose, is Moose Barnes.

"You again," he says. His voice is rough-hewn, like a splintered board after someone broke it in half. It's got a tremble to it. "Shit."

Then he grabs a hank of her hair, and begins dragging her down the hall, back out of Carrizo's office. She wills her muscles to move, tries to get them to do anything except hang off her body like moss off a tree—she starts kicking, reaching for him.

A door. Open. Her, thrown through it. The floor here is enameled concrete—smooth, the fluorescents above captured in it like liquid light. Metal shelves rise around like Erector sets. She reaches for one, tries to stand.

A fist pistons into her kidneys. She cries out, doubles over, curls up.

Moose growls at her, grabs her wrist, and slaps one of the shackles from a pair of handcuffs over it. It whiz-clicks shut. Then he secures the other end around one of the metal shelf posts. She feels him patting her down. Going through her pockets. "There. Stay here." He walks away carrying her phone and one of her shot-shells. He holds it up, stares at it like it's a piece of alien technology. "You got bullets but no gun. You're a dumb bitch."

"Not a bullet," she gasps. "Bullets are different."

"Whatever." He heads toward the door.

"Wait," she groans.

He turns back around.

"What the hell is this?" she asks. "Why you? You seemed . . . like just some dope jock asshole. But now . . ."

"I'm in deep." He looks lost. Swallows hard. He's strung out, maybe—way his back teeth grind. He's on something. Coke or pills or worse. "They, they got plans for me if I just . . . hunker down. You can't be here. You're gonna ruin it."

She sneers at him, "You killed her, didn't you? Samantha."

He winces like she slapped him. "She messed up. Okay? Wanted to end the partnership with Carrizo. And Carrizo . . ." But the words fall apart in his mouth and he just stares off, haunted by whatever's in his own head.

"So you killed her. Made it look like something else."

He makes a sound in the back of his throat. Something like a whimper. Then he hurries out of the supply closet, slams the door. Locks it.

She screams.

———

No phone. No way to call out. She should've sent the pictures of the drugs to Holger when she had the chance. Dangit! Shit!

All around her, the mostly empty shelves of the supply closet. Three sets of shelves. Far wall, which she can't reach, is home to staplers, hole punchers, paper reams, even a paper cutter—one of the ones that's shaped like an executioner's blade. *If I could get my hands on that . . .*

But the shelves are bolted into the concrete. Industrial manufacture. She shakes it, tries to pull them apart. They're solid.

Not much on her side of the shelves. Just cleaning supplies: Windex, bleach, paper towels, all that. She winces as she turns—her body still feels sore from the stun gun, and the pain that radiates out from her kidneys is its own special hell. *Maybe something's broken inside.* Did Moose hit her that hard?

She's got one hand free. She pulls at the metal cuff. It's tight. So tight. Almost cutting off the circulation to her hand.

Time passes. No idea how much.

Maybe I can pick the cuff lock.

She feels around her pockets for something, anything. She's never picked a lock in her life, but now she sure as hell wishes she learned. Wishes, too, that she'd brought a penknife or something with her. But she's got nothing.

Maybe one of the Windex bottles. She pops the top, pulls out the tube. The cleaning fluid stink fills her nose. She tries popping the tube in there, but the thing almost leapfrogs out of her hand. *Don't cry.* Atlanta blinks back tears. With a steadier hand she tries pulling apart the mechanism that forms the spray bottle part of it, and there's a little spring in there and—

Again it slips out of her hands, this time lubricated by the cleaning fluid.

"Dangit," she hisses, and kicks her boot against the shelves.

Clang, clang, clang. The shelves judder but don't budge. A bottle of bleach rolls off, thuds against the cement.

Bleach.

She thinks, *Doesn't bleach, like, eat through stuff?* No, no, not on its own. Suddenly she's chiding herself: *You need to pay better attention in chemistry class.* She's always saying how oh, ha ha, school is so worthless and they don't teach us anything worth a spit for use in the *real world*, but this sure feels like the real world and right now she needs a way to magically use bleach to get through these handcuffs.

Then she thinks—

Maybe there is way, after all.

———

Hours pass. By now, the banquet must be underway or done.

Atlanta leans against the shelf. She can't sit because the placement of the cuff doesn't give her enough leeway.

So, she stands.

Feet aching. Body hurting.

Then: footsteps.

She screams out for help.

The closet door unlocks, opens.

Help isn't here. It's Moose Barnes. He looks even worse than before, like all this is taking a toll on him. His hair is tousled. His face, slack, nose fat from where she elbowed him. Whatever he's on is wearing off. Which means he has to decide if he's going to take more, or go all the way down to the bottom.

She doesn't much care what he decides.

"C'mon, we gotta see Ty," he says, and he walks over, keys in hand.

Atlanta darts her own hand out. Grabs the Windex bottle off the shelf. It's no longer blue, because it no longer contains Windex.

There's bleach in there.

She starts spraying it at him—*fsst, fsst, fsst*—and he's swatting at it like it's a cloud of biting flies. He curses at her—"You fucking bitch!"—and then his words dissolve into a scream. "That burns! Shit! Shit that burns!"

Atlanta drives a boot into his crotch, hard.

The keys drop out of his hand with a clatter. He doubles over, and she pushes the keys toward herself with her boot—she strains to reach them, the tops of her fingertips tickling the key ring but not getting a hold. *Just a little farther* . . .

But then he's up again, and he pops her in the mouth with a clumsy fist. Her head rattles like dice in a cup. Bloodtaste fills her mouth, her lip is split. He comes in again, hands reaching for her throat—but she pitches an elbow.

Catches him for the second time in the nose.

He howls, staggering backward. Blister-red eyes. Snot and blood coming out of his nose. Lips slick with white spit.

Atlanta dives for the keys. This time she ignores all the pain, strains until she feels a tearing there—

Got 'em.

With her thumb she isolates the handcuff key, starts undoing it. The metal cuff springs open, her hand free, blood flowing back to the fingers.

Moose roars, comes at her like a storming bull.

She moves fast. Takes the Windex bottle again, slams its neck down against one of the metal shelves—hard enough the spray top pops off, bleach splashing out. Then she jerks the whole bottle forward—

Sending a gout of the stuff right into his eyes, nose, mouth.

He gargles, screams, heels skidding out from under him. On the ground he writhes like he's covered in ants, clawing at his face.

She pats him down. No phone. Not his. Not hers.

One of the phones on this floor has to be working.

Atlanta hurries to the door, throws it open. Out into the hall—

A hand catches her, slams her against the wall. "Hey, I know you," says a voice. *Flared collar. Hairy chest. Samantha's party.* The man who she whipped up on. The one who paid money for her. She tries the same trick as before—winging an elbow—but he kicks her behind her leg, and she drops.

He pins her, knee in the small of her back. Hand wrapped around her hair, pressing her face to the hard Berber carpet.

"Should've known once I saw the one, I'd see the other," Ty Carrizo says. Atlanta looks up from her vantage point on the floor, and here he comes down the hall. He's got Bee with him. She's still taped up, her hands still behind her back.

Carrizo has a gun to her head.

"I'm going to need you to let my associate, Mr. Shaw, put some duct tape over your mouth now. And around your hands. We're going to take a short trip, and then you're going to take a long trip."

Atlanta tries to lurch out of the man's grip, but he slams her back down.

"Added incentive—because I am all about incentivizing situations—is that I also have your mother. She is blissfully unaware of what's happening, but if you insist on making this more problematic for me than it already is, I will put a bullet in her, too." He smiles as the resistance goes out of her. "Good, good."

"Hold still, pretty girl," the man—Shaw—says, chuckling. He starts winding up her hands. Then tapes over her mouth. Tears, angry tears, run down her cheeks. "Maybe I'll get to play with you yet, get what I paid for."

Carrizo snaps: "You're being extrarude, Tom."

"Sorry," Shaw says.

"Barnes?"

Shaw stands up. Looks in the closet. "He's in here."

"Get him cleaned up. Get these two outside—take them out the *back* way, because soon enough we're going to have guests coming up here and this mess has got to be cleaned up by then. We'll use the blue pickup to drive them down to the garage. We can conclude our business there. I'll call Sigmund."

"You got it."

CHAPTER TWENTY-EIGHT

They sit her down on an oil drum, Bee next to her.

They're back in the garage after a quick trip in a rust-bucket blue pickup—a little one, like an old Dodge. The truck must be used to carry trash somewhere, because it stinks in there like garbage. Motor oil, too.

Right now it's just Moose and Shaw. Moose is in bad shape, whimpering like a whipped pup. His face looks bad. A red, blistered mess. He keeps saying to Shaw, "I can't see right. Something's wrong. I need to wash, I need to wash," and finally Shaw relents, tells him to go over to the office, to the sink upstairs, wash up.

It's enough of a distraction.

Atlanta hops up, and even with her hands behind her, starts to run.

Get to the door.

Shoulder it open.

Run to—

Shaw catches her in the gut with a knee.

She goes down, trying like hell not to throw up in her mouth.

He laughs at her, grabs the heel of her boot, drags her back to the oil drum, and just lets her lie there on the floor against it. "You dumb-ass," he says.

Through the front bay, here comes Carrizo. "Everybody gone home?"

"Empty, far as I can see."

"Good." Carrizo roams into view, shoves someone forward—

Mama.

Arlene. Not bound up, not taped. Like she came down here willingly, not sure what she was getting into. Carrizo pushes her forward and she says: "Atlanta? Baby?" The surprise on her face—the horror, too—is like a beacon of fear.

"Here's what's going to happen," Ty starts to say, but then interrupts himself. "Where the hell's my son?" He looks behind him.

Footsteps fast approaching.

Damon enters.

Venomous anger rises in Atlanta's belly. *He's in on it.*

"Dad?" Damon asks. "What's the rush, I was just—" Then he sees. The look on his face is pure confusion. He looks toward Atlanta. "Atlanta? I—" But then his gaze flicks elsewhere. Away from her. And toward Bee. "You."

You?

"Time to watch as I clean up your mess," Ty says.

"It's not . . . my . . . I didn't . . ."

"You dumb little fuckhead. I told you to use protection, didn't I?"

Damon, horrified, looks from his father, to Atlanta, to Bee, and back. "Please, Dad, this isn't right. Whatever this is . . ." To Bee he says: "I thought you were okay with it. I thought you were in on it."

Bee gives him a demon's stare as tears crawl down her cheeks.

The elder Carrizo growls through teeth clenched so hard it's like he's trying to eat his words: "I gave that girl to you as a present. I thought you could finally become a man, maybe *join* this family. And all you had to do was wrap it up. Not like I didn't give you a rubber."

"It broke. I was drunk. I thought—"

"Shut up. Stand there. Be a man."

Damon looks hollowed out—like he's just gonna break apart. Go to dust and blow away.

His father ignores it. To everyone else he says: "Like I was saying, here's what's going to happen." He gestures to Arlene with the gun. "Atlanta, you and your friend are going to go away for awhile. I've got a man who will fetch a very nice price for the both of you. Especially the pregnant one." Now, to Damon: "And here I guess I owe you that one—"

Damon cries out and bolts like a spooked horse. Running fast and, probably, far.

Ty Carrizo curses. "Shit." To Arlene: "Kids, huh?"

Arlene says, "You sonofa—"

He backhands her with the gun. She goes down. Crying. Bleeding.

"*Like I was saying.* You two? For sale. I'm going to sit here on your mother like a bird on a nest, and long as you two don't act up before morning, I will let her go. But you cause me any pain at all, I'll kill her."

Atlanta knows he's lying. He'll kill Arlene anyway. He's not an idiot. Not dumb enough to expect Arlene to just roll over, keep quiet. She's as good as dead, too.

Which means something has to be done soon. Sooner than soon. *Now.*

Her gaze flits around. She needs something. Some kind of advantage. Nearby: a forklift, with two forks sticking out. Not sharp. But might be enough.

"So," Ty says. "My friend should be here—"

Arlene must've come to the same conclusion Atlanta did.

Because she shrieks like a jungle cat and leaps, claws out. Ty yelps, staggering backward—her nails digging into his browline, leaving streaks of peeled skin. The gun in his hand goes off, the sound muffled.

Arlene shudders. Blood starts soaking through her white server blouse.

Mama, no, no, no—

Atlanta starts inchworming her way toward that forklift.

But apparently getting shot isn't enough to stop Arlene Burns. She grabs Ty's head and starts whaling on him something fierce, hard enough that he drops the gun.

Shaw's the one who stops her. Grabs her by the hair, throws her backward.

Atlanta scooches up against the forklift's tines. Starts getting the flat metal fork underneath the tape.

Outside, somewhere—an engine rumble. Accelerating.

Ty, moaning, staggering backward, yells: "Someone still here? Shit! Check that. Go. Go!" And as Shaw scoops up the gun and heads toward the mouth of the garage bay, Ty pulls his hand away from his scalp, finds it wet with red.

Mama lies on the floor, crying, bleeding, gut shot.

Shaw stops, stares outside. Calls out, "Someone in a pickup truck?"

Ty barks: "Flag him down. Find out who it is."

Atlanta starts *pulling hard*. Her wrists ache as her hands start to slip through the wound-up duct tape.

"He's not slowing down," Ty says. "He's speeding up—oh, shit!"

He dives out of the way just as a pickup truck leaps over the front ramp, slams askew toward the garage door, and rams into it. The whole building shakes. Cans and tools fall off shelves with a clamor.

Shaw scrambles to stand.

The pickup door pops open just as Atlanta's hands pull through the tape. She quick works to rip the tape off her mouth.

I know that truck.

Paul steps out of it and tackles Shaw to the ground. Again his gun clatters away. Then Atlanta thinks, *Gun*. Shotgun. The .410.

It's less than ten feet away.

She hurries on her hands and knees fast enough to get standing, then throws her body against the wooden pallets. Her hands dive down, find the cold steel and smooth wood of the Winchester.

It's up.

Paul knocks Shaw to the ground with a straight punch.

Ty Carrizo is bolting for the gun.

Boom.

Her shotgun bucks. Carrizo cries out, pulling back his arm like something just bit it—because something did. A scattering of birdshot. He howls, bleeding. Then he skids to a halt and goes the other way—toward the back door.

Paul calls out: "Arlene, oh, god, Arlene—"

Atlanta snaps at him: "Get her, get Bee, and get out."

"Come on, you come on, too."

She breaches the barrel, thumbs another shell in. "Go on!"

Then she turns to follow after Carrizo.

Time to hunt.

———

His trail is not hard to discern. Other animals might make it hard. From her class she knows, you might have to find a bit of fur here, some scat there, a footprint underneath a carpet of mulched leaves.

But Ty Carrizo leaves behind a spattering of blood.

And all she has to do is follow it.

She stalks through the open space. Night is settling in. Stars shine above. The air is crisp like a dead leaf in a closing fist.

Toward the tanks. Her feet crunching on gravel. No need to be silent now. He must know she or someone is coming.

And sure enough, there he is.

He bolts out from between two of the four tanks in a cluster—tanks as tall as barn silos, maybe bigger. Carrizo pounds limestone and she thumbs back the hammer, takes aim: *choom.*

His shoulder shakes as a flower of blood opens there.

But he keeps running.

And she keeps on following after, jogging now. Barrel break. Shotshell in the chamber. *Snap*—shut. Click of the hammer back.

Barrel up. Bead lined.

Bang.

His leg kicks out from under him, the birdshot taking him right below his ass-cheek. Carrizo drops to a knee. Then down to his hands.

Still not done. He scampers up. Starts hobbling away from her. Open. Shell. Shut. Hammer.

He turns hard to the left, heading back toward the garage area, away from the tanks—he's probably realizing now that it's open out here, *too open*, and that if he wants his own gun, he'll have to double back.

Bang.

His head jerks to the side. His ear goes to a bloody mess.

Her gun, it's not a killer's weapon. She knows that now. Killing him with this won't be easy. Killing a squirrel, sure. A man? Not so much. But she can whittle him down like a stick. This is surgery. Taking off pieces until he drops, broken and bloody, a cut of red, juicy steak for the police dogs.

He puts a little more pep in his step, screaming now, wailing.

One more shot should do it, she thinks.

Still pushing forward, she takes her time with this one. His back is dead ahead of her. Her boots carry her forth as she cracks the gun in half like a bone, putting one last shell in, closing it up, thumbing the hammer—

Now, she stops.

Gets a good bead on him. Figures: hit him square in the back. Take the wind right out of his sails.

Then:

Bang.

His head pops open like a kicked watermelon. A jet of red.

Ty Carrizo pitches face forward, legs kicking out against the stone.

I killed him.

But the hammer of her shotgun is still drawn back.

And there, in front of him, stands his own son. With the hand-gun in his shaking hand. Damon cries out. He throws the gun to the ground.

He runs.

PART FIVE: FUTURE PROOF

CHAPTER TWENTY-NINE

"Am I in trouble?"

Holger looks Atlanta over. "No."

"Good."

The hospital hallway stinks of antiseptic. And the white noise here is about to drive Atlanta buggy. Humming of machines. Air through the vents. The beeping and booping. Intercom calls from this floor and others. Someone coughing. Someone mumbling. The sound of a dozen televisions tuned to different channels.

"But we both know it doesn't all add up."

"What's not to add up?" Atlanta asks, knowing full well the answer. The lie she told was simple enough: She and Paul drove her mother to VLS that day to act as a banquet server. But Bee showed up, angry that Ty's son had done what he did to her. They kidnapped her and tried to make her shut up. Atlanta saw them taking her friend away, so she tried to stop them and got caught up in it, too. Then, for the most part, she told them the rest as it really happened. Paul said he was the one who took the shots at Carrizo with the .410, and Atlanta agreed.

"I don't need to tell you what doesn't add up." Holger shrugs. "It doesn't really matter anyway. Because that was one helluva bust."

Even now, a week later, the news is still talking about it.

A rape and prostitution ring run out of a national fracking company.

Bonus: guns, gambling, drugs.

And not just that—the slate of people attending when it all went down. They didn't catch any big fish like some presidential hopeful or whatnot, but they got a whole lineup of lobbyists, state senators, congressmen, and other moneymen.

All eager to take favors from Ty Carrizo.

Favors in the form of drugs or sex with drugged, underage girls.

They found girls there, too. Three girls from out of state. (Maybe once Samantha got dead, their *local opportunity* dried up.) Turns out, the girls were being kept on the fourth floor in a conference room, doped to the gills with pharmaceuticals most often found in a veterinary office.

Moose Barnes, they found upstairs. Blubbering. Half-blind from the chlorine. They got him squared away, taken to jail. Holger said he might not do much time—they had him drugged pretty good, and he'd agreed to roll over and throw some of the other folks under the bus.

Damon, well. He copped to shooting his father. He's not in jail, though. So far they're calling it *self-defense*. Bee said he'd agreed to a paternity test, despite his lawyer's recommendation to fight it.

"Fun times," Atlanta says with a sigh.

"I owe the bust to you."

"I just happened to be there."

Holger lowers her voice. "Same way you just happened to be there when Owen Mahoney was tied to a tree."

Oh, snap.

"I . . . I don't know—"

"I ran his gun for prints. Yours were on it. I didn't let that become a part of the file. Mahoney is scum, every inch of him. No reason to drag you down with him. But I know you're at the heart of all this."

"Can't prove it."

"Don't have to. I know it here," Holger says, and taps her temple. "And you know things there, too. You have good instincts. And also, *terrible* instincts."

"Thanks?"

"You ever think of being a cop?"

"Like, now?"

"No," Holger says with a laugh. "Training to become one."

"Oh, I dunno about that. I have been thinking about what's next, though."

"Work hard, graduate. The police academy awaits."

Atlanta shrugs. "I don't much like people. I'm guessing being a cop means working with . . . people."

"It tends to."

"I like animals. I was thinking maybe something with animals."

"Whatever you do, Atlanta, I just hope you manage to stay out of trouble. Whatever shitstorm comes blowing in, maybe next time stay inside."

"I will. Thanks, Detective."

"Cherry, remember?"

"Thanks, Cherry."

———

Later that night, Atlanta's sitting in the hospital room with her mother, watching HGTV. *House Hunters.* They're playing a drinking game—any time someone says one of the key bingo phrases, they take a drink. *Granite countertops. Man-cave. House with a view,* or *walkable to the beach. Stainless steel appliances.* A wife seeing a big closet and saying to her husband: *Okay, now where do you think your stuff will go?*

A couple looking at a condo in San Diego say one of the bingo phrases: *Double sinks.*

"Take a drink," Arlene says, her voice scratchy and deep.

Atlanta holds up her cup of Kool-Aid fruit punch, knocks it back.

Mama's drinking the heavy stuff: grapefruit juice. She *urps.* "Oh, god. This reflux is killing me." She groans as she sits up. As the show cuts to commercials, she says: "I can't wait to get out of here."

"You'll be cool with that?" Atlanta asks. "I mean, it's cozy in here. People bringing you meals. Every day's a new bouquet of flowers from Paul."

"That man."

"He kinda saved our asses."

"He's still on my shit list. Though lower down, now," Arlene says.

"Yeah, well. Same here, I figure."

Mama reaches out, takes Atlanta's hand. "I just wanna go home, but home isn't even home right now." She shuts her eyes, keeps on talking. "Will be soon. Insurance check will come in before long."

"That'll be nice."

Atlanta's mother's been in here for a week now. The bullet did a number on her innards, but not as bad as the infection that came after. They had a hard time dealing with it—had to run her through a few different courses of high-octane antibiotics. It's under control now, though, and her guts are stitched up inside and out. That means it'll soon be time. Time to return to normal life.

Much of a normal life as they could have.

Atlanta's phone chimes.

A text.

Shane: *How's your mom?*

Atlanta: *she's good thx*

Shane: *Come over tonight? We're at Josie's.*

Atlanta: *can't gonna hang with the mama bear*

Shane: *Cool. By the way: Bee is here.*

Atlanta: *cool cool she doin okay*

Shane: *I think so.*

Shane: *She says she loves you. I say we all love you.*

Atlanta: *aww love you too little burrito*

Shane: *You ruin nice things.*

Atlanta: *i know*

She sends him a poop emoji.

Arlene's eyes pop open again. "Hey. I've been thinking."

"There's a dangerous sentiment."

"Now, come on. You'll like this."

"Do tell."

"I say we pick up and leave."

Atlanta lifts an eyebrow. "Leave? Like . . . *leave* leave?"

"Darn tootin'. We pack up, pick up, hit the bricks. Insurance money will be enough to cover a new house somewhere cheap. Or maybe rent somewhere not so cheap. We can go . . . *well*, I don't want to say wherever, but lots of places. Better places. Where the people aren't . . . the same people."

Atlanta chews on that.

Get up and leave.

That was her idea all along, wasn't it? Earn enough money to skedaddle. "Maybe Florida," she says.

"See, there you go. Palm trees. Flamingos. Manatees."

"Manatees?"

"Sea cows, sure. I saw it on TV. They're cute."

"They look like big marshmallows."

"They do."

"Florida has old people, though. And any time you read the news it's always *a Florida man ate another Florida man*. It sounds like the zombie apocalypse down there."

"But with palm trees."

"True, true." She sighs. "I think I'd like to stay, though."

"You would?"

"Yeah. This is home. We've earned a right to stay here. I don't want to turn tail and run. For all the things that have happened . . . there's some good here, too. I found Whitey here. Shane, Josie, and the others. Maybe even Paul."

"Let's not get ahead of ourselves."

Atlanta shrugs and laughs a little. "I'm ready to stick it out if you are."

"I'm as ready as a rainbow, sugar pop."

Atlanta kisses her mother's hand. "I love you."

"Love you too, baby. Love you, too."

ABOUT THE AUTHOR

Chuck Wendig is the author of The Heartland Trilogy and the Atlanta Burns series for young adults, as well as numerous novels for adults, including *Star Wars: Aftermath* and the popular Miriam Black series. He is also a game designer and screenwriter. He cowrote the short film *Pandemic*, the feature film *HiM*, and the Emmy-nominated digital narrative *Collapsus*. Chuck lives in "Pennsyltucky" with his family. He blogs at www.terribleminds.com.